DANGER COVE

www.dangercovemysteries.com

DANGER COVE BOOKS

Secret of the Painted Lady
Murder and Mai Tais
Death by Scones
Four-Patch of Trouble
Deadly Dye and a Soy Chai
Killer Closet Case
Tree of Life and Death
A Killing in the Market (short story)
Killer Colada
Passion, Poison & Puppy Dogs
A Novel Death
Robbing Peter to Kill Paul
Sinister Snickerdoodles
Heroes and Hurricanes
A Death in the Flower Garden
Divas, Diamonds & Death
A Slaying in the Orchard
A Secret in the Pumpkin Patch
Deadly Dirty Martinis
A Poison Manicure & Peach Liqueur
Not-So-Bright Hopes (short story)
Tequila Trouble
Deadly Thanksgiving Sampler
Killer Eyeshadow and a Cold Espresso
Two Sleuths Are Better Than One
Dark Rum Revenge

BOOKS BY NICOLE LEIREN

Danger Cove Cocktail Mysteries:
Heroes and Hurricanes
Deadly Dirty Martinis
Tequila Trouble
Dark Rum Revenge

USA TODAY BESTSELLING AUTHORS
ELIZABETH ASHBY
& NICOLE LEIREN

DARK RUM
REVENGE

A DANGER COVE COCKTAIL MYSTERY
GEMMA HALLIDAY PUBLISHING

This work of my imagination is dedicated to my first grandchild, Reid. Though you aren't old enough to read...yet, I look forward to watching you and your imagination grow as a whole new world is revealed to you through story telling. Love, G-Mom.

Acknowledgements:

Special kudos to Lyona Helsely for helping Lilly name her very first pet. I appreciate your support and friendship over the years!

Thanks to my street team, Leiren's Lovelies, for your unwavering support and encouragement.

And last, but certainly not least, thank you to all the Danger Cove readers who love hanging out in this world as much as I do!

CHAPTER ONE

———

Sunday evening. The best night of the week. Most people aren't big fans of the day, as it represents the last twenty-four hours of freedom before the daily grind of work begins again. For the crew of Smugglers' Tavern, it represented the gateway to our day off.

"Hi, Lilly!"

I looked up from the bar and waved to one of Danger Cove's longtime residents, "Hi, Ms. Jordan. Thanks for coming in tonight." As bartender and now part owner of this fine establishment, it was my job to make sure everyone was having the best possible experience.

"Good evening, Lilly." Janiece Jordan smiled and waved as she took her seat.

The crowd was decent for a Sunday, especially since it was almost closing time. The ambiance of the nautical theme, dark wood, and comfy booths made Smugglers' Tavern the perfect place to unwind and relax.

Part of the perfection was the interaction between the crew. I smiled as Mandi, my best friend who also happened to waitress here, grilled our gardener, Abe, for a story about his sabbatical.

"Abe, come on. How hard is it to tell us just one story? You were gone for months. I know you were visiting your daughter, but you just *had* to have something exciting happen."

"I'm an old man. I try to avoid anything too exciting. Bad for the heart." He cut me a glance and winked. "Though, I've heard there's been no lack of excitement around here since I left."

I winked at him. "See what happens when you're not here to keep me in line?"

Abe's gray eyes twinkled. "Let's see. Since I've been gone, you, Miss Lilly Waters, have managed to be promoted from bartender to assistant manager, and now manager and part owner of the Smugglers' Tavern. I'd say you've done alright for yourself in my absence."

Mandi brought a drink order up to the bar. "Don't forget—she finally made her relationship with Tanner official. I've even heard her refer to him as her *boyfriend*."

Abe grinned. "Now that *is* news!"

I ignored the bait they were dangling in front of me. "Weren't you going to tell us a story, Abe?"

"Well, since you are the boss after all..." Abe's bald pate reflected the lights overhead as he leaned forward and beckoned all of us in the general vicinity to join him in a circle. "Are you ready?" he whispered.

Everyone nodded, not wanting to break the mood he was creating. His gaze darted around the room before settling on Mandi's wide blue eyes. "It was a dark and stormy night..."

Mandi stood up, crossed her arms, and laughed. "Abe, you can't start a story like that."

"I most certainly can." He laughed. "It was nighttime, and there was a storm brewing. How would you have preferred I started?"

She gazed up to the ceiling, deep in thought. "Something along the lines of...the evening sky loomed ominous on the horizon as gray clouds marked their presence with the clap of thunder and the resounding cracks of lightning."

Freddie, our busboy and New York transplant, brought a bin of dirty dishes up to the bar. "Not for nuttin', but can you tell we're taking a creative writing class in college? Mandi's getting an A, of course."

"Oh, I most certainly can tell. Perhaps I should let her tell the story then." Abe chuckled.

Before Mandi could reply, the door to the tavern opened, and Bree Milford, manager of the Ocean View Bed & Breakfast, stormed in and headed straight for the bar. "Hey, Bree. Everything ok?" I put a glass of water with lemon in front of her but knew that wasn't going to be her order tonight.

"Hey, Lilly. What's the new drink special? I may need three or four of them tonight."

I swear I could almost see the steam escaping from under her red hair. "The Dark and Stormy. It's ginger beer and dark rum. Some people like it with a lime, others with bitters."

She exhaled loudly. "Oh, I'm definitely feeling bitter. Serve me up one of those to try, and then we'll go from there."

As I mixed her drink, I slipped in an order of fries. Comfort food was definitely on the menu tonight. I placed the beverage in front of her and waited while she downed a few swallows. Once the tension ebbed a little, I decided to try to get to the bottom of her angst. "Wanna talk about it? I'm a certified barstool therapist."

She chuckled and then sighed. "Have you ever noticed that run-down, old motel just outside of Danger Cove?"

I narrowed my gaze and then grinned. "I make it a habit not to focus on scary buildings that I occasionally have to ride by on my bike."

Bree grinned. "Well, that eyesore you've been avoiding is quickly becoming the biggest pain in my...what is it you call it? Asteroid?"

I fought the urge to stick my tongue out at her. I really was trying to be more adult-like since becoming part owner. Bree tended to bring out the younger side of my twenty-five years, but I could tell she needed me to be ready to listen tonight. "Yes, a pain in the asteroid. Don't judge me just because my gram had a strict no-cursing policy."

This time my comment eased the worry lines on her forehead for a moment. "Not judging, just teasing."

Mandi made her way to the bar with an order. "Hi, Bree! Did I overhear you talking about Shady Pines? What's going on with it? That building has been abandoned for years now. I'm pretty sure it's haunted."

"If it's haunted, I want no part of it! No wonder I avoided it." I may risk my life from time to time in order to see justice prevail, but scary buildings that might be haunted—not my style.

Bree's worry returned, making its presence known on her normally cheery complexion. "Unless you're in the real estate market, you won't have to worry about it. The owner has finally decided to put it up for sale." She pushed her glass toward me and made a gesture indicating she wanted another. "And that *man*, Jack Condor, is planning on bidding."

Very few people in Danger Cove were fans of Jack Condor. I confess I might have been at the top of people who didn't like him, though Bree might now be vying for that position. "Why in the world would he want that run-down old building? I know he's been trying to purchase land and redevelop it into the modern, sleek look he fancies, but talk about your fixer-upper."

Bree's arms crossed as a scowl settled in. "Oh, he has plans for it alright. He told me he was going to buy it and make it into a nice little hotel that offers up a complimentary hot breakfast to the guests. He said it was high time the Ocean View had some competition. Ugh!"

Before I could respond, she continued. "You wanna know what's worse?"

I wasn't sure I did, but no way was I going to interrupt her tirade. "What?"

She used her thumb to gesture to a man and woman sitting at a booth in the corner. They'd been talking quietly and nursing their drinks for the past hour or so. "Those two, Adam Miller and Jessica Byers, are also real estate developers. I have no idea what their plans are for the place, but if they decide to return it to its full splendor, then I find it incredibly ironic that they're staying at *my* bed and breakfast while in town for the auction. I'm housing people who ultimately want to take business away from me."

She huffed out a good deal of exasperation and returned to her drink. I decided to let her have a moment before I tried to console her. I'd learned from my interaction with Mandi that even though the redheads in my life were pretty calm, when they did get upset, you needed to give them some space before trying to "fix" everything.

Instead, I ventured a glance over at the two people Bree had pointed out. They seemed cozy, but that could just be me looking through Tan-colored glasses. As Mandi had blabbed to everyone within hearing distance, Tanner and I were officially an item. It may have taken me a while to get with the program, but since that time, I had a tendency to see love in the air wherever I went. Even though I only got to see him on the weekends, as he was teaching fifth grade in Seattle now, we talked on the phone every night when I got home. He had blond hair, blue eyes, and a body that could make a girl forget her own name. At least this girl.

Before my vision became too dreamy, the door flew open, and none other than Jack Condor himself swaggered in. His beefy arms stretched the fabric of his blue and white jersey, making the pirate face on his chest look like it received a bad batch of Botox.

The rings on his fingers shone almost as bright as his teeth, which was saying something in the muted lighting. I stopped looking when I realized his pants were the typical polyester of baseball uniforms. Some things a girl just didn't need to see. "Well, there ya ladies are. Couldn't figure out why you weren't out supporting your community by playing on the DC Pirates softball team." He lifted the black and chrome aluminum bat like a sword. I was not surprised to see his initials emblazoned near the grip. Only someone as self-important as Jack would go to the trouble to have that done. "Took the Seattle Sluggers down in extra innings."

Bree's nose crinkled as though someone had just run their nails down a chalkboard. But a sly smile snaked across her lips before she tossed me one of her famous smirks. She spun the stool around to face her current arch nemesis. Obviously agreeing with me on the whole too small outfit, her finger traced a big circle in the air around him. "They probably finally threw the game because not everyone has a strong enough stomach to keep looking at this." She let out a little giggle/snort before continuing. "Which, coincidentally, is also why we won't join the team." She spun back around, the smile fading back into the whole chalkboard scowl as he began to chuckle.

"My, my, someone got up on the wrong side of the bed today." He leaned closer, a taunting smile on his face. "I bet you're worried someone is going to renovate that old roach motel and then you won't have to make up any beds because everyone will be staying there? Don't worry that pretty little red head of yours, missy."

The tension radiated from Bree, filling the room and thickening the air. Time to step in. I placed another drink in front of her. "This one's on the house—I went easy on the bitters since I know you enjoy a good, strong drink." I smiled to try to ease her aggravation. She relented enough to relax the tense lines around her mouth.

"Oh, I think I have plenty of bitter to go around." She took a quick sip and then faced Jack again and used her thumb to point to the other two real estate investors in the booth. "Maybe you should worry that not-so-pretty head of yours. Adam and Jessica plan on giving you a run for your money. They're in town for the same piece of property."

Jack's expression softened, revealing there just might be a heart buried under that barrel of a chest after all. "Like I said, you don't need to worry. I've talked to both of them. They have the same plans as I do. Tear down, clear the lot, and start fresh. I'm thinking some shiny new condos will do the trick. So you don't worry, and breathe easy. Ol' Jack ain't worried about them either."

"It's not them he should be worried about." A woman's voice edged into the conversation, though I couldn't see her behind Jack's large frame.

Apparently, Jack recognized her immediately without turning around. His complexion paled as his remaining swagger subsided. I swear I could see beads of sweat forming on his top lip. "It can't be…"

"That's right, Jack, darling. It's me. Camilla Cartwright."

I had no idea who Camilla Cartwright was, but Jack certainly did. She reminded me of Meryl Streep in *The Devil Wears Prada.* Her platinum blonde hair was short and wavy, but stern all at the same time. I guessed her age to be late twenties, maybe early thirties. She gave off a no-nonsense vibe tinted with high-class society that oozed affluence. Money certainly wasn't a problem she had to contend with.

Jack forced a smile to his face. "Camilla, what a surprise to see you."

She threw her head back as a shrill laugh escaped her ruby red lips. "Oh, Jack, I find you so amusing. You had to know I'd be here." Camilla handed her designer purse to a woman standing quietly next to her before moving into Jack's space. Personally, I never wanted to be *that* close to the man, but it didn't seem to bother her.

"Why is that?" he growled out between clenched teeth.

She walked her matching red-painted fingernails up his beefy bicep. I was immediately drawn to the pointed angle of each nail. Maybe she instructed the manicurist to give her claws? The arrogance in her voice interrupted my thoughts, "Because…if you want something, I see it as my job to take it away from you. Isn't that right, Serena?"

The purse-holding woman smiled, her long brown hair moving as one with her head. "Totally your style, and anyone who tries to stand in your way should know that."

Camilla smiled at her and winked. "See, Jack, even Serena understands that's how this works."

"Sounds like a playground bully to me," Bree offered as she twisted the barstool around to face Camilla.

The woman cut a sharp look in Bree's direction. "And you are?"

Bree forced what I was certain was a fake smile. "Bree Milford."

Camilla tilted her chin up, and the scrunching of her face gave me the impression she was trying hard to place the name. She turned to Serena. "Help me out, dear. You know how forgetful I am."

"Bree Milford runs the Ocean View Bed & Breakfast."

"Yes, yes, that's right. Pleasure to meet you, dahling. Quite a quaint little establishment you're running there."

Bree's face was drawn tight. I worried it might break. Though it went against my nature to help Jack out, I didn't care for Camilla's overall attitude or the fact she was making a spectacle of herself in *my* bar. I stepped closer to the group. "Can I get you something to drink?"

Her gray green gaze turned to me, and I received the up-and-down once-over. Maybe if she didn't like what she saw, she'd leave with a lot less fanfare than she arrived. I'd be ok with that. "Not this time, thank you. I need to head to Seattle and get settled in. Staying at a *real* hotel." She turned to Bree. "No offense, but I only stay in hotels with room service."

The tension slowly faded from my friend's face as she shrugged. "None taken. We prefer low-maintenance guests. No offense." She finished her statement with a bright smile.

Camilla appeared slightly taken aback at Bree's comment, but recovered quickly. "You'll have to worry about low guest count once I offer up some competition." She returned her attention to me. "Busy couple of days ahead of me. Perhaps my assistant and I will stop in for a victory meal once we put poor little Jack and your friend here in their place." She stepped closer to the bar and leaned in. "I don't like to lose to anyone, and I'm not about to start now. I always get what I want."

The hyena laugh escaped from her tiny throat again before she turned on her high heels and left. Serena lagged behind. I grabbed Bree's arm to keep her from vaulting after Camilla's retreat. I really needed to focus on finding new security.

Serena's voice was much quieter—and less grating— than Camilla's, but I could hear her speaking to Jack. "Look, you know how she is. Don't let her get to you. I heard your team won the game tonight. Lucky bat or glove?"

The tension released its death grip on Jack, and he nodded. "Thank you, young lady." He gripped his bat tighter and lifted it to tap his heart. "Luckiest bat a man could own." He sighed. "Maybe I should bring it with me to the auction."

Serena offered a smile and shrug. "It's not personal. She has her sights set on the place, so be prepared."

Jack hit his palm a couple times with his lucky bat. "Oh, I will. Thanks, Serena. Nice to see you again."

She nodded and then hurried out the door.

Jack turned and gestured to the drink Bree was downing. "I'll have what she's having."

Both Bree and Jack looked miserable, and there really wasn't much I could do to help. I delivered his drink and watched them both sip at the contents, staring off into space. All of this over the most run-down building I'd ever seen in the Danger Cove area. I didn't know much about real estate, but whether they demolished the property and rebuilt or tried to rehab it, I didn't understand how that could be profitable. Maybe when Jack was in a better mood, I'd ask him. From the sound of everything I'd heard tonight, that could take a while.

CHAPTER TWO

———

The next afternoon brought about a much-needed reprieve from the tension in the town. Everyone from the tavern was gathering for a good ol' fashioned barbeque at Abe's new place. The house itself was small, a simple cottage with a white picket fence. The backyard was amazing. I was pretty sure my old apartment would have fit inside his cedar-plank deck.

While we waited for Bree to arrive, Mandi and I had held our own in the cornhole toss against Abe and Freddie. As Abe played his turn, Mandi leaned in closer to me. "Did you notice the purse Camilla was carrying last night?"

I shrugged and offered a small smile. I didn't really want to revisit those events. "I noticed she had a purse. Does that count?"

Mandi chuckled. "You get half points for that. It was designer. Not like one of those that I could afford if I saved for a few months and bought on clearance. Hers would cost more than I make in a year!"

"I understand. Honestly, though, if I'd saved for that long, I can think of so many different things I'd choose to spend that money on. But, hey, to each their own, right? Besides, Camilla obviously can afford it."

Mandi rolled her eyes. "Or she's in debt up to her eyeballs."

"Yeah, let's go with that."

We finished up the game of cornhole with Clara and Tara, our twin chefs at the tavern, emerging triumphant in the finals. When Freddie's stomach started growling louder than the sound of the waves crashing into the rocky cliffs nearby, he stood and moved next to the grill.

"Not for nuttin', Abe, but that grill is almost as big as the one in the kitchen at Smugglers' Tavern." Freddie's eyes reflected the gleam of stainless steel as he ran his hands appreciatively over the hood. Abe patted him on the shoulder. "Thanks, Freddie. Why don't you grab the burgers and brats and let's fill the inside?" He lifted the cover to reveal a large cooking area divided into two levels. A metal container was on the side, maybe for heating a liquid? I couldn't be sure as no one, including myself, had ever considered me a domestic goddess. Unless you counted microwave skills. If that was a category, Martha Stewart and Betty Crocker better look out.

The picnic table hosted a variety of side dishes, compliments of Tara and Clara. I'd brought the soda and...

"Here's dessert." Bree offered with a small smile as she stepped into the backyard.

I decided not to comment on her tardiness. "Hey, Bree. How are you feeling today?" I took the bag from the Cinnamon Sugar Bakery—yeah, Bree wasn't blessed with domestic gifts either.

She shrugged. "A little rough. I think someone may have overserved me last night."

My spine stiffened. "You had two...I..." I took the responsibility of my job very seriously. I'd seen bad things happen when people had too much to drink.

The corner of her mouth upturned a tick. "Relax. It wasn't you. Uncle Eddie and I may have spent some time with the tequila bottle after I left the tavern."

"Oh..." I moved over to my purse and retrieved a bottle of aspirin. I handed a couple to Bree with a bottle of water from the cooler.

The uptick morphed into a full-fledged smile. "Thanks, Mom."

Mandi joined our group. "Hi, Bree. You look like..." Mandi's face revealed a struggle, striking the perfect balance between polite and honest.

Bree rescued her with a chuckle. "Like I was run over by a truck."

You had to love that Bree was comfortable with brutal honesty. Mandi stopped for a moment, lost in thought, and then grinned. "I don't have recent numbers, but I do know that the number of people affected by accidents involving large trucks has been steadily increasing the past few years."

Bree chuckled and pulled Mandi into a hug. "Thanks, my trivia-loving friend. You always know how to cheer a girl up."

I grabbed a water for myself and Mandi, and the three of us sat at the picnic table while Freddie and Abe cooked the meat. After a few moments, I decided to broach the subject everyone was avoiding. "Did you talk to your parents about the auction? Since they're technically the owners, I'm sure they'd want to know what's going on, even if they are recovering after following Bon Jovi on his last concert tour."

Ignoring my question, Bree busied herself with peeling the wrapper from the water bottle. I waited. Mandi did not. "While Bree is deciding whether or not to answer your question, can I ask when you're going to hire a replacement for Tanner?"

It was my turn to ignore a question. I'd interviewed several people as a through-the-week replacement for my security. Since graduating from college, Tanner had accepted a teaching position in Seattle. He came home every weekend to visit his family and spend time with me. Since I had to work every weekend, he continued his work as security at the tavern so we could at least flirt with each other from across the room. I couldn't help the dreamy smile that crept onto my face when I thought about all the time we spent together *after* work.

Mandi sighed. "And now she's off in Tanner Land. Once you make your way back here, I'm reminding you that you have to fill that position soon. Freddie and I can't handle the dining room and security, not with as busy as we've been lately. Last night was a perfect example of how quickly things could get out of control."

Bree tossed the wrapper into the trash with flourish. "At least you have to worry about being busy. I'm worried we're not going to be busy enough to keep everything going. I appreciate the fact most of the real estate developers aren't interested in reviving Shady Pines, but Camilla made her intentions pretty clear last night. Even Uncle Eddie is worried." She chuckled. "Of course, his solution was a little more extreme than the average person's."

I held up my hands to stop her. "We probably shouldn't hear this, as we don't want to be called as witnesses at his trial."

Mandi laughed. "I'm going to side with Lilly this time. You have to love how strong his protective instincts are over you though."

Bree nodded. "He's definitely got my back. Don't worry, though. I made sure he understood we'd have to use normal channels to deal with this. Though..."

Mandi and I leaned in. "Though what?"

"I want to go over to the motel today and check it out. Maybe I'm missing something. Honestly, I don't even think an HGTV star would tackle this project. There has to be more to this."

My head moved up and down, indicating agreement. Jack had told us that Jessica and Brian's plans were the same as his—to demolish the building and use the property for their own purposes. Despite what Camilla had said, I couldn't wrap my head around the benefit of renovation. Unless she charged a small fortune to stay there once it was complete, I had no clue how she could make any profit, much less the ones she bragged about last night.

"You have to come with me." Bree's urgent whisper left no room for disagreement.

This time my head moved in the opposite direction. "Scary old building, reportedly haunted. You can't be serious, Bree."

"You owe me."

I looked to Mandi to see which side of the friend equation she was going to come down on. I prayed our BFF wavelength would land her solidly in my corner. Mandi sucked her bottom lip between her teeth—not a good sign. Finally, she answered. "She's right. You owe her."

"Want to share how you arrived at that conclusion?"

Occasionally, I was sorry I asked certain questions. This would have been one of those times. I listened as Mandi recounted the number of times Bree had helped me out or provided intel to assist with the capture of a bad guy. As much as

I hated to admit it, she was right. I huffed as I pulled my blonde ponytail tighter. "Ok, I owe you. But, if I go with you, the score is back to even. Deal?"

Bree's triumphant (and relieved) grin kept me from being too annoyed at her victory. "Deal."

"Mandi, you're coming, right?" I turned to my traitorous-yet-right best friend.

She laughed. "No way. I'm not going anywhere near that haunted old place. Besides, someone has to stay behind to help clean up from our cookout and tell the police where to find your bodies."

"You are so funny. Remind me to give you bathroom duty next week."

Before she could answer, Clara and Tara called out. "The food is—" Tara began.

"—ready. Come and get it," Clara finished.

Their twin connection was pretty cool, though you did have to get used to it taking both of them to tell you something. "We're coming. I'm starving. I can't wait to eat…what I hope isn't my last meal." The last part was said in a much lower voice for Bree and Mandi's benefit.

Abe did his best to keep Bree engaged in conversation, but it didn't take a highly observant person to realize her mind was elsewhere. "Lilly, might I speak with you for a moment?"

"Sure, Abe." I joined him over by the grill. "What's up?"

He handed me the keys to his truck. "You girls go do what you need to do before it gets too dark."

"But…how?"

His kind, old eyes crinkled with his smile before he winked. "Benefit of being a retired schoolteacher—not much gets by us, and we hear everything."

That did seem to be a perk of being a teacher—certain senses were on steroids. Apparently, that didn't go away with retirement. "Ok, but we can take Bree's car."

This time his gaze narrowed, and I was transported back to middle school and caught passing a note. "I'd prefer you take my vehicle. That way you will need to return it and I can ensure your safety. I'd prefer to go with you, but as I'm certain you will fuss about that and I have to make sure Freddie shares the food with the girls, this is the next best thing."

I couldn't help myself—I gave him a quick hug. I'd really missed him while he was away. I'd never met my grandfather, so Abe was like the grandpa I never had. "Thanks, Abe. You're the best."

He squeezed my shoulder. "Don't forget your go bag. Be safe, and hurry back."

This was one time I had exactly zero issues with following instructions regarding my safety. I confessed it amused me both Tanner and Abe referred to a backpack that contained a flashlight, bandages, glow sticks, knife, and other safety related gear as my *go bag*. They had been watching too much *NCIS* if you asked me. I prayed that none of those items would be called into service during our visit. That was not how I wanted to end my day off.

CHAPTER THREE

———

Shady Pines could very well be the creepiest building I'd ever seen. This was before even considering any paranormal figures that might be lurking in the shadows. From a distance, ominous vibes oozed into the hazy cloud that always surrounded the property. Chills crept along my spine, eliciting a shiver through my body as we approached the run-down remains of what might once have been a classy place. The dwindling rays of sun loomed behind the darkening clouds, adding to my apprehension. I chanced a quick look at Bree to see if the scene ahead of us caused her any concern. The grim determination on her face indicated she had far more at stake in investigating this place than I did. For her, I would keep putting one foot in front of the other even though every fiber of my being pleaded with me to turn tail and run. Hey, sometimes retreat was the better part of valor.

Though it was difficult to tell for sure in the twilight evening, the chipped paint, missing siding, and rotted wood indicated a bright day would cast this building in no better light. Deep breath in. Deep breath out. I could do this. Once at the door, I noticed a real estate agent lockbox on the door. Oh darn. Guess we'd have to leave. I pointed to the giant padlock and whispered, "Looks like we'll not get that look inside after all."

Bree smirked and pushed on the door. The large wooden barrier creaked as it gave way under the gentle pressure. That totally didn't go as I'd planned.

"Looks like someone else is here already. Time to see if there's any more competition I need to be aware of."

The inside didn't look any better than the outside. Old, dusty, and partially rotted furniture littered the lobby area.

Doorways on each side led to corresponding corridors for rooms. The elevator—obviously out of order—was frozen in place with its doors half-open. A sign over a door right next to the elevator indicated the stairs to the second floor.

"Should we split up?" Bree murmured as her head maintained a constant swivel.

"Should I have your head examined?" Seriously, she had gone completely off the deep end if she thought I was going to let her out of my sight.

She chuckled, the first one I'd heard from her today. "Just kidding. Relax. Let's head to the west wing. Then we'll check out the other side before heading upstairs."

Always thorough—that was my friend Bree. "Sure. Whatever. Let's just make this quick."

We had only taken a few steps down the corridor when a scraping noise seared the silence we'd been enjoying. My hand immediately dug into the go bag and retrieved the can of Mace. It wasn't much, but at least it was something. "I suppose you're thinking we should investigate the source of that disturbance," I whispered.

"Exactly. It's better to know, don't you think?"

It was official. She'd lost her mind. I huffed. "Fine. Lead the way."

Bree smiled. "You've got the Mace. You lead the way."

Ugh. The score would not be even after this—she would most certainly owe me. A lot. "If I die, you're explaining all of this to Tanner."

"Deal."

"And my parents."

She rolled her eyes. "Ok. I'll make all the necessary notifications, Miss Drama Queen. Now can we go?"

My teeth managed to clamp on to my tongue, preventing a sarcastic remark being leveled at the woman currently responsible for this scenario. We tiptoed through the lobby, my extended arm brandishing the Mace leading the way. I'd managed a few steps down the corridor and turned to check the first room, when my hand encountered a solid object. A warm—breathing—solid object.

"Hello." The man smiled before noticing my weapon. He raised his hands. "Hey now, no need for that. I ain't here to hurt nobody. Ain't fixing to get myself hurt neither."

He was tanned and bald like Abe except there were more wrinkles on his forehead and face than on my cotton dress when I forgot and left it in the dryer. Just a note, the "wrinkle prevent" setting only works for so long.

"What are you doing here?" Bree was now acting large and in charge. Guess she didn't need Mace to confront an old man, only to confront the scraping noises we heard earlier, for which I hoped he was responsible.

He leaned against the doorframe and studied us with curious eyes. "Not sure how that's any of your business, missy. What're you doing here?"

"I…the door…it was open." Somehow she managed to retrieve a bit of her earlier bravado. "And my name is Bree, not missy. I'm here to check out the property. It's being auctioned tomorrow. Are you a prospective buyer?"

He chuckled at her statement as he shook his head. Glad others were finding the humor in this situation. "I'm just passing through. I'm down on my luck, but happen to know the owners of this ol' place." He stepped aside to let us see inside the room. A sleeping bag and backpack occupied the floor.

My heart grew heavy for this man I'd just met. Life could take you on some twists and turns you didn't plan. During my cross-country trek from New York to Seattle, I'd stayed in some pretty sketchy places. None quite as run-down as Shady Pines though. The sun continued its descent outside, and what light we had would fade soon. The desire to say good-bye and finish this little exploration expedition continued to build in the pit of my stomach, but my manners prevailed. I moved the Mace to my left hand and extended the other in greeting. "I'm Lilly. We're taking a quick look around, and then we'll be out of your hair. You may want to look for another place tomorrow though. Like she said, there's going to be an auction."

A leathered hand took mine and shook it. "Billy. Billy Nester. Appreciate the heads-up, Lilly. No need to be worryin' about me. I can take care of myself."

Billy sounded like he might have grown up in the South. His tanned skin made me think he'd spent a lot of time outdoors. If Billy wasn't worried about the impending auction, I wouldn't be worried about Billy. "Understood." I looked at Bree, who was still sizing the man up, if her intense gaze was any indication. "C'mon, Bree. Let's let Billy get some sleep, do what we came to do, and get out of here."

After another moment of scrutiny, Bree nodded. "Yeah, let's go."

We headed for the stairs. Wanting to be prepared for when the sunlight disappeared, I exchanged the Mace for a flashlight. I intended to do the quickest walk-through in recorded history. The stairs creaked with each step. I prayed the rotted wood didn't extend to this particular part of the motel. I thought that maybe if we fell through, Billy would help us if I promised him a hot meal. We made our way to the end of the corridor. There was a breeze wafting in our direction, adding to the compounding chills I'd had since we stepped through the door.

I did a slow arc of the flashlight through the room to find the source of the breeze. A broken window proved to be the culprit. I'd almost exhaled a sigh of relief, when the beam of light dropped a few inches and revealed a ghostly white, unmoving female body.

"Bree!" Was there such a thing as a screamed whisper? If so, that was what I'd just emitted.

"Not good. We should check and see if we can help."

She was right. I really, really hated when she was right. "Fine, but this time *you* are leading the way."

"You're such a wuss," she teased but headed in the right direction.

I used the flashlight to survey the length of the corpse. No chest movement to indicate the person was sleeping. Only stillness. As illumination fell across her face, I gasped at the sight as recognition dawned. I'd only met the woman a day or so ago, but she'd made an impression. She'd taunted Jack and posed a threat to Bree's family business. Bree pressed two fingers to her neck and shook her head. "She's dead." She looked up at me, fear clearly displayed on her face. "Camilla Cartwright is dead."

CHAPTER FOUR

———

"What are we going to do?" I knew the right thing to do, but sometimes fear affected the decision-making part of my brain and pointed out that the right thing wasn't always the smart thing. *We should call for help. Go get help. Something to do with help. That was the right thing.* Instead, I envisioned an eight-by-ten glossy of the disapproving glare of Detective Marshall. He and I had a speckled past, thanks to what he deemed my sticking my nose in where he didn't feel it belonged.

I stood by the belief that it was *my* nose and I only had to stick it into his business when he wasn't taking timely action…at least in my opinion. He disagreed. Thanks to his eating pizza the first time he'd tried to lock me up—yeah, there was more than one time—I lovingly referred to him as Detective Pizza Guy. Never to his face though. I might have interfered, but I wasn't stupid.

While I was navigating the tricky trail between doing what was right and doing what was smart, Bree had retrieved a flashlight from her purse and was looking around the area. She directed the light to the floor underneath the window. "Look."

I silenced the argument in my head and focused where her light shone. "I don't see anything."

"Exactly."

It took a moment for me to arrive at apparently the same conclusion she had. "There's no glass on the floor."

"Right."

"So, what does that mean?" I didn't mean to be short, but there was a dead body that needed to be tended to.

Bree shrugged her shoulders. "I don't know, but I find it curious."

I slowed the whirring in my mind and surveyed the entire scene. "Her purse is gone. It was designer."

"Didn't know you were into high fashion."

"I'm not, but my BFF Mandi brought me up to speed at the barbeque before you arrived. She mentioned that Camilla's purse cost more than she would make in a year."

"We need to get out of here." Now that discovery time was over, Bree was ready to leave.

"We need to call the police."

"I really hate it when you're right." She held the flashlight close to her face and cut me a look.

"Ditto, but you know we can't just leave her here."

"Do you really want Detective Marshall to know we were here?"

No. I really didn't. After a few seconds, I totally ignored the fact there was a good chance our prints would be found somewhere. I also reasoned there was no way to know how many prints they would have to sift through first. As a result, I compromised to buy us time. "We'll call and tell them we were going to come by and check the place out when we noticed the door was open. We can suggest they look into it. They should find the body, right?"

Bree nodded. "One would hope. Let's get out of here."

"What about Billy?" I hated to state the obvious, but he knew we were here.

"What about him? He's not supposed to be here either. He's not going to say anything." Bree started to move toward the door.

She made a valid point. I started to follow her, when thanks to my sweaty palms, my flashlight slid from my grasp and fell right next to Camilla's outstretched arm. I knelt down to pick it up, entirely too close to her face for comfort, and my nose (the one that couldn't help stick itself where it didn't belong) registered a sickly sweet smell. If that was what designer perfume smelled like, I'd take a pass. Please and thank you. I grabbed the light and started to stand, when I noticed something in or on her hand.

Closer inspection revealed words scrawled on the palm. I remembered Camilla mentioning she was forgetful. Writing something on your hand would be a good way to make sure you didn't forget. I might have done that a time or two myself when I was in a hurry.

I looked closer at the words—three words, to be exact: *skinny.punt.older*. Ok, now that was just weird. I'd double-check with Mandi, but I was confident this was *not* high fashion. *Stranger Things* didn't have anything on this woman.

Bree nudged me with her knee. "Lilly, let's go! I've had enough of this place."

Valid point. "Ok, I'm ready. You don't think Billy…" I let the inference hang in the musty air.

"I don't know, but I suggest we not stick around to find out." Her grip around my hand tightened as she pulled me from the room. For the record, if Bree was ready to leave, so was I.

We hurried down the steps and out the front door. Just before we exited, I stopped, effectively halting our progress. "We need to check to see if Billy is still here."

"You have lost your mind, woman. Why in the world would we do that?"

She was right. I probably had lost my mind. The curiosity kitties that lived inside of me clawed in demand that we know if Billy had bothered to stick around. If he hadn't…

"Because we need to know. Camilla deserves that."

Bree's snort resounded in the empty space. "I bet Jack Condor wouldn't agree."

I pulled on her hand, leading her to where we'd first found Billy. "Since when do we care what Jack Condor thinks?"

"Valid point."

All noise stopped as we tiptoed back down the corridor. I let my flashlight lead us into the room. "Billy? We were just heading out. Wanted to say good-bye." If he really was the killer, I was totally lame—and a sitting duck. If he wasn't, I won the manners award.

The room was empty. All evidence of Billy Nester gone. For some reason, that made me more nervous than him being there. Bree whispered what I'd refused to think.

"Great. If he is the killer, we've now seen his face and know his name."

Yeah, so far I'd managed to do neither the right thing nor the smart thing. If I were playing for the DC softball team, I'd be batting zero. "Let's get out of here."

We exited the door, leaving it just as we'd found it. Once back in Abe's truck and down the road a bit, I pulled off to the side. My hands trembled as I dialed the Danger Cove Police Department. They should probably be on speed dial, but really what did that say about a person who had to call the police that often?

"Danger Cove Police, this is Minerva Taylor. How may I help you?"

I was relieved that the new admin answered the phone rather than a member of Danger Cove's finest. I'd not had much interaction with her—yet. "Hi, Ms. Taylor. This is Lilly Waters. Bree Milford and I were just over at Shady Pines. We were going to take a look around but noticed the door was already open. We thought we should report it."

"Isn't that the place that's up for auction tomorrow?"

"Yes, ma'am."

"Was the key in the lockbox?"

She asked a valid question. One I could venture a guess at but would rather not speculate. Since Camilla was inside—dead—one had to assume she'd entered with the key. Of course, that made me wonder how and when Billy got in. "I'm not sure."

"Did you not have a code for the lockbox?"

Ugh. I didn't want to lie, but I didn't want to expound on the truth either. "Since the door was open, I didn't look to see if the key was there."

There, not a lie but not exactly the truth, the whole truth, and nothing but the truth...so help me God. I could sense she was going to ask me another question—one I could not skirt easily around. I decided to be proactive. "I'm sorry I'm not more helpful, but I think you should send someone over to check it out."

With that request, I cut the connection. I turned to Bree, who was scowling. "What?"

"You just had to put my name in there?"

I chuckled and put the truck in gear, heading toward Abe's house. "I most certainly did. You got me into this mess, and I am not going down in the sinking ship alone."

"Some captain you are."

We rode the rest of the way in contemplative silence. Right before we turned into Abe's drive, Bree twisted in the seat to face me. "They're going to figure out we were there."

"I know. It may take some time, but despite all our attempts to be prepared, we failed to wear gloves. You'd think we'd have learned by now."

I pulled into the drive and put the truck in park. "Detective Marshall is going to pop that vein in his neck when he finds out."

"I know."

She sighed heavily. "It won't take long for them to figure out I could be a possible suspect."

Bree was right. She had motive, at least in the eyes of some. Camilla would represent competition for the Ocean View Bed & Breakfast. She had means. Though I had no idea what actually killed Camilla, Bree was perfectly able to hold her own in any kind of fight. And, most disturbing, she had opportunity. She was late to Abe's cookout. Depending on the official time of death, none of us there could vouch for her whereabouts. Hopefully, someone besides Uncle Eddie could provide an alibi. I turned to face her, sharing my sympathy at her situation as best I could with an expression.

"I know."

CHAPTER FIVE

―――――

I confess I hadn't slept much after our visit to Shady Pines. Images of Camilla's body, still and pale against the dirty floor flashed before me every time I closed my eyes. I didn't think she was a very nice person based on the little interaction I'd had with her, but no one deserved to go out like that.

Mornings were rarely my favorite time, but not even a strong black tea made a dent in my desire to ignore the world and crawl under the covers for another six or seven hours. I needed to find some energy and find it fast if I was going to make it through the day.

"Morning, Boss!" Mandi's chipper voice pecked at my brain faster than Woody Woodpecker. Ugh. You knew it was bad when the only analogies you could recall were from old-time cartoon characters. It only reinforced that urge to return to bed and channel Porky Pig with the timeless "That's all folks."

But duty and friendship called. I forced a smile from somewhere in the emotional reserve bank. "Morning, Mandi. Why are you so happy this morning?"   ▾

Her body vibrated with energy. I spent a second or two wondering if I could siphon some of that into my nervous system.

"I wouldn't say happy."

"What would you say then?" I managed to unlock the back door and get the lights on in the kitchen before she bustled ahead of me and started the teakettle. At least she was putting that energy to good use.

"Didn't you hear?"

"I live alone and don't listen to music or the radio, so I haven't heard anything really this morning." That was the truth—

most days. My activities yesterday prompted me to text Bree the moment my eyes could focus. She'd filled me in on some updates, but Mandi was having so much fun, I didn't want to provide the spoiler alert. My smile was tiny, but genuine. "Well, except for my BFF's voice as we engaged in a guessing game even before the kettle whistled."

Mandi crossed the kitchen and gave me a quick hug. "Sorry, I keep forgetting you need at least three doses of caffeine before you function. No more games, just information. The auction for Shady Pines has been postponed."

Bree had learned of the delay through official channels since she was listed among possible buyers. Curiosity made me want to learn if Mandi had any unofficial news. "Really?"

She moved closer and lowered her voice even though we were the only two in the room at the moment. "They found Camilla Cartwright in the motel last night. Dead."

When I didn't immediately reply, she clarified. "Murdered."

"Wow." It was a lame wow, I confess. I'd never been good at faking it.

Being my best friend, it didn't take more than a microsecond for her gaze to narrow, her arms to cross, and all that energy to focus directly on me. "You knew already!"

"I didn't know what tidbit you were going to share at first. I did learn about the auction this morning. Bree texted." I retrieved two cups and the necessary tea bags to get our standard breakfast started.

I watched her out of the corner of my eye as she processed what I'd said and, more importantly, what I hadn't. She was crazy smart. I'd be lucky if I'd bought myself even thirty seconds. "But you knew she was dead."

Not wanting to confirm or deny, I poured the hot water into the cups and handed her one before making my way into the office. Her footsteps were only two paces behind me. "Holy moly. You and Bree were there…"

The papers on my desk were suddenly very interesting. Without a doubt they required my immediate and full attention. My hope was Mandi's sense of responsibility would kick in and she would get started on her pre-open routine. She allowed me three sips of tea and a slight shuffling of the papers before she spoke.

"You called the police, right?"

"Yes."

"And reported the body?" She leaned forward, honing in on her prey (aka me.) Absently, I wondered if this was how a deer felt when they sniffed trouble in the air.

"Not exactly."

A dramatic sigh escaped. "Lilly Raine Waters! Have you learned nothing? Are you crazy?"

Her use of my full name brought my gaze to hers, and I couldn't help but smile. "Ok, Mom…" I was going to explain our reasoning when she continued.

"You have to tell them what you saw and when you saw it."

"Now I know you're the crazy one. Do you have any idea what Detective Marshall will say if we admit to being at the scene of the crime? He'll arrest Bree and me before his pizza from Gino's has even been delivered. And you *know* how fast they can get your order to you."

Before our discussion could continue, loud pounding at the front of the restaurant returned our focus to the business at hand. "What in the world?"

I started to barrel through the front door but remembered the not-so-small detail about a murderer being on the loose. Hurrying back to the office, I grabbed the Mace that had been my protector last night at the haunted motel. This time, I moved quickly, but quietly. When I arrived, the front the door was standing open, and Mandi was grinning from ear to ear. I offered my best motherly scowl. Though, to be honest, I had no idea what that looked like. My parents had been absent for most of my life, only rejoining in the last year or so. My gram had raised me. Now the Gram Glare—that was something to be reckoned with.

Her giggle gave me the impression my stern face needed a lot of work. "What is so funny, and what is going on?"

Mandi pointed to Abe. With all the glaring, I hadn't noticed him. He was smiling too. "Will someone please tell me what's going on before I put my Mace to good use?"

Abe's blue eyes twinkled as he fought to contain his laughter. He turned to the building and finished tapping in the nail with his hammer. "This is what's going on."

His brightly colored *Help Wanted* sign would definitely draw attention. "This really isn't necessary. I'm going to hire a new security person. Tan hasn't been gone *that* long. It's not like we draw a rowdy crowd, especially not on the weeknights. I did call the *Cove Chronicles* last week and place an ad in the Help Wanted section. I've received some résumés—just haven't made calls to set up the interviews."

Abe slid the hammer into his tool belt and draped his arm around my shoulders and offered a squeeze. "The ad is a start. I'll leave the sign up, but it's time, my girl, for you to make those calls."

I shrugged out of his loose embrace. "I know. I will." I couldn't explain why I hadn't been able to pull the trigger on this hire. My record was fifty-fifty. Freddie had been my one good hire, and the person I'd hired to replace Abe during his absence—not so good. Terrible, even. Maybe there was some worry which way the scales would tip this time.

"Mandi, will you give us a minute?" Abe's baritone voice had a way of calming nerves while getting things done. Must be a by-product of all those years teaching.

"Sure thing. I'll get started on the morning checklist."

Once we were alone, Abe leaned against the building. "Does this have anything to do with Mr. Montgomery?"

Abe had been a supporter of my relationship even before I was. He'd always had a soft spot for Tanner and liked him even more after he decided to become a schoolteacher. I reviewed my motivations—well hesitations—a little more in depth. "I don't think so, but there might be a small part of my subconscious that suggests this is me replacing him." I shrugged. "A girl can't be held responsible for what happens in the basement of her brain, can she?"

After a few moments of prolonged silence, he smiled gently. "No, but she is held responsible for letting that keep her from what needs to be done."

A heavy sigh escaped my partly pouting lips. "I know you're right. I just don't want to screw up and hire the wrong guy. My track record is a little iffy."

He shrugged. "So hire a gal."

I'd not considered hiring a gal—woman—but this was the twenty-first century. No rule said a woman couldn't provide security. Truthfully, the more I thought about it, the more I liked it. And I knew Freddie wouldn't complain. He and Abe would be swimming in a sea of hormones, but I had faith in our team. "Good point. Maybe I'll do just that. I promise I'll make the calls to all the applicants and set up interviews for today. Thanks, Abe."

His chuckle made me smile. "All in the job description. Now back to the garden and greenhouse for me. I'll be in to help with the lunch rush."

The morning prep work provided routine and a sense of calm. Everyone was right. I needed to hire someone. Although the idea of hiring a woman appealed to me, the curiosity kitty clawed at my conscience to maybe try and find Billy Nester again. He'd said he was down on his luck. Maybe if I offered him a job, I could learn a little more about him.

The rational part of my brain—a part I was proud to say had been expanding, even if only in small measures—reminded me he could potentially be Camilla's murderer. And, I was convinced she was murdered. There was nothing "natural causes" about the way her body was positioned on the floor. Sadly, I'd actually seen enough dead bodies at this point to be somewhat of an authority on the matter. A small chuckle escaped the serious nature of my thoughts. I bet the Danger Cove Police Department might have a word besides *expert* to describe my ability to inadvertently find trouble.

Regardless of my expertise, logic said hiring Billy would be a considerable risk. Still…I wanted to consider it. Even if I didn't hire him, I planned to put together some food for him and take it by Shady Pines this evening after the dinner rush. He probably wouldn't be there—*especially if he had killed and robbed Camilla*—but if he was an innocent bystander, I didn't want him going hungry on my watch. I'd been there before, and it was not something I'd wish on anyone.

As promised, I'd made the calls and set up a number of interviews. Since we were typically slower in the morning, I'd opted to have them come in sooner rather than later. The first guy showed up, and my first impression was not positive. His massive muscular build brought to mind the word *beefcake*. He deserved a fair shot, though, so I cleared my brain of those references and invited him back to the office for an interview.

"Please have a seat. Mr....?"

"John Jacob, little lady."

The urge to finish the phrase in a singsong voice nearly overwhelmed me. The "Jingleheimer Schmidt...his name is my name too" lyric was hanging on the tip of my tongue. My irritation over being referred to as a "little lady" provided the necessary control. While I wasn't model height, at five feet six inches, I was far from little. "Lilly."

"I'm sorry?"

I was too. Sorry I'd decided to interview this man. "My name is Lilly, Mr. Jacob. Why don't you tell me about your experience?"

He stood up and removed his jacket, revealing a muscle tank top. He moved through a series of poses as though first prize in the Mr. Universe competition was at stake rather than a security guard position. His poses were impressive, but truthfully I worried he would frighten some of my patrons. I could just imagine the look on Janiece Jordan's face if he called *her* "little lady."

I clapped my hands once he finished. "Very impressive, Mr. Jacob. I'm not sure how relevant that is to your skills as a security guard. Although we have a beach not far from here, we are a ways from Venice Beach."

John flexed again. "All you need to know is that one taste of these guys"—he demonstrated the strength in his biceps again—"and everyone will fall in line."

All I needed to know was that I wasn't hiring him. "I have no doubts about that. Unfortunately, here at Smugglers' Tavern, we prefer a more subtle approach. Thank you for coming in."

He shrugged and put his jacket back on. I wouldn't swear to it, but I'm pretty sure he kissed his biceps as his arms came close to his face. Definitely not the kind of personality I wanted to add into the team mix here.

Three interviews later, my head hurt and I was no closer to finding the replacement I needed. Mandi poked her head in. "Lunch rush is starting. You want me to see if I can call someone to come in and cover so you can keep interviewing?"

"No! Please, no..." I offered a pitiful smile. "I need a break from the HR department and need to get behind my bar. I promise I have more scheduled for later. I just can't take one more man showing me his "guns" before lunch. Besides, Ruby is on a yoga retreat right now in Seattle."

Ruby was a friend of my former boss and now silent partner, Hope Foster. Ruby and Hope had been together for years, and thankfully, Ruby was still in the area. From time to time, she'd help me out when we were short staffed or during the busy season. Besides being pretty good behind the bar, she'd been doing her best to teach me meditation techniques to calm the fairly constant beehive of activity in my mind. Let's just say she was a better bartender than I was a student.

"Ok, but if you change your mind, I can make some calls."

"No worries. I really need a break. I'll be right out."

Once Mandi left, I pulled my cell phone from the desk drawer and texted Tanner. *You sure about this teaching gig? Finding your replacement has been challenging.*

I didn't expect a response but hoped he might be on his lunch break at the school. A moment later, my phone buzzed.

You aren't replacing me as your boyfriend already, are you?

LOL. No! You're stuck with me now. Though there was a lot of muscle parading around in my office today.

I'm happy to be stuck with you. Just trust your gut. The right person will show up soon.

Thanks. Have fun with the kids.

Thanks. Don't have fun with the muscle men. Love you.

Love you too.

"Lilly!" Mandi's urgent call broke the lighthearted nature of my moment of peace.

I put the phone away and headed toward the front. As I started through the kitchen door, I ran smack into Mandi. "What's wrong?"

"Detective Marshall is here to see you, and he is not happy."

CHAPTER SIX

———

Now was as good a time as any to put to use some of the meditation techniques Ruby had been trying to teach me. My patience was stretched thinner than tequila on Cinco de Mayo, thanks to the interviews I'd been forced to endure. Now I had to deal with the ultimate beefcake. If he was showing up at lunchtime demanding to speak with me, you could bet the worm at the bottom of the tequila bottle that he wasn't asking for recommendations for his next cocktail party.

Deep breath in, hold it for ten seconds, deep breath out. I repeated it three times as Ruby had taught me. She assured me this activity sent signals from my body to my brain that good times were coming. I think the signals hit some negative neurons on the trip because in no way, shape, or fashion was this interaction going to go well.

"Afternoon, Detective Marshall. Are you joining us for lunch today?"

The vein in his neck pulsed with power. Not a good sign since I'd said nothing but hello. "I have no time for lunch, Miss Waters. There's a murder to solve." He managed to cross his thick arms and narrow his gaze, the intensity of a laser, with me centered directly in the firing range.

Water spots on the glasses sitting in front of me demanded my attention. I grabbed a towel and focused on my distraction rather than meeting Marshall's mutinous mug. "Mandi mentioned that this morning when she told me about the auction being postponed."

I heard, rather than saw, his frame descend onto the barstool with a thud. His fingers circled the glass I'd just cleaned and removed it from my grasp. "Let's not play games. I'm tired, hungry, and in no mood for your verbal variations of the truth."

"You haven't asked me a question yet. So far you've grumbled, complained, and called me a liar." I crossed my arms—a much easier task for me than him, I might add—and decided to have a go at my stern face again. Moment of truth. He was far better at glaring than I was ever going to be.

He leaned forward, the smell of pizza on his breath. Either he was lying about being hungry, or he'd had something Italian for breakfast and not bothered to brush his teeth. "What were you doing at Shady Pines last night?"

Valid first question. Now I was sorry I'd pointed out he hadn't asked me any yet. "We wanted to check out the competition."

"Who's we?"

Since I'd mentioned Bree's name when I spoke to Minerva last night, my guess was this was a truth test. Well, look out, Pizza Guy. I was about to get an A on this test. "Bree Milford and I."

"Why were you there?"

"Bree wanted to see what all the fuss was about. It could represent some serious competition for the Ocean View." Two for two. Take that.

"What did you see when you were inside? Before you answer, you should know that CSI is in there now dusting for prints."

If you missed one out of three questions, did that mean you failed a test? I'd managed to evade the lie last night on the phone. In person, much harder. Perspiration dotted my upper lip, and I had to fight the urge to wipe it off.

"Lilly, could we steal you for just a moment? There's a crisis in the kitchen that demands your attention." Abe's calm voice worked its magic once again. Even managed to knock Detective Marshall's hostility down a notch or two.

I chanced a glance at Marshall. "Ok if I deal with this? Promise to be back in a few."

He sighed. "Sure."

A small—very small—pang of compassion poked at me. The man *was* just trying to do his job. "How about I grab you something to eat from the kitchen? I'll ask Clara to put it in a to-go container."

"Thank you. That would be great."

I nodded and made my way to the kitchen. Besides his all-time favorite food, I happened to know he enjoyed a chicken parmesan sandwich, probably because it was as close to pizza as we offered on a regular basis. "Hey, Abe, what's up? Your timing was perfect."

His sapphire eyes sparkled. "I know."

Recognition dawned. "You rescued me, didn't you?"

The smile faded slightly. "I'd say this is more of a reprieve than a rescue. Perhaps you should call Ms. Milford to determine the best way to proceed?"

"Thanks, Abe. I'll do that now." I started toward the office, but stopped. "Tara, can you whip up a chicken parm with pasta to go for Detective Marshall?"

"Sure thing. I'll have it up in a few."

A moment later, Bree answered her phone. "Hi, Lilly. What's up?"

"My blood pressure."

"Uh-oh, what's wrong?"

"Detective Pizza Guy is here. He wants to know what we saw when we were inside Shady Pines. He also mentioned that CSI was in there now processing the scene."

"Crap."

"That about sums it up, yes. I'm not good at lying. I'm decent at avoiding the truth, but not at outright lying."

Bree chuckled. "Good to know for future reference."

"Let's consider how mad he'll be if I find some creative way to avoid telling him about our involvement. If our prints are found…"

"That vein in his neck is going to erupt with more power than the Mauna Loa volcano in Hawaii."

"Ok, I'll tell him. If I don't make it, tell Tanner I love him and everything I own is his."

"I'm a little hurt by that. Don't you want your friends to have anything?" Bree teased. She dealt with stress a lot like I did. Mine typically fell more in the sarcasm spectrum, but the end result was deflection.

"Like any of my possessions are worth fighting over. Let's discuss who gets what if and when he kills me."

"You know he'd claim justifiable homicide as his defense."

This time she succeeded in making me laugh. "That he would. Ok, I gotta go."

When I made it back to the bar, Detective Marshall was gone. I called Mandi over. "Where'd he go?"

"Tara had just brought his sandwich out when his radio buzzed. I couldn't make out what they said, but it must've been important. He gave me some cash to cover the sandwich and said to tell you he'd be back."

Just like the Terminator. Once I told Detective Marshall the truth, he'd probably exterminate me. Well, until then, there was work to be done. "Ok, thanks. Probably for the best. Gives me a little time to put my affairs in order."

"You're so dramatic," Mandi teased. "Your first order of business…"

"I know. I know. Working on it." Besides a love for trivia, Mandi also happened to be relentless in the pursuit of what she felt was important. That probably explained why her parents were getting back together. Mandi believed from the beginning they'd find their way back to each other. She'd been right.

I checked on all my customers and had just started looking over some more applications at the back bar when a woman walked in. Her casual style and striking beauty caught my attention. Her long black hair shined in the artificial lighting and framed a perfectly proportioned heart-shaped face. Her tall frame was covered in black jeans and a white shirt with three-quarter length sleeves. The look was completed with high-top Converse tennis shoes. She slid onto the barstool with ease, her gaze taking in all of her surroundings in a serious survey.

Before I could get over to her, one of our regulars, Tucker from One Man's Trash, our local salvage store, flagged me over for a refill. Out of the corner of my eye, I saw a man—probably a tourist—approach our newest patron. It was obvious he was hitting on her by the smile he was sporting, the invasion of her personal space, and the touching of her arm and back. It was also obvious, to me at least, that she wasn't interested. I listened to Tucker and nodded while I watched the situation unfold out of the corner of my eye. I give the guy credit for his persistence, but his ability to take the hints she was dropping was abysmal. With each attempt, despite her polite protests, he kept getting closer and more brazen in his touch. The moment his hands started to roam where they shouldn't, I smiled at Tucker. "I'll be right back."

"Groovy." Tucker nodded, his dreadlocks moving in tandem with his head.

It only took a few steps to get to the other end of the bar, but by the time I got there, the man had been sufficiently subdued with one of those twist-their-hand moves you see in karate movies, which had him bending low to avoid further pain.

"It's not polite to put your hands where they're not invited. Understood?" The woman's voice was low, calming, and surprisingly nonthreatening. More like a mother explaining to her child why it's important to eat your vegetables.

"Yes," the man hissed through his clenched teeth.

She turned his hand just a fraction more, sending him even lower. "Is that any way to talk to a lady?"

He grunted. "Yes, ma'am. I understand."

The moment he answered, she released his hand and offered him a smile. "Thank you. Now, please, enjoy the rest of your meal."

He shook his arm and nodded to both her and me before returning to his booth. I turned to the woman, who'd started talking before I could say anything. "I apologize if I overstepped. I'd tried the pleasant, subtle decline of his invitation for drinks and a *fun* time at his place."

I couldn't hide my smile of admiration. "No apology necessary. I'm sorry I didn't get over here fast enough and you had to deal with that on your own. I'm trying to hire a new security person. As a matter of fact, my next interview must be running late." That did not bode well for him.

She extended her hand. "Actually, I was right on time. Sam Sheraton."

My face heated, and I could feel the red creep up. "I'm sorry. I just assumed…"

Sam waved off my apology. "This time I have to apologize. My name is actually Samantha Olivia Sheraton, but many times when I put that on an application for a security position, I suspect I'm eliminated due to"—she offered a rueful smile—"lack of experience. I keep trying to explain to people it's difficult to get experience when no one will hire you."

The fact her initials spelled SOS, the worldwide recognized call for help, did not escape me. "Well, based on what I saw a few minutes ago, I'd say whatever experience you have is the kind we're looking for. We rarely get rowdy patrons, but occasionally it happens. I prefer to have it handled with the same quiet, calm de-escalation techniques you chose to use on Mr. Overzealous."

The dark brown of her eyes lightened with a spark for just a moment before the reserved façade descended again. "I have a black belt in tae kwon do. Master Kim believed in teaching everyone self-defense."

Sam was definitely our gal. "Why don't you come on back and fill out some paperwork. The hire will be probationary until the background check comes back. You ok with that?" I'd been burned once before, and even though I liked her, I wasn't going to let that get in the way of my due diligence. The safety of my team, the tavern, and the town demanded I be sure Sam had no dark secrets in her past.

Sam nodded. "More than ok. If you hadn't insisted on a background check, as your new security personnel, it would have been on it as my first recommendation."

Freddie, who had been lurking in the corner watching our exchange, chuckled. "You know, Boss Lady, I think she's gonna fit in perfect here."

I grinned and gestured for him to come over. "Sam, this is Freddie, our busboy, tech guy, and token New Yorker. Freddie, this is Sam. Our new Monday through Friday security."

Freddie, who reminded everyone of a young Joey from the television show *Friends*, moved his bangs out of his eyes and smiled. He extended his hand. "Welcome to the team. You got any questions, you let me know."

"Thanks, Freddie. Come on back, Sam. We'll do the paperwork, and then I'll introduce you to the rest of the team."

Thirty minutes later I had made the rounds with Sam and gone over the basic details of her job. She had just moved to the area a few weeks earlier and was currently staying in Hazlitt Heights. Mandi had been thrilled and had already invited her over for dinner. There might have been the tiniest part of me that was jealous, but I told that part to sit down and shut up. Mandi and I both had other friends. This was not a big deal. Plus, since I'd moved out to my own place, we didn't get to see each other as much outside of work. Guess that was a part of growing up.

The rest of the lunch crowd thinned out around two in the afternoon. I was checking inventory when Vernon came in. He'd been coming in every day since Ruby had been away. He'd always get one meal here and one to go. "Hi, Vernon, enjoying your last couple of days of eating whatever you want before Ruby gets home?"

He plopped onto a barstool and grumbled. "I swear that woman is gonna kill me with her healthy lifestyle." A small grin emerged, just on one side of his mouth. "I may have to find more retreats to send her on the next time I need to replenish my grease and sugar levels."

Vernon and Ruby fussed at each other like an old married couple, except they weren't married—at least not as far as anyone knew. Vernon said he was a retired schoolteacher, but I suspected there was a lot more to his story. He had a lot of contacts in law enforcement—contacts that had been very useful for me over the past year or so—for someone who had a career in education. Just sayin'. "What can I get you today?"

He shook his head. "Actually, I'm heading to Seattle with some buddies tonight. Hitting up our favorite steak house. I'm also stocking my system with red meat before it's back to turkey and tofu."

"You want a drink then?" I didn't mind Vernon coming in and just hanging out, but he wasn't usually the come-in-for-no-reason type.

Vernon leaned in. "Just stopped in before I left to tell you the preliminary autopsy report came back on Camilla. Her parents are rolling in dough, so they greased the gears at the coroner's office and got things expedited."

No surprise about Camilla coming from money. Everything about her exuded wealth. "What did they find?"

"A puzzle."

I knew those three words on her hand would be important. Though, it didn't seem like something a coroner would focus on. That typically fell under the police department's purview. "What kind of puzzle?"

"There was evidence of blunt force trauma along with petechial hemorrhage."

I knew I'd heard that term before, probably from the television crime shows. "Isn't that caused from suffocation?" Medical school had never even been on my career radar. Bugs and blood were two things I did my very best to avoid.

"Most likely, yes. It can also be caused from coughing, holding your breath, vomiting, or crying."

Since it didn't seem likely she'd coughed herself to death, suffocation provided the most likely option. I couldn't imagine how horrible being deprived of oxygen would be. I drew in a large breath for good measure and exhaled slowly. "So did she die from suffocation or from blunt force trauma?"

Vernon patted my hand and shrugged. "And there's where the puzzle comes in. Their job right now is to determine the actual cause of death. It will be important to know if the blunt force killed her or if suffocation provided the means."

"Definitely a puzzle. You'll keep me posted?"

"If I hear anything. Gotta run, kiddo. Keep your nose clean."

The more I thought about it, the more I agreed with the confusion. Was she hit on the head and then suffocated? That was the most logical, wasn't it? Of course, that assumed murder fell under a logical progression. Despite my curiosity spiking, I gave myself a stern lecture that I should just let it go and *not* get involved.

Yeah, like that was gonna happen.

CHAPTER SEVEN

———

Adam Miller stormed into the tavern and announced his arrival with a slam of the front door. I started to say something, but I noticed Sam move quickly behind him. Her hand on his back slowed his pace, and he came to a stop as she spoke something low near his ear. Whatever she said brought his angst level down about five notches. He exhaled slowly and then resumed his journey toward the bar. I caught Sam's gaze and sent a small smile to indicate I was pleased. She nodded in return and then restarted her surveillance of the room. During the day and through the week typically wasn't a high risk for security, but something had our guest riled up.

"Hi, Adam. What can I get you today?"

"Your signature drink and some Irish nachos. I'm looking for comfort food." He pulled out his cell phone and started using his thumbs to convey his agitation to whoever the recipient of the message was.

I made him a Dark and Stormy after putting his order in. "You want to talk about it?"

"Time is money. I'm here for the sole purpose of acquiring the land that Shady Pines sits on. Now they've postponed the auction." Each word was punctuated with disbelief and dismay.

"Well, someone was murdered."

"So they say." He tipped his glass up and drained half the contents.

"You don't think that's the case?" I wasn't going to share that I'd seen the body and was pretty confident whether it was blunt force trauma or suffocation, neither would qualify as an accidental death.

"I think CSI should have finished up and the rest of us should be allowed to get on with our lives. Camilla was not a nice person. She had no friends or real associates, only people who owed her favors. She made plenty of enemies. It may take them months to sort through all the people who would want her dead."

Adam's sympathy—or lack thereof—was astounding. It made me wonder where he might fall on that list of people. "Why would someone kill her here, just a day before the auction? They would have to know she would be found almost immediately and an investigation launched."

He finished off his drink and shoved the glass toward me with a gesture for another. "Sometimes people don't think before they do stupid things. Sometimes people push every single button you have. Sometimes…they don't know when to stop."

Made me wonder if he was talking about himself or Camilla. "My gram always wondered who *they* were," I confessed with a smile. She never let me get away with a generic *they* when I was trying to justify my own actions.

He leaned forward and looked from side to side. "Jessica hated Camilla."

Jessica was the woman Adam had been with at the bar the night Camilla had made her grand entrance. She was interested in acquiring Shady Pines too. I tried to remember if I'd noticed Jessica saying or doing anything while Camilla was here or after she left. All I could remember was how cozy she and Adam were. "Why did she hate her?"

The drink was sipped much slower this time, as though he was hitting the pause button in order to formulate what he would say next. A grin appeared. "Why do you care? Are you trying to be a modern-day—and much-hotter—Columbo or Sherlock Holmes?"

The hair on my arms came to attention at his words. I didn't appreciate his tone, his compliment (such as it was), or his reference. Time to cool this man's jets before he tried to take off. I grabbed his empty glass and put a water in front of him. "I'm simply making conversation. You brought the subject up. I can move on to another customer if you don't want to talk."

The grin flip-flopped as his face turned red—not from embarrassment, but from anger. Before he could give me a piece of whatever rational mind he had left, Jessica stepped in beside him and slid her arm around his waist. "Hey, baby. Sorry I'm late. Have you already ordered?"

"Yeah," he grumbled. "I was just going to grab a table."

If Jessica was fazed by his lousy mood, she gave no indication. "Go ahead. I'll place my order and then just have them deliver it to wherever we're going to sit. Ok?"

Her demeanor and tone managed to calm him again. He had a temper that apparently needed a pretty woman with a quiet voice to talk him down. Since Camilla's voice was anything but quiet, it made me wonder.

"Ok." He offered me one last glare. "I'll take another drink too. Have the redhead bring it."

I squashed the urge to stand at attention, salute, and yell, "Sir! Yes, sir!" However, I was in no mood to require Sam's services again so soon. It was only her second day, and I didn't want her running for the hills—at least not until the weekend, when Tanner would be here. "Sure thing. I'll ask Mandi to bring it over to you when it's ready." Which, by the way, was going to take me a sweet minute. My power to placate wasn't going to be used on someone who couldn't stay calm for more than five minutes.

Once he made his way to the table, Jessica smiled apologetically. "You'll have to forgive him. He's upset about the delay of the auction."

"What can I get you to eat and drink?" I would forgive him, just not right away. My irritation level bordered near the red zone, so it would be at least fifteen to thirty minutes before we entered the forgiveness range.

"I'll take a BLTA and a hurricane."

The hurricane brought back some fond memories of when I first came to Danger Cove and started at the Smugglers' Tavern. I'd come a long way, baby, but knew I still had so far to go. "Sure, one bacon, lettuce, tomato, and avocado sandwich coming up along with a hurricane."

While I placed her order and made her drink, my curiosity kitty clawed viciously at my ankles. I needed to find out what to feed those kitties so they'd stop bothering me. Oh right—information. Best way to get information was to ask. "Are you not upset about the delay of the auction?"

She shrugged her shoulders. "It's a minor inconvenience, I suppose. Since I'm planning on making Danger Cove my home, I plan to make use of the extra time to scope out houses and potential office spaces. The cost of living is much more reasonable here than in Seattle."

"That's true. If you're looking for a real estate agent to help you, I know someone. Unless you're planning on living at Shady Pines." The mere thought of that alone gave my goose bumps the chills, but who was I to judge?

Jessica grinned and took the drink I'd placed in front of her. "Shady Pines, demolished and rebuilt, was my first plan, but seeing as how I currently make my living as a real estate agent, I think I can handle a plan B without sweating it. Thanks for the offer though."

Oh yeah, right. I'd forgotten that little detail. She was already at the booth with Adam by the time I'd recovered from my oops. I'd hoped to ask her about the nature of her relationship with Adam, but now wasn't the time. If they really were a couple, he'd hit the lottery jackpot. Jessica's dark complexion, charcoal eyes, and hair styled like she was on the front page of a fashion magazine put her leagues ahead of Adam. He was attractive in way, I supposed. His shaved head only made his oversized ears more pronounced. There was a chance his smile would ease the stern set of his jaw, but so far he'd not graced us with anything resembling humor. Maybe he was rich, and Jessica found that attractive? Oh well, to each their own, right?

Other than keeping a covert eye on Adam and Jessica, there wasn't much to do right now behind the bar. Remembering my promise to myself to be more thorough in my background checks to ensure I'd make the right personnel decisions, I decided it was time for a field trip. "Hey, Mandi?'

"Yes?" Mandi grabbed some glasses for refills and headed my way.

"Can you guys handle things for a bit while I run some errands for the tavern?"

Her head cocked to one side. "Everything ok?"

I handed her the refills. "Yes. Just going to visit Attorney Pohoke to get his advice on the best background search company."

"Maybe he can do them?"

"Maybe." I grinned, "Won't know until I ask."

She chuckled. "This is true. No worries, we can handle things until you get back."

With that detail handled, I double-checked with the kitchen staff to make sure they didn't need anything and then headed into downtown. My new wheels consisted of a motorized scooter. I still wasn't ready for the hassles of owning an automobile. I barely managed to keep up the maintenance on my bike. A scooter was enough of a leap for me for now.

The afternoon sun delivered a much-needed dose of vitamin D. I really needed to get out more. All too soon, I arrived in front of Attorney Pohoke's office on Main Street. I'd been in here a couple of times and always appreciated the effort he went to in order to put his clients at ease. The large door opened with an effort and allowed beams of light to shine on the dark furniture and softly lit room. A soft chime announced my arrival.

A moment later, the man who'd saved me from the police more times than I cared to admit, entered the room. "Good afternoon, Miss Lilly. To what do I owe this unexpected visit?" His initial smile faded as he added, "You're not in trouble again, are you?"

My chuckle eased the worry lines around his eyes. "No, not this time. I'm actually here in an effort to be proactive and *not* get myself in trouble again."

His rich laughter dispelled a little of the darkness hanging around after the discovery of Camilla's body. "Now that's something I love to hear from my clients, though I suppose it's bad for business." He held open the door. "Come on back to my office and fill me in."

After providing me with a glass of iced tea, he sat behind his desk and folded his liver-spotted hands in front of him. "What can I do for you?"

"I want to do a better job with background checks for new employees. Can you make some recommendations, or is that something you could do?"

He leaned back in his chair so far I feared he might tip over. He scratched his chin for a moment before he finally spoke. "Some of my corporate clients like to use LexisNexis."

"Lexis what?"

He grinned and sat up. "Come over here so you can see my computer screen. I'll show you."

This sounded super cool. Since I was a visual learner, the chance to see something in action always appealed to me. As I stood close to him, I could actually see the veins in his scalp through his fine white hair. "Ready when you are."

He moved some papers around until he found a yellow sticky note with scribbles on it. He held it up, triumphant. "Here we are. Username and password. Don't tell my wife this is how I remember things." He shook his head. "There are entirely too many of these things one is required to remember. If they'd allow it, my username would be my name and the password, well..."

"Password?" I supplied with a grin.

"Exactly!" His fingers carefully pressed the required keys to allow him onto the website. There I could see the services offered to LexisNexis customers. "You can learn a host of valuable intelligence about individuals, and they also offer deep-dive background checks. Those are typically more for witness verification and other larger-impact scenarios. That may be more than you're looking for."

Or it could be exactly what I was looking for.

"Let me see if I can find some pamphlets provided by companies about similar services. I know I have some back in the file room. Give me just a minute."

He wasn't gone two seconds when temptation taunted me from the little yellow note shining brightly amongst the piles of paper. I shouldn't, but I could see these two bits of information coming in handy. Besides a background check on Samantha, I could do some research on Bree's competition. Before my imaginary good angel could launch a significant argument, I pulled my phone out of my back pocket and snapped a picture of the sticky note.

"Here you go. I hope some of this will help." Mr. Pohoke handed me some pamphlets.

"Thank you so much. I really appreciate it." I started to leave but thought of one more thing Mr. Pohoke could do. It was something I could pay him for and would help alleviate my guilt a little about lifting his password. "Could you run a title search on the property at Shady Pines?"

"I suppose I could. Is there a particular reason? Are you looking to invest?"

That would be a big fat no. I'd already been there one too many times. "No, but I guess I'm curious as to what all the fuss is about. I'm also going to share the info with Bree since I know she has an interest in what happens with the property."

His gaze combined elements of concern and curiosity, but he nodded his head. "I'll start the search today and email you the results."

"Thanks. Just send a bill for that along with your time today."

He smiled. "Always happy to oblige a paying customer. Thanks, Lilly. Have a nice day."

* * *

When my dinner break finally arrived, I decided to call Tanner. He would be home from school now. After a few rings, he answered. "Hey, Lilly. How's things?"

"Hey. Sorry if I'm bothering you. I just wanted to hear your voice."

"Everything ok?"

"One of the potential investors in town for the auction was murdered yesterday."

"Shitzu, that's not good. Do they know who did it?"

I totally loved and adored that he'd adopted my replacements for the curse words. Personally, he didn't have anything against cursing, but he did it out of respect for my gram. She would've loved him too. "Not yet, but Detective Pizza Guy is hot on the case."

His chuckle made me smile. "And how do you know that?" He paused for just a split second before continuing, not even giving me a chance to respond. "Tell me you're not involved."

Ugh, this was not where I wanted this conversation to go. "I hired your security replacement."

"Don't think I don't know what you're doing here. I'll play along for now though."

"Just because you're curious," I teased as I leaned back in my chair and closed my eyes.

"I am curious. He better not be hotter than me."

"Well, the person has beautiful chocolate drop eyes, long dark hair, and moves that have already put two men in their place."

Now he was laughing. "So even if *she* is hotter, I don't have to worry. That's what you're telling me."

"I'm telling you Sam seems to be amazing." I noticed the ever-growing pile of paperwork on the corner of my desk.

"Just seems to be?" The tone of his voice hinted more than idle curiosity. He was diving deep.

"I'm doing the background check."

"I hope one that costs more than twenty-five dollars."

"That lesson has been learned. I'm going to secure a full report. My confidence is just a little shaky. This part-owner stuff carries a lot more responsibility than just serving up drinks. You know I didn't go to college."

"Are you feeling left out since Mandi and Freddie are going to college?"

He didn't hit my insecurity nail on the head, but he was pounding close by. "Do you think I should go to college? Business school?"

"I think you've done an amazing job managing the tavern while Hope is gone. I also know she is an excellent judge of character. She wouldn't have offered you part ownership if she didn't think you could handle it. If *you* want to go back to college, then I think you should. You gotta do what makes you happy. Except breaking up with me—that's off the table completely."

This. This was why I'd finally taken the leap and made him my boyfriend. He always knew exactly what I needed to hear. "Thanks. I appreciate the advice and support. I should probably get back to work." I might have also been avoiding answering his previous question about my involvement with the murder.

"We'll talk tonight. That should give you time to get your story straight with Mandi or Bree or whoever else you might have been with when you managed to get yourself into trouble again."

I half expected him to finish the sentence with "young lady" or some other dad-like response. He liked to fuss at me about my involvement about as much as Detective Marshall. Though I enjoyed Tanner's fussing a little more. But he knew me. Knew me and still loved me. That had to count for something. "Love you."

"Love you."

I was just about to head out to the bar to finish out the evening, when the phone rang. "Smugglers' Tavern, this is Lilly."

"Hey, Lilly, it's Vernon."

"Oh hi. Are you coming in this evening? We're closing in about an hour, but for you I'd keep the kitchen open."

"I appreciate that, but Ruby is home from her retreat, so it's back to tofu and tapas for me." The last words left his mouth with a tone of distaste. I couldn't blame him. Though I enjoyed some tapas, tofu and I had yet to become friends.

If he wasn't calling to place an order, that meant something must have developed in the case. "Did you hear something from the coroner?"

"They can't be certain until tests results come back from Seattle, but they're pretty sure Camilla was hit on the head with a smooth, probably round object."

"Did that kill her?"

"Still determining. If that did come first, not too hard for the killer to finish the job. Suffocating an unconscious victim is much easier. They don't tend to fight as much."

Or at all.

"Thanks for letting me know."

"No problem, kiddo."

The thought that someone was possibly roaming around Danger Cove who was capable of knocking someone in the head and then suffocating them lodged a lump in the center of my throat. We could wait for official results, but that sequence of events was the one that made the most (and terrifying) sense. I swallowed hard and tried to think happy thoughts. "Sure thing, Vernon. This is one situation I want to stay as far away from as possible."

For the first time in a long time, I truly meant that.

CHAPTER EIGHT

———

It was after eleven by the time I arrived at my home. It wasn't much, but it had been considered a move in the right direction by all my friends when my lease ended at Hazlitt Heights. Blake Glover of Glover Rentals had scoured the coast to find me a nice little place to call my own. After an exhaustive search, he'd struck gold. A cute little two-bedroom home, painted sky blue, complete with a porch and white railing. I'd even splurged and put a glider out front. Occasionally, Tanner and I had a few moments on Sunday to relax before he headed back to Seattle and I headed into work. Since I was on the other side of Danger Cove now, too far away to ride my bike, at least at night, I was grateful for my cherry red moped. Other than that, all the furniture and decorations remained the same as they were in my one-bedroom apartment—which made the house look very, very empty.

A long shower did nothing to ease my mind. Every time I closed my eyes in an effort to relax, images of Camilla's body filtered through, along with what the last few moments of her life must have been like. I crawled under the quilt my great-grandmother had made and tried to read a romantic comedy. My eyelids had just started to descend, when I heard a noise that sounded like someone had knocked something over in my backyard. Usually my neighborhood was very quiet. I was probably the rowdiest one here, and that was only when the gang from the tavern was over for pizza.

My heart rate started beating in an allegro rhythm, fast but not too fast. My moderately successful rock star father had made it a goal of his to teach me one new musical term when we spoke on the phone each week. He would be proud I remembered, even though I admit to being more than a little scared at the moment. Fishing through my purse, I managed to find the Mace. The flashlight was by the back door. Have I mentioned how much of a Boy Scout my boyfriend is? He considered it his job to help me safe-proof my new home and be prepared for multiple eventualities. Right now, I was very thankful for his thoroughness.

Because I was on the outskirts of town, streetlights were few and far between. Even if there had been one in the front yard, I wasn't sure it would have had enough illumination to do anything more than cast eerie shadows. Definitely didn't need or want that. I slipped through the sliding glass door as quietly as possible, keeping the beam of light low and willing my heart rate to slow. Maybe I'd learn the word for that next week.

The backyard wasn't big, just enough for a picnic table and grill—not that I would ever use a grill. The trash cans sat over to one side. My adrenaline paused for a moment as I realized I hadn't put my garbage cans out last week to be emptied by the garbage company. The fear ratcheted up a notch as I heard more sounds of scratching and rustling from over there.

My curiosity warred with my fear. Part of me wanted to go inside, lock the door, and call Mandi to come over and spend the night so I wouldn't be alone. The other side of me told me to stop being a chicken and go find out what it was. That side, of course, won the battle. Curiosity always won out with me. Something I should probably work on. Moving on tiptoes to aid in my quiet approach, I ninja'd my way across the yard until I was only a foot or so away. I lifted the beam of light, and two demonic green eyes met me.

I screamed.

The owner of the eyes meowed and took a leap from the top of the can squarely in my direction. Something tiny and sharp scratched my skin, making me drop both the Mace and the flashlight in order to have my hands free to grab the body of fur currently fastened to my chest.

Apparently not wanting to go down without a fight, the cat twisted and turned, trying to evade my grasp. I tucked the animal in a better hold against my chest—paws and claws secured. The moment I made the transition, the cat calmed and snuggled further into my embrace. Awww, now why did he or she have to go and do that? "Hey, you, what brings you into my yard?"

The low growl didn't come from the cat's mouth, but rather its stomach. "Meow."

"You're hungry. I bet my full trash can called to you with its smelly siren song, didn't it?"

"Meow."

Don't tell Tanner, but I might have just fallen in love. "Let's get you inside and rustle up some tuna. Lucky for you, I'm not much of a chef, and tuna salad is one of my favorite dinners."

I adjusted the cat and grabbed the flashlight. I'd have to come back for the Mace. Once inside, I filled a bowl with water and put some tuna on a small plate. While I made dinner, the cat—my cat—was investigating. I watched from the corner of my eye the blur of orange as he methodically visited every corner and over, under, and around what few pieces of furniture were in the living room. I sat the plate and bowl down by the back door. All investigation stopped as he darted to the food. The way he inhaled the tuna reminded me of Freddie on his lunch break. I swear I'd never seen anyone eat quite so fast.

He was about halfway through the tuna when he stopped. His ears perked up, and he stared at the door. "Meow."

This meow sounded different from the others. This was a *hey, something's not right out there, and as the human, it's your job to check it out* kind of meow. Ok, technically I didn't speak cat, but his body language told me all I needed to know.

When I didn't move right away, the meow moved into a low growl. Maybe this cat was part dog? "Ok, ok. I'll go check it out." I grabbed the flashlight and fought the urge to hit myself over the head with it when I realized the Mace was still outside. Out there with whoever had my cat all riled up. I was going to have to name him, but that would have to wait.

I turned the living room light off. No sense in letting whoever was out there know I was coming. I was already at a distinct disadvantage. Tanner would be disappointed in my lack of preparedness. I looked down at the cat, staring out into the darkness, his bushy tail still evident in the dim lighting from the kitchen. "You got my six, right?"

No response. Not even a little meow. Guess he figured he'd done his job with the early warning system. I was on my own for the actual encounter. "Ok, tuna is on the top shelf. Good luck with that."

Still nothing. He and I were going to have to work on our communication. Delay tactics over. Time to face the music. I slid open the door once again but didn't close it all the way. Just in case the cat decided to put those claws to good use. *Note to self: clean the wounds on my chest and arms and put triple antibiotic on them before bed.*

I made my way to the back of the yard, once again by the trash cans. They looked untouched. Absently, I wondered if there were any wild animals besides cats running around these parts. The beam of the light stayed low, guiding my feet and looking for the Mace. The prize had just come into illumination, when I heard a deep voice. "Don't be scared, Lilly."

Nice try, but it didn't work. I started to run toward the house, but the long arms of my intruder caught me before I managed three steps. My mouth opened automatically to allow the surging scream a route for escape. The captor must have sensed my next move, and rough, weathered hands covered my lips. "Please. Don't yell. It's me, Billy Nester. We met the other night."

My body tried to relax at this news, but my brain sent out every warning klaxon known to man to fight as muscle memory kicked in from a self-defense class Mandi and I had taken together at her mother's insistence.

With a long exhale, I let my body go limp. The action had the desired effect, and I slid right out of his hold. The moment I hit the ground, the flashlight became my weapon of choice, and I swung it hard against his shin. That created distance between us as he hopped backward out of the swing arc of my arm. "Why'd you go and do that? I di'n mean you no harm."

Finding my feet, I managed to stand and direct the beam of light at his face. The guilt vise wrapped itself tightly around my heart as I took in his appearance. The wrinkles sagged around his dirty face, and the pain-laced despair in his gaze nearly stopped my breathing. If he was a murderer, he was the saddest one I'd ever met. "I'm sorry…" I knew I shouldn't be, as he was trespassing, but I did feel sorry. Sorry for him.

Billy's head shook slowly and waved off my apology. "I'm the one who's sorry. I wanted to talk to you outside the tavern, but you were off in another world when you left. I hate to bother folks."

Common sense kicked in, and I decided not to share with him that I'd been distracted about how Camilla had died. If he was the killer, he already knew. "What did you need?" Maybe if I dealt with him quickly and efficiently, I could get back to my scaredy-cat.

He wrung his hands and shook his head. "It's nothing."

I realized in an instant he must have been looking for food in my trash can. Compassion replaced fear. The man was down on his luck. I had no proof he'd killed Camilla or even stolen her purse. Innocent until proven guilty—that was how we rolled here in the good ol' US of A, right? "Are you hungry?"

He started to walk away. "It's not your problem. I'll be on my way. Sorry I scared you. Ain't no reason to be scared of me. Was just gonna ask for some of your scraps."

"Hold on, Billy. Come to the back porch and wait for a few minutes." Part of me wanted to give him a hug, like I had the cat, and invite him in for some food. The other part remembered all the stranger-danger lessons I'd been taught as both a child and adult. Common sense said to provide the food and don't be foolish.

"You ain't gonna call the cops, are ya?"

Valid question under the circumstances. "No, I promise. I'll be right back." I hustled inside and grabbed the to-go box Tara had prepared for me before I'd left work. It had a grilled chicken sandwich and some homemade kettle chips in it. I also grabbed a ten from my purse. Once outside again, I handed Billy the box and the cash. "It's not much, but if you're hungry, there's not much better in town than Tara and Clara's cooking. The money is for whatever you might need. I know it's not much, but I don't carry a lot of cash. Sorry."

Tears glistened in his eyes. "Thanks, Lilly. That's very kind."

Although tonight wasn't the time, I did want to ask him a little more about anything he might have seen out at Shady Pines. "I know what it's like to be hungry. I try very hard to keep that from happening to anyone I come in contact with if I can help it."

"I'll find a way to repay you. Ol' Billy's gonna be back on his feet in no time. I got a plan."

"Well, when you do get back on your feet, you just pay it forward, ok? That's all the thanks I need."

He nodded and started to walk away. "Hey, Billy?"

"Yes?"

"If you stop by the tavern tomorrow night after we close, I'll be sure to have another meal for you."

"Thanks, Lilly. I best be on my way now."

With those words, he faded into the darkness. I stood and stared into the night for a few minutes wondering if Billy truly was friend or foe? Meowing at the back door redirected my attention. Oh sure, *now* he wanted to come out. I slipped through the door, careful to not let him escape. As I scooped him into my arms, he immediately settled down. A few scratches behind the ear and he was purring with a contentment that made me more than a little jealous. Wouldn't it be nice if humans could get a little scratch on the head and moments later we'd found our center?

After a quick survey for fleas or any other evidence of nastiness, we climbed into bed. The two surges of adrenaline had left me drained. "What shall we call you?"

The cat looked up as though he understood we were about have a conversation about an important matter. "What about Tucker? He owns One Man's Trash, and I found you on my trash can."

"Mee-ooo-www." The sound conveyed very clearly he didn't want that to be his name.

As I considered the events of the day and what I knew about the cat, I gazed into his eyes. He obviously liked to investigate, and he'd sensed danger before I did. The memory of the grumpy real estate agent, Adam Miller, accusing me of trying to be Sherlock Holmes, floated to the surface. Oh, I was going to show him a Sherlock Holmes like he'd never seen before. If he was hiding anything, I was going to find out.

If I was going to be Holmes, then my cat... "How about Watson? What do you think of that?"

He purred loudly and circled a spot on the bed a few times before plopping down right against my thighs. "Meow."

Watson it was. Tonight we would sleep. Tomorrow, Sherlock Holmes and Watson would be on the case.

CHAPTER NINE

———

Truth time. I totally hated leaving Watson to go to work on Thursday morning. Was this how parents felt when they left their babies at day care for the first time? Since my mom was definitely not typical mother material, I wasn't sure I could accurately judge, as she'd never shared what her emotions were the day she'd dropped me off at my gram's and headed off to tour the United States with the love of her life.

I decided I'd leave Watson with some parting instructions. No time like the present to work on our communication. "Ok, I've left you a plate of tuna. I promise to find some cat food for you—tuna flavor if you prefer—soon. I'm also going to need to get you to a vet for a checkup. I've already grown quite fond of you, but you should know I hate bugs. So we need to make sure you aren't harboring any little stowaways. Also, if you are an able hunter and could find and dispose of any multi-legged creatures in the house, that would be most appreciated."

Watson managed to lift his head, barely, from the pillow on the couch. "Meow."

I took that as a yes. It was either that or a *will you please go to work so I can catch up on my cat naps?* kind of reply. We'd go with a yes.

* * *

When I arrived at work, everyone was already getting started for the day.

"Little late, aren't you, Boss Lady?" Mandi teased as she handed me a cup of tea.

"If by late, you mean on time, then yes." I took a sip of the tea. Mandi and I were the non-coffee drinkers, so we looked out for each other and always made sure hot water stood at the ready in case of an emergency, we were thirsty, or just wanted to enjoy the finest caffeinated beverage around. "Thanks for the tea. Perfect as always."

"You're welcome. So why are you on time today?"

"I had some visitors in my backyard last night."

My statement got Mandi's full attention. "Oh? What kind of visitors?"

"One was a friend. The other I'm not sure about." I should just come right out and tell her, but somehow forming the words to explain I was within a foot or so of a potential murderer whom I gave my dinner to didn't sound reasonable.

"Tell me about the one you aren't sure about first." Mandi's keen gaze narrowed in as she sensed the importance of what I was about to share.

I gestured for her to follow me into the office, and I shut the door. No one else needed to hear this. "You know that Bree and I were at Shady Pines earlier this week."

Mandi nodded, but said nothing.

"While we were there, we met a man named Billy Nester. He's apparently down on his luck and was sleeping in one of the rooms downstairs. We exchanged pleasantries, and then Bree and I left to check out the rest of the motel. A few minutes later is when we discovered Camilla's body."

The firm line of Mandi's mouth had opened in what I guessed was a mix of shock, surprise, disbelief…the list goes on. "Do you think he killed Camilla?"

I shrugged my shoulders. "I don't want to believe that he did, but…"

"But what?"

A sigh escaped as I realized how stupid my actions last night were with regard to personal safety. "But when we came back downstairs to leave, Billy was gone."

Mandi leaned back in the chair, one hand covering her mouth as her head shook. "And this man was in your backyard last night?"

"Yes."

"What did he want?"

"Food. He was hungry."

Her expression softened somewhat. "Did you give him any?"

I nodded. "Along with the cash I had in my purse so he could get whatever else he might need."

Several moments of silence stretched between us as she processed everything I'd shared. "You know he had opportunity. He had to have been there."

For some unknown reason, I wanted to defend Billy—or at least my belief in Billy's innocence. "That still leaves means and motive. I don't think he and Camilla ran in the same circles. And, we still don't know the cause of death."

"True, but even if there is a chance he's the killer, you don't need to be hanging out with him. I know you want to help, but, Lilly…"

My hands went up in defense. "I know. I know. Right now, can we keep this between the two of us?" I also knew that now wasn't the time to mention I'd invited him back to the tavern tonight for some more food. "Now that we've got my poor judgment out of the way, don't you want to hear about my new friend? He's very cute."

My desire to lighten the mood and direct attention away from my lack of discernment prompted my decision to tease Mandi a little. Her gaze snapped to mine. "Does Tanner know about this new *friend*?"

The way she stressed the word *friend* almost made me lose it. "Not yet. It was late when we got together last night, and after everything that happened with Billy, I decided to wait until he gets home tomorrow night to share."

My BFF knew me well, so I could tell by the confusion on her face that she wasn't sure how to take what I'd been dishing out. "What does he look like?"

"Well, he has the most intense green eyes, and his orange fur is fairly clean and shiny for someone who's been living outside for who knows how long. He's also very light on his feet—all four of them."

By the time I finished, she was chuckling. "Not cool, Lilly."

I stood and moved around the desk to pull her into a hug. "Probably not, but it was fun. You know I'd never cheat on Tanner."

She punched me lightly on the shoulder as she moved toward the door. "Well, if you ever do decide to cheat, you better not let me find out about it, as Tanner will be my first call."

"You know me better than that. It takes me forever to commit, but once I do…"

"Hopefully, it's for forever," Mandi finished.

I wasn't sure I was ready for that long term of a commitment, but I was happy where things were. That, in and of itself, was progress. "So now that we've cleared the air about all my late-night guests, let's head back out and get started on our morning routine.

Everyone was waiting when we returned to the kitchen.

"Was Mandi telling you she had us up early talking about that Camilla chick's murder," Freddie shared before moving aside his container of wrapped silverware.

Not only had my BFF not mentioned this, she'd spent the time asking me questions instead. "Let's head out to the dining area to finish our prep and continue this discussion."

A few moments later, we were all at our respective areas. "Ok, so what about the murder did you discuss?"

Mandi slid onto a barstool and grabbed some fruit to slice for garnish. "Well, now that we know the cause of death— sorta—we were trying to figure out who might have done it."

My curiosity prompted me to ask, "So what have you come up with?"

Freddie moved to the bottles of liquor he'd brought in earlier and started to restock the shelves. "I think it was that dude, Adam. He's got some serious anger issues. Camilla wanted the same thing he did. Maybe she said somethin' to him like she did to ol' Jack and he decided to wipe that condescending smirk off her face."

Sounded like Freddie wasn't a big fan of Camilla either. Even though I didn't have an opinion—yet—I chimed in. "Bree shared with me she thinks it might have been Jack Condor as well. She said she's never seen him as angry as he was when Camilla was taunting him." It was no secret that most of the townspeople weren't big fans of Jack Condor. Since coming to the area, he'd been trying to "upgrade" all the locations we felt made Danger Cove the cozy little place that it was, which did not go over well.

Mandi dumped the fruit into the bins while shaking her head. "No way. He's a hothead, but he's motivated by profit. He may harm someone financially or even emotionally by destroying a building they love, but I've never heard of him being physically violent."

Her statement was reasonable, but I'd also learned that everyone has a breaking point. We don't want to admit this and rarely speak of it out loud, but I believe there's at least one thing that could make a person do things they never thought they were capable of. My gram, God rest her soul, was one of the most peaceful people I've ever met. I had no doubt, though, that if someone had ever threatened to hurt me, she would've done anything in her power to prevent that. There was a reason the law contained a self-defense provision. "So who do you think could've done it, Mandi?"

Abe walked in from the kitchen about that time. Based on the perspiration beading on his forehead, I'd guess he'd just delivered some freshly picked vegetables to Tara and Clara. I poured him some iced tea and handed him a bar towel.

"I think it could've been Jessica Byers," Mandi offered.

This caught me off guard, along with Freddie. He spoke up before I could say anything. "No way. She's too hot to kill anyone."

Everyone laughed. "Pretty sure being hot isn't a defense, Freddie. You learn that in your statistics class?" Mandi teased.

"Wow, that sounds hard. What other classes are you taking, Freddie? I hope it's an easy one to go along with stats." I couldn't help but be impressed with my friends who were taking the leap to higher education.

"I'm also learning about cool programs out on the web, both good ones and bad ones, and how they influence society. Youse guys know I like that better than a bunch o' numbers that make my head hurt." His face lit up like a sugar addict in a candy store. "You gotta let me show you some of this stuff, Boss Lady. It's off the charts."

It was almost time to open, so I wanted to get everyone's opinion on this round of whodunnit. "Sure, Freddie. Sounds like fun."

Freddie smiled, "Thanks! I know you're gonna love it."

It was hard to ignore his enthusiasm for learning. I turned to Sam, who'd been quietly standing at the door, observing our conversation. "What about you, Sam?"

She smiled. "Sure, I'd love to see Freddie's way cool stuff from his class."

I grinned. "I'm sure we can include you whenever the time comes. I was referring to who you thought might be our person of interest?" It wasn't a fair question, as I had no idea what she knew about the circumstances of the murder, but I was curious to hear what she'd say.

Sam smiled. "Honest?"

"Of course, that's how we roll around here." Or at least tried to.

"I think we should let the police do their job and stay out of it. No sense asking for trouble."

Smart, but not as much fun as the guessing game we'd been playing. Abe tossed me his towel and put his glass in the dishwasher at the bar. "I think Sam is right." He turned and winked at me. "Trouble seems to find some of us anyway, doesn't it?"

I nodded. "Whether we ask for it or not. Ok, everyone, Sam and Abe are right. We need to let the police do their jobs, and Sam, if you'll do the honors of unlocking the door, we'll set about doing ours. Have a good day, everyone."

Before I could contemplate how to find out what the police were doing to solve the murder, Camilla's personal assistant, Serena, walked in. She sported a navy pencil skirt, white blouse, and a red suit jacket. A little dressy for the tavern, but maybe it felt normal to her...and I was certain she could use a little *normal* right now under the circumstances. Even in the dim lighting of the bar, I could see the forlorn look on her face. I had no idea how close she and Camilla had been, but this whole ordeal couldn't have been easy on her, even if they only had an employer-employee relationship.

"Good afternoon, Serena. Can I get you something to drink?"

At the mention of her name, she glanced up, and her face registered a small spark. "You remembered my name?"

I shrugged and smiled. "I always appreciate when people remember my name, so I try to return the favor. Plus, Gram always said it was important, and she was one of the smartest people I knew."

The dark cloud over her features lightened the tiniest of bits. "She must have been very proud of you. I understand you're part owner of the tavern."

The skin on the back of my neck prickled at her comment, forcing the tiny hairs to straighten. Why would she know about the ownership of the tavern? Why would she care? I decided to play it cool. "I certainly hope so."

I put a glass of water in front of her. "May I ask you a question?"

"Besides my order?" Serena smiled.

"Oh yes, what would you like?" Service then snooping, that was the proper order.

"Burger and fries, vodka and cranberry. Make the vodka a double. It's been a difficult day dealing with all the details after Camilla's death, including giving my statement at the police station."

I entered the order and made her drink. Once she had a chance to enjoy a couple sips, I resumed the snooping portion of my job description. Oh, it was in there—fine print…at the bottom.

Before I could ask, Serena sat her half-empty glass down. "Camilla almost always had me check out the businesses in an area she's looking to invest in."

Since she'd volunteered the information, I decided to try to get all my questions answered. "Why?"

"In case she wanted to acquire additional property. It's business, not personal."

Serena had said the same words to Jack that first night I'd seen her. I wasn't sure if it was to convince herself or the people she was talking to. This certainly felt personal to me. Hope and I loved Smugglers' Tavern and would never sell, especially not to an outsider who didn't appreciate the town and its people as much as we did. "If you say so. How'd it go at the police station?"

She hesitated for a moment, but after another sip, she answered. "It went ok. I gave them the list of possible suspects I'd prepared."

She prepared? Guess she *did* make her living as a personal assistant—making lists were probably under the skills section of her résumé. "Always good to be prepared. We were discussing earlier who we thought might be capable of doing such a terrible thing. Can I ask who made the top of your list?" I had no idea if she'd answer, but she'd been fairly forthcoming, so worth a shot.

Abe brought out a plate of food and set it in front of Serena. "Here you go, young lady." He touched my arm before heading back into the kitchen and gestured for me to follow him.

I double-checked that Serena had everything she needed, as well as my other patrons, and then stepped through the double doors. "What's up, Abe?"

He pointed to my office. "Phone for you. It's Ms. Milford."

Bree calling me in the middle of the workday? That couldn't be good. She knew I kept my cell phone on silent unless I was on break or out running errands. This had to be very important if she called the office phone. "Ok, thanks, Abe. Can you keep an eye on the bar for a few?"

"Of course."

I took a few deep breaths before answering. "Hello?"

"It took you long enough!" Bree's irritation came through the phone crystal clear. This set my heart to racing, as Bree rarely got irritated and never, that I could remember, at me.

"Sorry. I had to take care of a couple customers before I could get back here. What's wrong?"

"Detective Pizza Guy is on his way to Ocean View to provide me an escort to the station for questioning."

Shitzu. Guess I now had the answer to who was at the top of Serena's list. I wondered if she'd mentioned Jack or not. From the way she tried to console him after Camilla's taunting, it appeared she had a sweet spot for him despite her employer's lack of fondness for the man. "What do you need me to do?"

"Can you send Mandi over to watch the front desk? I'm expecting a new guest this afternoon, and I can't be sure I'll be back in time. I know it's asking a lot…"

She also knew I'd move heaven and earth to help her out. She, Mandi, and I did what we could to support each other. I knew my boyfriend Tanner's younger sister wouldn't mind helping out. "Of course, no problem."

"Thanks. I'll keep you posted."

"Are you going to mention the interaction between Jack and Camilla that first night at the tavern?" It was a fair question. I might consider sharing that info with them if the situation were reversed. My guess was once they learned Bree and I had both been in the motel the night Camilla was killed, they'd bring me in for questioning just for old times' sake. They might think I had a motive if Camilla had also looked into possibly making an offer on the tavern.

The audible sigh told me she'd run over that same question a time or two since she'd received the call. "No, I don't think so. He's a jerk. I can't stand him, but that's not who I am. If the police can't figure out he had as much, if not more, motive than me, then the good Lord help us all."

Bree was good people, no doubt about it. "Agreed." I hesitated for a moment.

"What?"

"You may not throw the police the Jack bone, but if it comes down to you or him, I'm going to use my good arm and toss him into the ring as best I can." I know I'd mixed my metaphors. I couldn't stand by and let my friend get railroaded just because Serena may (and I shuddered at the thought) have feelings for Jack. Her list, in my opinion, wouldn't be much of a list without his name near the top.

"Thanks, Lilly. I'll call later."

I hoped she could call me later. "If you use me for your one phone call, don't worry. I'll call Attorney Pohoke for you."

"If I only get one call, I'm calling Uncle Eddie. He can stage a prison break for me."

She laughed, but I could tell she didn't like being in this position. Heck, no one would. I certainly didn't. "Tell him I'll furnish the tequila!"

We disconnected the call. I went ahead and texted Tanner's sister, Ashley, to ask her to come in until closing time. She had proven a great asset to the tavern. She filled in whenever we needed some extra hands. Hopefully, Mandi would be back long before then, but best to be prepared.

I took a few more deep breaths before heading back to the bar. It might have helped a little. One final long exhale before stepping through the doors. "Thanks, Abe. I can take it from here. Appreciate your helping out."

"No problem. Ms. Serena here was telling me she'd been working for Ms. Cartwright since college."

"Wow, you must've had some great connections." Since most of my experience was at bars and fast food, up until my introduction to Smugglers' Tavern, those types of opportunities hadn't really come my way. I was ok with that.

I noticed my BFF heading toward the bar. I needed to get her over to the Ocean View as soon as possible so Bree wouldn't worry. Before Serena could tell me about her job history, I added, "If you'll excuse me for a minute."

I caught Mandi at the silverware station with a fresh batch of utensils. "Can you head over to Ocean View? Bree needs you to cover for a bit."

The smile on her face fell faster than Freddie's bangs when he ran out of hair gel. "Bree's in trouble, isn't she?"

"The police just want to ask her some questions. No way did she do this, so we have to trust it will all work out."

Mandi nodded and looked around the room. "You'll be ok here?"

"Ashley is coming in to cover. We'll be fine. Bree said she's expecting a guest. I'm sure she'll leave the details for you if she happens to be gone before you get there." I reached into my pocket and pulled out the keys to my moped. "Here, take my ride. It'll be faster."

"Thanks, Lilly."

Without another word, she headed out the back to grab her things and be on her way.

Freddie came over. "Everything ok with Mandi?"

The chocolate in his eyes darkened as he asked the question. Though they'd never officially dated, between going to school together and hanging out a lot in their free time, I suspected he had feelings for her that went beyond coworkers and even friends. They'd figure it out eventually. "She's fine. Bree needs her to cover for a bit. Ashley's on her way in."

He nodded. "Gotcha. I'll watch the tables and help out wherever needed until she gets here. Don't worry, Boss Lady."

"Thanks, Freddie. You're the best."

By the time I made it back to the bar, Serena was doling out cash for her check.

I gave her the change she was due. "How long are you planning on staying in Danger Cove?"

"The police want me to stay at least a few more days in case they have any follow-up questions. One of Camilla's associates is due in today. He is going to monitor the situation with the auction and determine if a bid is still necessary."

I remembered Adam saying Camilla didn't have associates, only people who owed her favors. Made me wonder what she might have had on this person. "Will he or she be staying here in Danger Cove?"

Serena's gaze darted around the room before narrowing to settle on me. She cocked her head to the side. "What difference will that make?"

My smile was meant to put her at ease again. "None at all. Just wanted to extend an invitation for a meal here if they were going to be close by." I also wanted to meet this person and maybe ask a few questions, but that information wasn't necessary to share with Serena.

The wary expression on her face relaxed as she nodded. "I'll be sure to extend the invitation."

"Thanks. Hope you can enjoy the rest of your stay. Come visit us again soon."

A short time later, Ashley arrived. She wore her normal faded, ripped jeans along with a dark T-shirt. Her jewelry caught my attention. "Hey, Ashley, thanks for coming in. That's some interesting bling you've got on your ears."

She rolled her eyes at me. "By interesting, I take it to mean something you wouldn't be caught dead in."

The dangling earrings resembled a small cluster of tiny balls with silver leaves. Hot pink dots adorned each blue orb. It worked for her. "Not my style, but they look good on you."

She laughed and waved off my comment. "Fair enough. Where do you need me?"

I wanted to put my newly ill-gotten LexisNexis credentials to use and then try to check on Bree. "I need to catch up on some paperwork. Can you and Freddie handle things on your own for a bit?"

She nodded. "Go. Do your manager thing. Freddie and I got this. Right, dude?"

Freddie looked up from the table he was clearing with a grin and nod. "Dude."

How sweet. Pet names—or something. Anyway, they had the dining room covered. I just needed an interim bartender. I motioned to Sam to join me. "How's it going?"

Sam grinned. "Pretty rowdy for a Thursday evening, I think."

I loved that she felt comfortable enough to joke around with me. I decided to tease a little in return. "Hopefully you won't have to use one of those fancy moves on any of our regulars."

"Let's hope that's never necessary." She took a cursory glance around the room.

I liked how vigilant she remained, even on what we both knew was a slow security night.

Once her gaze returned to me, she asked. "Did you need something or just realize I needed a break from boredom due to this well-behaved crowd you've got here?"

"Actually, I have some forms and data entry that require my attention. Your résumé didn't mention bartending skills, but I figured it couldn't hurt to ask."

"I bartended during the summers when I was in college. I'm rusty but can hold my own for a little while as long as you're close by to field the tough ones."

I removed my apron and handed it to her. The way she held it out with two fingers and the look of disdain on her face made me think she was about as domestic as I was. "You'll thank me if it keeps from getting cherry juice on those cute white jeans of yours."

Sam chuckled. "Aprons are practical, just not flattering."

She slipped the flower-trimmed black apron around her petite waist. While not a normal accessory for security, Sam pulled it off with flair. Remembering her initials, I decided to try them out as a nickname. "Not bad, SOS. Not bad."

She laughed. "Hey, save the code for a real emergency. We don't want to invite bad juju."

Couldn't argue with that logic. "You're right. We'll save that nickname for emergencies. Ok, I'll be back in about fifteen."

In the kitchen, I grabbed some tea, iced this time, before heading outside to my favorite bench. I knew it was probably too soon for there to be any updates, but I wanted to reach out to Bree just in case. I sipped the tea as I dialed her number. As I suspected, it went straight to voicemail.

Hi, it's Bree. Leave me a message...and no, I won't pass anything along to my mom. Stop enabling her disregard for technology. Thanks.

Her message made me chuckle despite the seriousness of the moment. "Hey, Bree, It's Lilly. Call me back and let me know what's going on. If I don't hear from you in the next hour, I'm calling Uncle Eddie and we're planning a jail break. And calling your mother!"

Since my phone was already out, I decided to take another look at the one photo I'd taken at the crime scene. Maybe there was something there that could help Bree get released.

It only took a few moments of scrolling through photos of Watson to find the one with the words scrawled on Camilla's hand.

I studied them intently for several minutes. *skinny.punt.older.* Honestly, what kind of message was that?

"What are you focused on, young lady? It better be cat videos and not half-naked men." Abe's teasing voice startled my concentration.

"What? No, too much going on." I handed Abe my phone. "Here, see for yourself. This is what has captured my attention the last few minutes."

His long, angled nose scrunched up in an adorable fashion before he handed my phone back to me. "If I didn't know better, I'd say that's a picture of one recently deceased Camilla Cartwright."

"You're right, but how could you tell that just from the picture of her hand and arm?"

Abe took my phone again and enlarged the picture. He pointed to her bracelet. "I remembered the bracelet. In my gambling days, I learned to notice all the details. And"—he shrugged—"I might have bought my fair share of jewelry back in the day." He grinned and then pointed to Camilla's wrist. "That bracelet is from Tiffany, their HardWear collection, if I'm not mistaken. Probably runs over three grand."

The surprise on my face was genuine. "Abe, you are a man of many talents. I had no idea." My surprise morphed to confusion.

"What? Surprised this old man has a few tricks up his sleeve?"

I shook my head and smiled. "Nothing about you surprises me anymore. I'd originally thought robbery-gone-bad might have been the motive for killing her, since her purse was gone, but no thief worth their merit would have left the bracelet behind."

Abe nodded. "A rookie thief might, not realizing its value. Or maybe he or she was in a hurry and didn't have time to grab the jewelry."

"You're right. That's possible. It's also possible this wasn't money motivated."

"Lilly, my dear, most things in this world are money motivated in one way or another. Sometimes it's just not as obvious as a designer purse or jewelry." He pointed to the three words *skinny.punt.older* on the picture. "Any idea what that means?"

"Not a clue." I sighed.

"Have you asked the Google about it?"

I giggled at Abe's question. "*The* Google?"

He shrugged. "Technology and I aren't on the best of terms. Besides, you knew what I meant. Have you typed those words in the... What is it called?"

"Search engine?"

"Yes, that's it."

"Not yet, but I will." I typed the words separately and hit Search on my phone. Within seconds four hundred eighty-four thousand results appeared. Fantastic. That would take all night. I read the first result to Abe. "How thin is too thin when you get older?"

"I'll let you know when I actually get older." He laughed.

"You're never getting old!"

"What's next?"

"Eeeww! Something called skinny granny videos."

Abe leaned over with interest. The moment he saw that caption belonged to a site that started with an *X*, he backed away. "I don't think that's it."

I closed out the browser. "It's ridiculous, and I have other things that require my attention. Thanks for the company, Abe." I leaned over and bumped my shoulder to his. "Let me know if you want me to send you the link to those granny videos."

"Lilly!" His face flushed with embarrassment.

I laughed all the way back to my office. At the computer, I brought up the website for LexisNexis and entered my ill-gotten username and password. First, I typed in Samantha's name and brought out the file with her résumé. The employment history matched, with her last employer being a jewelry store in Everett, Louisiana. I looked up the number and dialed.

After a few rings, a woman answered. "Jewels Fit for a Queen, this is Sally. How can I assist you today?"

"Hi, Sally, my name is Lilly Waters. I'm calling to do a reference check on Samantha Sheraton."

There was a long pause. "She listed us?"

Technically, she hadn't. "I apologize. I'm new at this. I believe it's called verifying employment."

"The owner isn't here right now. She will have to pull the file and call you back with the exact date she…left."

My face twisted into a grimace. I really liked Sam, but depending on the reason she *left*, it could change everything. There was something in Sally's voice that made me hope she wanted to say more. I forced a quiet breath to calm my nerves and planted a smile on my face. "No worries. I'm just trying to wrap up my paperwork. Were you there when Sam quit?"

I heard a door shut. "She didn't quit. They fired her. It was about a month ago," Sally whispered.

"I appreciate your telling me, Sally. I promise this stays between us. Will you tell me why they fired her? Sometimes personalities clash, and it's no one's fault really..."

The silence stretched as I waited for an answer. I could almost envision her pacing as she decided how much to tell me. Finally she spoke. "Sam's good people. I never believed she had anything to do with the missing diamonds."

"Diamonds were stolen?"

"We believe so, yes. We import our loose diamonds from Canada. Sam was responsible for overseeing the transfer and securing them in the safe. When an inventory count was done, a few were missing."

"Did they charge her with the crime?" I hadn't got that far in my search yet, but Sally could save me some time.

"Of course not. She didn't do it!" Her voice registered indignation. There was a long exhale. "Sorry. Sam was—is a friend of mine. I hated she had to leave."

"So even though she wasn't officially charged, she was responsible for security."

"Exactly. You have to believe me that there's no way Sam dropped the ball. I don't know what happened, but Sam is innocent. Give her a chance."

"You're a good friend, Sally. Thank you for sharing the information you did."

I disconnected the call and leaned back in my chair. I'd have to ask Sam about it. If she stole the diamonds, why only a small amount? Sally had said a "few," which wasn't an exact number but implied less than several—however many *that* was. Maybe Sam thought they wouldn't notice? Didn't seem likely, but it was all I could come up with at the moment.

Speaking of Sam, I needed to get out there and relieve her of bar duty. My research of the other real estate agents would have to wait until later.

My favorite member of the police force, Officer Richie Faria, was sitting at the bar. I nodded at Sam. "Thanks for helping out. I'll take it from here." I put a soda in front of him. As a complete opposite to Detective Pizza Guy, Faria was lean, despite his love of chocolate chip cookies. Maybe because they were the only sweets he really liked. His hair was blonder than mine (I'm sure that's because his was natural), and he stood about four or five inches taller than me. Overall, your average boy-next-door kinda guy. Today, his appearance was a little frazzled. "Afternoon, Officer. Can I get you something to eat and ask for some advice?"

He rubbed his head and sighed. "Sure, Lilly, as long as it doesn't take too long. I need to get my turkey burger and parmesan fries to go."

"Of course. Should I ask Tara to throw in a couple cookies for you?"

At the mention of his favorite, the corner of his mouth inched upward just the slightest. "Yeah, that'd be great. Thanks."

After I put in the order and refilled his glass, he lifted his hand and waved it like he was gesturing for me to continue. "Ok, out with it. What advice do you need?"

He really was in a hurry. Usually we'd take our time with conversation, especially when I was looking for info. "I need to ask someone a difficult question, but I'm not sure the best way to go about it. I really like this person, but depending on their answer, it could change things."

Faria's head shook. "No disrespect, Lilly, but I don't want to get involved in matters between you and Tanner."

"What?" I wasn't sure who was more surprised—me or him. "This isn't about Tanner."

His lips parted, and a huge breath escaped before he smiled. "Whew, ok. I know you and I are friends, but I thought that was going too far." He took another drink of his soda. "To answer your question, I've found the direct approach is the best. Sincere, honest, and straight to the point. You know me. I don't like to play games."

He was right. Anytime he'd had to question me, that had been his approach. "Fair enough. I'll go with that plan. Thank you."

"No problem. Wish everything was that easy." He used the palm of his hand under his chin to turn his head. I could hear the bones in his neck crack. Figured I'd try the approach he'd suggested on for size. "You wanna talk about it? As a bartender, I'm licensed by the state."

"You're a licensed therapist?" The question was asked along with an arched eyebrow.

My chuckle transformed his frown into a nice smile. "No, just licensed to dispense alcohol. However, after years behind a bar, you pick up a thing or two just from listening to people."

"You are a good listener. I'll give you that." His expression showed him lost in contemplation. What he was thinking about, I had no clue. Direct and to the point, here we go. "Things not going well with the investigation?"

He leaned in. "You could say that."

I could, and technically I did. My hope had been he would say more. "Serena was in earlier and said she gave a statement. That had to help."

His glare told me I could be tiptoeing into none-of-my-business territory, but he'd told me to be direct, so I was simply following instructions.

"It provided some possible suspects," he admitted with the return of his frown.

I returned his glare, as he and I both knew one of my besties was being questioned as a result. "You and I both know Bree didn't do it."

"We have to question the people who have motive. You know the drill."

I knew it, but that didn't mean I had to like it. "As long as you question *everyone* who did. From what I've picked up, that list of people should keep you and the rest of Danger Cove's finest busy for a while."

"Are you trying to help my headache or make it worse?"

A pang of compassion surfaced. I knew the police were doing their job. I had to believe that the justice process would see Bree released sooner, rather than later. "Sorry. You know how protective I can get. You've shared you're focusing on the motive, but what about the means? That's one of those three items necessary to convict someone, isn't it?"

"Don't go all *Law & Order* on me, but yes, that's part of the process."

"So knowing what killed her could help narrow your large suspect pool, right? I also heard through the town grapevine there was some blunt force trauma involved."

This time he rolled his shoulders to relieve the pressure. "Who told you that?"

"I have to protect my sources." I shared the info with a small smile and a shrug. Vernon was really my only source. That made it extra critical to protect him from getting into any trouble and subsequently cutting me off from the info stream.

When he didn't add anything right away, I decided to prompt him. "It can't be easy to narrow down which blunt object was used. Kind of like finding a needle in a haystack."

His head shook. "Worse. Like trying to find a needle in a stack of needles. The processing of the crime scene and possible objects at Shady Pines provides more needles than a sewing convention."

"Or the killer could've taken whatever it was with him."

His head snapped up, and his mouth twisted. "Don't remind me. One step at a time. A witness would really help, but those seem to be in short supply too. Your source doesn't happen to have any they could share, do they?"

Clara brought his food out. "Here you go. Hope you like it."

Faria smiled. "Always do. Thanks."

He paid his bill and started to get up. "Richie, wait." I gestured for him to join me at the end of the bar by the server station.

"What's up?" He leaned closer, already suspecting I had something to share that other ears shouldn't hear.

"Let me check with my source, see if they know anything else I can share."

"I don't want you to get involved. Just let us handle it, please."

His frustration over their lack of progress made me want to tell him about my being at Shady Pines the night Camilla died and the fact that Billy might have witnessed something. Once Bree was released, I'd talk it over with her and determine the best way to proceed. Faria sensed my hesitation. "Do you know something you're not telling me?" His gaze was direct but held a hint of compassion and concern.

"Does it sound crazy to say I'm not sure?"

He continued, "Just tell me. Whatever it is, we'll figure it out together. I've always had your back, haven't I?"

He was right. He had. "Ok, here goes. Please don't be angry at me, and remember you asked me to tell you."

Faria nodded, but I could see the frustration lines marring his normally smooth forehead. I exhaled slowly and shared. "I met someone who may have been at Shady Pines on the first floor when everything went down with Camilla."

His gaze narrowed. "How do you know this person wasn't the murderer?"

Case in point, I didn't. "I don't think he is, but I can't say for sure. He's homeless right now and is coming by the tavern tonight at closing time for some food. What if you meet me here right before then, and I'll introduce you." I gestured to his attire. "Maybe lose the uniform. Seeing a cop may spook him."

"I'll do as you ask this time, as it may be the only lead we have. Heck, he may be the killer. Bottom line, I need him to talk to me rather than you. After this, you stay out of it. Deal?"

He was asking a lot since Bree was at the top of their suspect list. If nothing else, I'd supply him with a few more names of people they should talk to. People like the other real estate agents, Adam and Jessica, and even Jack Condor. Any one of them had just as much, if not more, motive than Bree. "No promises, but I'll try."

CHAPTER TEN

———

The next hour or so crept by interminably slow. We had the normal number of customers, but my mind was focused on closing time and my introducing Billy to Faria. I hoped I hadn't made an error in judgment by sharing this information. I liked Billy, and my compassionate side hurt for the hand life had currently dealt him. But the fact remained that he could be the only witness to provide any details regarding Camilla's murder. Or, as Faria pointed out, he could be the killer. Either way, I held the belief that it was my civic responsibility to connect him with Danger Cove's finest. I'd also make sure he had food. That represented my duty to mankind—to help out whenever I could.

Closing time arrived, and the small bit of sandwich I'd eaten earlier was flipping around in my stomach like a ten-year-old at a trampoline park. Faria had poked his head in and signaled to me he'd be hanging out in the beer garden at the side of the tavern. After finishing up my nightly routine at the bar, I headed into the kitchen.

Tara was wiping down the already gleaming stainless-steel workstation. "Oh hey, Lilly. The to-go box you asked for is in the fridge. I put two sandwiches in there and extra chips just as you requested." She grinned. "Tanner coming home early this week?"

I laughed but didn't answer her question. I steadfastly avoided lies of commission but was still working on the lies of omission. Who knew that little c made such a difference. Tara probably wouldn't care that the sandwiches were neither for Tanner nor me. For some reason though, I didn't tell her. Maybe it was my way of not getting her involved. I couldn't be sure.

"Thanks, Tara. I appreciate it. Why don't you head out, and I'll finish up in here."

"You sure?"

"One hundred percent." I was also one hundred percent sure I didn't want her to be in the vicinity just in case Billy didn't take kindly to meeting Officer Faria. "Would you mind heading out the front and making sure the door is locked?"

"Sure thing. See you tomorrow morning."

Once the closing tasks were completed, I checked my phone. There was a text from Mandi. Bree had finally been released from her inquisition. I shot off a quick text asking Mandi, if she wasn't too tired, to meet at my place for a debrief. I'd like to talk to Bree as well but was certain she would want to catch up on business at Ocean View and then crash for the night in her own bed.

The to-go box along with a couple bottles of water were deposited into a plastic bag while I forced the gymnasts in my stomach into a rest period. The cool night air whispered across the damp strands of blonde and brown plastered to my forehead. I must've worked up more of a sweat than I realized. Or, my nerves were responsible for the increase in moisture production. Either way, a hot shower was in order when I got home.

There was no sign of Billy, so I sat on the bench and waited. A few minutes later, the rustling of the bushes to my left triggered an eruption of pinpricks along my neck and arms. "Billy?" I offered in a stage whisper. I wanted Faria to know someone was approaching me.

"Hi ya, Lilly. Was just waiting until the coast was all clear." Billy's frame cut through the foliage with minimal effort. One hand remained behind his back, a move that put the nerves already at attention on high alert.

"Have you been here long?" Not sure why it mattered, but I was curious. And I really wanted to know what he had behind his back.

"Long enough."

I had no idea what that meant, but I wanted to give him the food, introduce him to Faria, and then get the heck out of dodge. I picked up the bag and handed it to him. He grabbed it with his free hand. "There are a couple sandwiches in there, chips, and a couple bottles of water."

His blue gray eyes glistened in the artificial lighting. "That's very kind."

A rustling noise from the side alerted Billy to Faria's presence. The gratitude in the older man's eyes turned accusatory as he took several steps back. "You set me up! I thought I could trust you."

"You can, Billy. I promise. I want to help you, and I think you might be able to help my friend Richie here."

Billy cut a glance in Faria's direction. "You police?"

Faria nodded. "Yes, but you aren't in any trouble. As a matter of fact, you may be the one person who can help us."

Nicely done, Officer. Put him at ease. Enlist his help. I started to think about Watson as Faria explained to Billy that they needed his help to learn who might have wanted to hurt Camilla. I'd just about got all my nerves back to an at-ease status, when Billy moved in my direction again. I regretted zoning out while Faria talked, as I had no idea if Billy was mad or glad at this point.

Billy set the container down on the bench. He was less than a foot away from me. The only thing keeping me in place was knowing a policeman was right there. The pounding in my heart hadn't quite gotten the full message, so it continued beating a conga rhythm against my chest. It made it hard to concentrate.

"I was gonna share this with Lilly. If she trusts you, I will too."

At that moment, he moved the hand he'd been holding behind his back around front to allow both of us to see the contents.

My gaze widened as I stared at the blunt object that could prove to be the proverbial smoking gun. The initials clearly displayed in the smooth wood left no question who this item belonged to. There, in Billy Nester's dirty hands, was Jack Condor's bat.

CHAPTER ELEVEN

————

"Billy!" I wasn't sure who was more shocked, Officer Faria or me. "Where did you get Jack's bat?"

"Whose bat?" The confusion on his face seemed genuine. "I found this in your dumpsters over there when I was scrounging for food earlier." He gestured to the bag I'd given him and blushed. "I didn' know you'd be giving me a meal fit for a king."

Faria had slipped on some latex gloves. Maybe he always carried around a pair in his pocket for situations like this. Or…maybe he knew my penchant for trouble finding me and tossed some in his jacket as a just-in-case measure. Whatever the reason, I was glad for them now. He spoke softly to Billy as he held out his hands. "Why don't you hand me the bat?"

Billy lifted the bat as though it were King Arthur's sword and he was presenting it to the Knights of the Round Table. Faria took it by the ends and shot me a look. I might not be able to read Detective Marshall—other than when his face turned red and his anger was squared directly at me—but I knew Faria. We both knew there was no way Jack would've tossed his bat unless there was very good reason to do so. *Like it was a murder weapon.*

At the thought of Jack's choice of locations for disposing of the alleged weapon, my features turned a fiery red. How dare he involve, or worse, implicate me or a member of my staff in this matter. That really pistoled me off. He could've tossed it in the ocean, and then even if it was found, the likelihood of DNA still being evident would be slim. Ugh! Why couldn't people think things through all the way? I stopped myself as I realized how ridiculous my logic was. Wanting someone to get away with murder to avoid my headaches with law enforcement… Not my finest moment.

"Billy, I'll need you to come down to the station so we can fingerprint you and use that to eliminate your prints on the bat from others that may be there."

Billy looked from Faria to me and then back to the bushes he'd emerged from. I could see the desire to run playing across his gray eyes as though they were part of an HD movie, or was it 4K that was now the best? I'd have to ask Freddie. Whether Billy was the actual murderer or not—and right now the odds were leaning toward Jack—he needed to be convinced to cooperate. I reached down and handed him the food. "I'm sure they'll let you take this with you. I've known Officer Faria for years now. He's open-minded and fair. I don't think you did this, but we need to follow the process to let the police arrive to the same conclusion. Ok?"

The old man's hands shook, and tears glistened in his eyes. I felt like a heel. And not one of those pretty, tall, slender ones that made men drool when you walked into the room. No, this was an old clog of a heel that had taken advantage of someone's situation to coerce them into showing up at your back door squarely in a trap you'd set. In all fairness, I'd had no idea Billy would have a bat with him, but still…

Billy looked up to Faria. "I didn' hurt no one. I was just hungry." He pointed to the end of the bat. Some blood and other fibers that I didn't care to guess their origin were on the end. "I saw that and wanted to give it to Lilly in appreciation for her helping me out. Was tryin' to be helpful."

Faria sat the bat aside and moved next to Billy. He put his hand on his shoulder. "You are being helpful. You've provided the first real lead we've had. I don't think you would have killed someone and then revealed the possible murder weapon." Faria offered a small smile to go along with his soft words. "That wouldn't be very smart."

Or…it was incredibly smart if he knew the weapon would throw the scent away from him and onto another. I didn't know Billy well enough to know if his blood ran that cold. I doubted it though. "Just go with Officer Faria. Let them take your prints, and give your statement. Everything will be ok."

Billy nodded and followed Faria to his car with only one scared look back. I consoled myself that there was a good chance he'd at least have a warm, reasonably comfortable place to sleep tonight. Faria and I both had a soft spot for people, even though he didn't bend or break the rules (like I did from time to time). He might be able to convince Billy to rest there for the night and give his statement in the morning.

Speaking of this night, I needed to get home. Watson was waiting, and Mandi would be there to fill me in on the latest gossip from Ocean View. I'd almost forgotten that I'd let Mandi borrow my moped and wasn't looking forward to the long walk home, but when I rounded the building to the parking lot, my transportation was there under the lamppost, gleaming like a new penny. Mandi's bike was missing from the bike rack. She must've done an exchange before heading to the apartment she shared with her mother. Best BFF ever.

I reached into my purse for the spare key and headed in the direction of my home. For some reason, my moped became possessed and turned down the road toward Shady Pines. It was the last place on earth I wanted to be, but that run-down piece of property was causing our town a great deal of trouble. Since I'd recently committed to Danger Cove being my home, I took that personally.

I stopped just outside of the illumination circle of the lone streetlight that stood about fifty yards from the front entrance and turned off my headlight to get a better view (and hide my presence.) To be honest, I wasn't sure what I was looking for—maybe just understanding of the allure and appeal of the property. Had someone killed Camilla so they could own this deathtrap?

My breath shuddered as I saw a flashlight beam emerge from the back corner of the building and start to move quickly in my direction. I shut off the engine of my moped and walked it backward to seek cover in the line of trees along the side of the road. My heart paused as I saw the figure jogging into the circle of light. It was Sam, my potential diamond-stealing security personnel. What in the good Lord's name was she doing out here—by herself—at night? I ignored the fact that I happened to be out here—at night—by myself too. She stopped, still jogging in place, looked around as she felt her wrist. I assume she was checking her pulse. Her gaze traveled across my hiding place, but didn't stop. A moment later she moved on.

Once she was out of sight, I allowed my heart to pick up the pace again. Time to go home.

"What's a nice girl like you doing in a place like this?" Adam's voice resounded loudly in the quiet night, spiking the adrenaline in my system to dangerous levels.

I spun around to see how close he was to me. I instantly regretted turning off my moped and not changing into tennis shoes when I left work. Running would not be an option in the adorable little flats I'd been wearing today.

"What are you doing here?" I purposely didn't respond in kind by asking what a nice guy like him was doing here, as I didn't believe he was a nice guy.

He gestured to his pants and a sweaty T-shirt. "Out for a run, when I spotted you hiding in the trees. Thought I'd come over and make sure you were ok."

Based on his attire, it was a reasonable statement. Was nighttime jogging a thing now? "I appreciate that. I just thought I'd drive by this place before heading home. Still trying to understand what all the fuss is about."

He closed the distance between us, which led me to start my moped. Depending on how fast he could run, it might not make a difference, but the purring motor made me feel better. "You have a good vantage point from the tree line?" His arms crossed, and the smirk on his face told me he didn't believe my story. That was ok. I wasn't sure I believed his. The fact Sam had been out jogging at the same time didn't escape me either.

I moved away from the trees and back out onto the road. He held up his hands as though they were a camera lens he was looking through. "You have to see the potential in places. You're only looking at the surface. Sometimes there are gems hidden in plain sight. You just have to know what you're looking for."

Right now, I was looking to make my escape. "Guess that's why I didn't go into real estate. Bartending is easier. Nothing hidden. No agendas. No reason to kill anyone." That last one I threw in for dramatic effect.

The smile disappeared from Adam's face as his gaze locked on to mine. "You'd be surprised the reasons people have for killing."

It was no surprise that I wanted this conversation to end. "I'd rather not think about that. Now if you'll excuse me, someone at home needs me. Enjoy the rest of your jog, and be careful." I hit the gas and moved as fast away from Adam as possible. There was something about that man that made me uneasy. I also wondered at the reasons he might have for killing someone—namely Camilla.

Watson was asleep in the center of my bed when I arrived home. He lifted his head slowly, as though it weighed fifty pounds. In reality, I'd put it close to a half pound or less. I mean, let's be honest—he couldn't weigh more than ten pounds total, so how much of that could realistically be his head? "Hey, Watson, did you have a good day?"

"Meow." He yawned and shot me a look that said I'd just disturbed his perfect nap.

"I'll take that as a yes." I quickly changed into yoga pants and a tank top. I pulled him into my arms and hugged him close. He snuggled in and rubbed his head under my chin, the purring instantly calming my spirit. We walked together into the kitchen. Since I'd given Billy my dinner, Watson and I would need to share dinner.

My stomach growled, signifying I'd really need to put Watson down so I could make us both some dinner. I'd just started to release him, when the doorbell rang. The sound of barking dogs filled the house. I'd forgotten about the doorbell since no one ever rings it. My friends usually knock and then walk right in. The sound startled Watson, and he used my arms as a springboard to the floor and back to the safety of my room. The scratches he left in his wake matched the ones on my chest from last night. "Who is it?"

"It's Mandi. My hands are full. Can you open the door?"

I grabbed the ointment I'd left on the counter from the previous day and applied some to the scratches as I made my way to the door. "Be right there."

Once the door was open, she lifted the contents in her hands up with a big smile on her face. "Surprise. Mom sent litter box, litter, and all the necessary items to feed your new friend."

I pulled Mandi into a quick embrace. ""Please convey my thanks. That was so incredibly thoughtful of her. Thank you for bringing it over."

She released me from the hug. "Of course. That's what besties and their moms do. Now let me meet this new mystery man in your life."

Watson and Mandi got to know each other while I made tuna salad sandwiches for dinner.

Once dinner was made, I put a sandwich in front of Mandi. "So tell me about your afternoon at Ocean View."

"It was pretty uneventful until the new guest came in."

"Tell me about him." I put a spoonful of tuna on Watson's plate and then returned my attention to Mandi and to my own sandwich.

Mandi stood up and lifted her chin, stuck out her belly— well as far as Mandi was able to—and replied in a haughty voice. "David Charles Winchester the Fourth arrived at the Ocean View Bed & Breakfast at approximately four thirty in the afternoon. He was less than pleased that a bellboy was not available to bring in his three suitcases."

"Three? How long is he staying?"

"Until Tuesday I think."

"Three bags for five days? That's almost as bad as my mother."

Mandi laughed. Even though my mother had spent most of her life on the road with my father and his rock-and-roll band, she'd always believed that didn't mean you had to travel without the comforts of your home. More than one roadie had complained about the personal luggage they'd had to haul around in order to keep her happy.

"How is your mom?"

"Mom is mom. You know how she is. Always fussing about one thing or another." I grinned. Mostly she fussed about decisions my dad made about the band.

"Those two fight like a married couple—they should just go ahead and do it."

I didn't think that would ever happen, but you never know. "Tell me more about Winchester the Fourth."

Watson had finished the tuna and was now circling Mandi's legs. Yeah, she was totally in. Mandi reached down and picked him up and resumed the affectionate petting she'd been doling out earlier. "He was an odd duck."

"Can you be more specific? Did he say why he was here?"

Mandi shrugged. "I asked him the standard business or pleasure question, but he sniffed and looked down his very long nose at me and reminded me my job was to see to his comfort, not ask a million questions. He further shared that it was neither my business what he did while he was here nor where he went after he left."

"Sounds like a pompous pain."

My comment elicited a chuckle. "Most definitely. Anyway, from his registration information, I know he's from New York, so he's a long way from home. The identification he provided was a passport, which I thought was odd."

"Maybe he's headed to Canada after this? We're not that far from the border." I poured an iced tea for Mandi and myself and brought them to the table.

Mandi reluctantly put Watson down. "I suppose it's a possibility. He doesn't have to worry about me asking any more questions though." She smiled down at Watson. "I may have to talk Mom into getting a cat."

My arms were lifted for her inspection. "I'd recommend getting it declawed before he or she scars you for life."

She sat down across from me and grabbed her phone. "I'm going to google if a cat scratch can actually scar you."

My eyes rolled, and I couldn't help but smile. "How about Googling about Mr. Winchester to see what you can learn?"

There was a sigh, but she nodded her head. "Ok. I'll save the scratches for later."

My sandwich disappeared faster than a jet on David Copperfield's stage, so I initiated a hunt for more food while Mandi searched through cyberspace. A bag of marshmallows left over from s'mores last weekend was all I could find. "Hey,

Mandi, maybe next time your mom could send food for me." I laughed and held up the results of my find.

"I don't suppose there's any graham crackers or chocolate left?"

"That would be a no and an are you kidding?"

"Right. There's never any chocolate left. Ok, hand over some fluffy sugar and I'll share what I've learned."

After the appropriate amount of sugar was consumed, she sipped her tea and then started to share. "The only thing I could find is a LinkedIn page that shows he works for a company called BARAG."

"What kind of place is that?"

Mandi's thumbs worked the images and links on the screen of her phone before her nose scrunched up. "The best I can come up with, it is a group of investors, but there aren't a lot of details about what they invest in, who the investors are, etc."

"Well, we can assume Mr. Winchester is one of them, right?"

The blue of Mandi's gaze settled on mine. "I'm not sure we can."

"What makes you say that?"

"Investors typically have a lot of money, or they at least need to look like they are wealthy. People want investors to be successful before they turn over their hard-earned dollars. Mr. Winchester may have acted like he had a lot of money, but he certainly didn't look the part. Plus..." She leaned forward as though she was going to share a secret.

Mandi had an eye for details, so if she noticed something, I'd be willing to bet big on any hunches or observations she made. "Plus what?"

"Only the large suitcase contained clothes. Trust me, I lugged all of them to his room. The others felt very heavy. I could hear some metal clanging, so I know it wasn't shoes or any of the normal things you'd pack for a trip." There was a pause, before she amended. "Well, anything a normal person would pack for a trip."

"Any thoughts?"

She shook her head. "None so far, but I'll keep thinking about it."

That was good enough for me. "So while we have our thinking caps on, I need to bring you up to speed on what happened at the tavern and on my way home tonight to see if that adjusts your prior assessment about who might have killed Camilla."

I filled her in on my interactions with Faria and Billy and the introduction of the bat as evidence. I ended with my run-in with Adam. I decided to keep the Sam appearance to myself for now. Not that I didn't trust Mandi, but since they were coworkers, I didn't feel it was appropriate. Once finished, I resumed eating marshmallows as I waited for her to process. I was about ten mini mallows in when she sat up straight. "Well?"

The intensity of Mandi's expression bored through my sugar snack. "I still don't think Jack did it. I think Billy might have."

CHAPTER TWELVE

———

Mandi left about thirty minutes later without really providing what Watson and I felt constituted a valid reason for putting Billy to the front of the suspect line. I turned on my side and stroked Watson's fur as he started to settle in for the night. "Let's think about this, Watson. Billy was the only one we know of that was in that old motel around the time Camilla was killed, but that doesn't mean there weren't others, right?"

"Meow."

Sounded like agreement to me, so I continued. "That just means he could've had opportunity. We have no idea if he had the means."

This time Watson cocked his head to one side and offered a quizzical look. "Ok, he did have possession of Jack's bat, and he could've been lying about when it came into his possession. I'll give you that much."

My concession mollified him, and he resumed his curled-up position with his head tucked near his paws. Not wanting to be bested by a cat, even an adorable orange one, I made my final argument. "But what about motive? Lots of other people had motive to kill Camilla. We don't know of any motive Billy had." Of course that didn't mean there wasn't one—just that we didn't know it yet.

I sighed.

Watson yawned and closed his eyes. At least one of us could sleep. He was so adorable curled up there next to me. I snapped a picture with my phone and then sent a text to Tan with the photo. *Thought you should meet the male I'm sharing my bed with tonight. Hurry home so you can meet him.*

It took several minutes before a response came in. I noticed the time and felt guilty for waking him. It *was* a school night. *He's pretty cute, but I bet I'm a better kisser.* He followed the message with a smiley emoticon, a heart, and an emoji blowing a kiss.

I returned his text with a smile and heart along with, *You are definitely a better kisser! Get some rest. I'll see you tomorrow night. Sleep over?*

He replied simply with a smiley with its tongue hanging out. Boys! I'd just about put the phone down to try to sleep, when the text beeped again. *I'd love to sleep over, and I love you. See you tomorrow.*

With those warm thoughts and Watson purring softly beside me, I closed my eyes and slept better than I'd slept in days.

* * *

The next morning, I hadn't been at work for more than an hour when the grapevine came to life with news of Jack's arrest. Guess Billy must've been able to provide a reasonable and believable alibi. Bree came in shortly before lunchtime. She shuffled in, to the barstool at the end of the bar. I put water and a menu in front of her. "You don't look very happy for someone who was released on her own recognizance."

She graced me with a roll of her eyes and a slight grin. "I'm pretty sure you have to be arrested to be released, but I appreciate your being as relieved as I am about my freedom."

"If you're relieved, then why do you look like you have the weight of the world on your shoulders? You did get to sleep in your own bed last night rather than a narrow cot."

"Because she doesn't think Jack did it," Mandi interjected as she handed me a drink order.

Bree turned in her seat. "You don't think he did either, even though they found his bat?"

Mandi crossed her arms. "They don't even know if it's the murder weapon yet. How can they arrest him?"

Since I'd been the only one of the three of us to actually see the bat when Billy turned it over, I couldn't help but add,

"The end of the bat did have substances I'd rather not speculate about on it. I know that doesn't guarantee it was the murder weapon, but it has to be a top contender. The police obviously feel good enough about it to arrest Jack."

Bree's mouth fell open and what sounded like a surprised gasp sounded from her lips. "Since when are you a big believer in our justice system? You usually lead the crusade against the keystone cops."

As much as I hated to admit it, she might have had a point. "I'm not saying you're wrong about Jack, but maybe the police got it right this time. It's not like you're Jack's biggest fan either."

Bree's chin tilted up a fraction. "I'm not, but that doesn't mean I want him going down for murder. You should go talk to him."

This elicited a snap of my gaze to hers. "Why on earth should I do that? I've been instructed not to meddle in affairs that don't concern me on a regular basis. You've even shared that wisdom with me a time or four."

She huffed and pointed on the menu to what she wanted. "You have this nose for getting at the truth, even if it's by accident sometimes." She winked and smiled with the last few words.

As I handed Mandi the drink for her order, my bracelet clanged against one of the beer tap levers. Bree pointed to the bracelet that had two matching charms on it. Each charm had etchings on it that represented my family's crest. I'd had my gram's since she'd died, and the other—my grandfather's—was returned to me a year or so ago. It was among my most treasured possessions. Bree clasped a charm between her thumb and forefinger. "I bet your grandparents would want you to at least hear what Jack has to say."

That was low. Really low. Even for Bree.

But she was right. My grandfather fought for what was right in Vietnam, and it had cost him his life and future with a woman who loved him more than life itself. My gram always stood up for the underdog. "You do recall Detective Marshall has questions for me. Questions he will ask if I show up like a gift basket on his front door."

She nodded. "I know, but it's not like you can avoid him forever. It's not that big of a town. Might as well face your foe."

This was more like a lamb walking straight into the lion's den. "Ok, I'll go talk to Jack on my lunch break. *If*"—and I stressed that word—"they'll let me see him. We also have to assume that Detective Pizza Guy will let me go once I'm there. I may end up in the cell right next to Jack for obstruction of justice or some other charge Pizza Guy comes up with."

Bree's face lit up, and the dark shadows around her eyes lightened a bit. "You are such a drama queen, but I love you and appreciate your doing this. Now, where's my food? I'm starving!"

Thoughts of Jack Condor filled my brain as I went about my day. What would I say to him? I didn't like him. Didn't want to see him. Didn't want him to be guilty. That last part bugged me. I wasn't sure why, but it was true. Maybe there was a small—very small—part of me that sided with Bree and Mandi about his innocence. When my break finally arrived, I shrugged on a sweater and made a general announcement to the team. "I'm heading out for a bit. I'll have my cell on me if anything comes up or you need me." I stopped in front of Mandi. "If I'm not back in an hour, you should probably call Attorney Pohoke for me."

I headed out the front door. Sam put her hand on my arm. I looked up into her concerned gaze. "I'm not entirely sure what's going on, but my advice to not get involved still stands. It's none of my business, but I wouldn't feel right if I didn't at least warn you again."

My head nodded, and I bit back my question about her whereabouts the night Camilla was killed. There was zero reason to believe Sam was involved, but the timing of her showing up at the tavern felt a little too perfect. Instead I smiled, and my voice dismissed her concern. "It's just a friendly visit. No worries. Can't get myself into trouble at a police station, right?"

Her lips twisted as she shook her head. "Something tells me you can find trouble wherever you go."

"That's where you're wrong." I winked and offered a small smile. "Trouble finds me. Thanks for looking out for me though. I feel safe knowing you and your jujitsu are standing guard."

Sam laughed and waved me off. "Yeah, something like that. As long as it does the trick, doesn't matter what it's called, right? Be back soon, or I'll send the cavalry after you."

With a salute and a smile, I headed downtown to see Jack.

The Danger Cove Police Department hadn't changed since I'd moved to the area. Based on the décor or lack thereof inside the interrogation room and other key areas, my guess was it hadn't changed since the seventies.

Faria was heading out the door as I was heading in. "Lilly, what brings you here?"

My smile did its best to be charming and innocent all at the same time. "Friendship."

He raised an eyebrow. "Since when are you friends with Jack Condor?"

"How do you know it's Jack I'm here to see? Maybe I wanted to check on Billy." I'd assumed they had released him after they got the information they needed, but I hadn't seen him, so my statement was reasonable.

He crossed his arms. "Billy left after a good night's sleep and a hot breakfast this morning. Felt it was the least we could do for his help. So I know you're here to see Jack, because he's the only person in here right now who isn't employed by the police department."

The man had a point. "We're not friends—not really. But my friends, Bree and Mandi, are convinced he's being framed or something along those lines. My goal is to learn if they're right or not."

His chuckle should've irritated me, but instead my heart warmed for the friendship we'd formed from our shared experiences (mostly him trying to keep me out of trouble with Detective Marshall). The smile faded moments after it started. He moved in closer and lowered his head. "I might side with your friends on this one."

Great. It was now three to one in favor of Jack's innocence. I inwardly sighed. Ok, maybe three and a half to the small part of me that ignored the nice, neat way this was tied up. Some presents were just too good to be true. "I appreciate your sharing that with me. I don't know what they expect me to do, but they wanted me to talk to him. Can I see him for a few?"

He nodded. "Just a few though. He's allowed visitors, as he's just being held on the suspicion of murder at the moment."

This was news—different news—than what Mandi had told me. "Wait, why? I thought he'd been arrested for the murder."

"All the i's have to be dotted and t's crossed. The Cartwright family is not someone you want to screw things up with. They've paid for expedited testing of the DNA found under Camilla's fingernails. Once that comes back as a positive match, we'll have enough for the arrest. The timing for how long he can be held without a charge varies, but typically something needs to happen in seventy-two hours. We expect the DNA results to be reported by tomorrow at the latest."

"And if it's not a match for Jack?" If he really was innocent, I wouldn't have to be involved at all, as my friends and even my not-really friends would all be in the clear. No Lilly-based intervention necessary. That sounded like music I could relate to.

"Doesn't mean he didn't do it, but certainly makes it harder for the district attorney to get a conviction. Depending on what the results showed, we would have to widen the scope of the investigation, but he'd still be a prime suspect."

That made sense. Though, unless the bat knocked her unconscious first, I couldn't envision her not fighting off an attacker. I'd seen enough crime shows to know DNA under the fingernails lent itself to being a primary way to identify the guilty party. "Fair enough. I better get in there before you-know-who comes back and shares his extreme displeasure with us."

"No need to be so hard on him, Lilly. He's a fair man. He worries about you getting hurt when you insist on getting involved."

The desire to argue stood on the tip of my tongue ready to springboard into action. I showed restraint, though, because I knew that Richie was a fair, respectful, and good man. He saw past the *way* Detective Marshall went about things and focused on the *why*. Maybe I could do that if I wasn't primarily on the receiving end of his blustery temper. "We'll save that discussion for another day when we have more time."

Richie smiled, nodded, and let me back to the visitor area. Jack's normal haughtiness had hightailed it and left him dejected and deflated. "Hey, Jack."

Jack looked up, and then his gaze darted to Faria, who stepped outside the door. "Hey, Lilly. You come here to rub my nose in all this? Kick a man while he's down?"

Time to add drama king to dejected and deflated. "No, I came here because, for some strange reason, there are people who believe you didn't do this. They asked me to come talk to you so we could hear your side of the story."

My words forced his chin up from the floor, where it had been dragging. "Who?"

"Does it matter?" Really, what was up with this guy? Someone believed in his innocence. At this point you would think that would be a welcome gift regardless of the source.

"What about you? Do *you* believe I'm innocent?"

Never one to lie—not about the important stuff anyway—I shrugged my shoulders. "I'm undecided, which is why I'm here to talk to you."

He leaned forward, a little life coming back into his sails. "I didn't do it, Lilly. I swear to you."

"Can you explain your bat?"

"Someone took it from the back of my truck. I mean, this is Danger Cove. It's not like I locked the bat up or anything. I loved it, but at the end of the day, it was just a bat. I tossed it in the truck after I left the tavern that night. I headed over to Ocean View to wait to talk to Bree."

Bree hadn't mentioned this. "What did you want to talk to her about?"

The paleness in his cheek blushed pink. "I wanted to let her know I'd decided not to move forward with my plans for Shady Pines. I was still going to go to the auction and try to drive up the price."

"To hit Camilla where it hurt..." I supplied.

He nodded. "Yes, that...that..."

"Woman?"

Jack grinned. "Not the word I was going to use, but sure. That woman had made my life miserable on several occasions. I wanted some payback." His smile faded. "But I didn't want her dead."

"So did you speak with Bree?" If he was with her, she could possibly provide him with an alibi based on the time of death."

Any air that had found its way into his lungs escaped in a large sigh as he lowered his head. "No, I'm not sure how late she was at the tavern or where she went after, but I got tired of waiting and left."

"Was your bat in the truck when you left?"

"I didn't look. I assumed it was, but maybe someone had already taken it."

Someone like Billy? He had a way of moving in and out of the shadows without being seen. It was a possibility. "Were there any other prints on the bat?"

Another drawn-out sigh. Seriously, who knew Jack Condor could be so dramatic? "None that they've told me about. Other than the guy that claims he found it in your dumpster." He lifted his head from those giant forearms of his. "But if you were going to go to all the trouble to frame someone for murder, you wouldn't bother leaving prints, would you?"

Valid point. "No." I chewed on my bottom lip for a moment, trying to determine where to go with this next. "When was the last time you saw Camilla?"

"I saw her briefly at Shady Pines the night she died."

That wasn't good news. "Did you argue?"

"Not really. She taunted me—again. I was tired, so I left. I swear the woman thrived on making life miserable for others."

"Who else might have wanted her dead?" If I was going to start my own little investigation and risk the wrath of the DC police department, I at least wanted a good starting point.

He chuckled. "Besides everyone she met?"

I crossed my arms. "Narrow the field for me, Jack. We don't have much time before either the auction takes place and all other possible suspects leave town, or they charge and arraign you for her murder."

My words hit their mark. He sat up and closed his eyes. I assumed that meant he was thinking. "Her biggest rivals in the real estate market are Adam Miller and Jessica Byers."

"Not you?"

His big head shook. "Not really. I only got into the ring when she came around this area. Adam's and Jessica's reaches are wider. I'm more of a niche-market kind of guy."

"Ok, I'll start looking into them more. What about Billy Nester?"

His head tilted to one side as his lips pursed. "Who?"

"The guy who found the bat. I don't believe he was involved, but I wanted to see if you knew something about him that maybe I didn't." If Jack didn't know who he was, then Billy might be the next person I run a search on. Unless he was a ghost, there should be some intel on him.

Jack rubbed his face with his large hands. "Camilla made enemies wherever she went. All she cared about was the next big score. Money was her motivator. I'd heard rumors she was looking to move into another league."

"What does that mean? What kind of leagues are there in real estate?"

He shrugged and settled back into the chair. "Not in real estate but in investments that would net her a larger return."

"Such as?" I didn't want to appear stupid, but I had no idea what he was talking about.

"Such as, I don't know for sure. They were just rumors. Music to my ears, though, as I hoped that meant she would move away from my playground."

Understood. It sounded like I might have to cast the net wide to capture all possibilities. My head started to hurt. Three knocks were heard through the door. I turned and saw Richie hold up all five fingers. I nodded. I had one more question to ask Jack, and it wasn't about leagues or playgrounds. "Do the words *skinny*, *punt*, and *older* mean anything to you?"

This time he managed to scrunch his entire face up. If there had been a cowboy Cabbage Patch doll, Jack could've been the model. "I think it means you've lost your mind."

As I considered how long this current crusade for the truth might take me, I couldn't disagree. "Ok, Jack. A simple no would've sufficed."

I started to stand, but he grabbed my hands. The intense look in his eyes gave me pause. "I know I don't have many fans around here. I get that. But I swear to you on everything I treasure in this world, I did not kill that woman."

And, contrary to everything I wanted to think about Jack...I believed him.

CHAPTER THIRTEEN

———

Friday brought about a bevy of business at the tavern. There were a lot of people hanging around town waiting for the auction. I still couldn't understand what people saw in the rundown old place even after my multiple visits. I didn't understand, but I intended to find out. There was no way in Hades I was going to go there at night, but I wanted to take one final look around the place to see if any grand revelations or insights occurred. The ticking clock inside my head added to my anxiety. On one hand—we'll call it the minute hand—was Jack's timetable. The DNA was expected back by end of business today. Even if the science got him released from custody, Officer Faria had made it clear that it wouldn't completely exonerate him.

On the other hand—the hour marker—was the auction. It had been scheduled for Sunday afternoon. Once the auction took place, there was a good chance the killer would be gone for good. I was assuming, of course, the killer hadn't already left town. I understood Camilla had made many enemies over the years, but my gut told me Shady Pines played a role in this whole *Murder, She Wrote* scenario. If I couldn't figure it out, maybe I'd need to pay Elizabeth Ashby a visit. Sometimes she saw things others didn't. She'd certainly helped me out in the past.

After the lunch rush, I handed the apron strings to Abe. "You sure you don't mind covering for a bit?"

"You're giving me a Friday night off. I don't mind covering for you." His gaze narrowed. "Though I worry about where you might be headed in the middle of the day."

I patted his arm. "A place that it's better to visit now rather than the middle of the night after we close. I could say I worry about you going out on a date with Agnes Thermopolis."

The blush on his tanned cheeks rose to cover his bald head. "How did you know?"

I laughed. "I didn't, but I do now."

The shaking finger he pointed at me didn't even have an effect, since the twinkle in his sky blue eyes diminished the glare he tried to add to it as well. "You are sneaky."

"Go easy on her. Love hasn't been kind to her in the past." Agnes and I had become friends about a year ago after the local paper did an article on both of us. Agnes, the former receptionist at the police station, had won the lottery. The death of her husband, even though their marriage had been more about money than love, had caused her a lot of grief.

"It's a little too soon for talk of love. This is only our first date."

"Just watching out for both of you. I know you and Lady Love haven't gotten along well in the past either."

This time Abe laughed. "My trouble has always been with Lady Luck."

"They're distant cousins. Just be careful—for both of you." I firmly believed Abe had put his gambling days behind him, but access to the kind of money Agnes had could be tempting.

He nodded. "I promise. Slow and steady. We'll see where it goes. And, Lilly?"

"Yes?"

"You don't need to worry. I'm a changed man." The sincerity in his voice left no doubt in my mind he spoke the truth.

Abe and I had been down some rocky paths together, but in the end, he'd been there for me and I'd been there for him. "I believe you. Well, now that we've covered that topic, I should be going. I'll be back as quick as I can."

Shady Pines presented a less intimidating picture during the day, but still eerie enough to make all the heebie-jeebies dormant in my system to start dancing the tango. I could almost see a dark, foreboding cloud hanging over the structure. Most likely my imagination had engaged in creative license with my vision, but the goose bumps responded and began to surface all over my skin.

The buzzing of my phone brought me back to reality. A quick check of the caller ID made me smile. "Hi, Mr. Pohoke, to what do I owe the pleasure of your call?"

"Hi, Lilly. You asked me to run a title search on Shady Pines, so I wanted to call you with some information."

The man had perfect timing. "I'm all ears."

His chuckle kept me smiling despite the topic of our conversation haunting me just a few feet away. "As suspected, the title is all clear. There are no liens or legal notices against the property."

"Guess that's good for prospective buyers."

"Yes..."

"You have additional information?" It wasn't like him to hesitate, so I prompted him to make sure I got the full story.

"Well, it's not official information."

"Hey, you know how curious I am. I'll take any information you can give me."

"My uncle is quite the storyteller, and he's lived here in Danger Cove his whole life. He loves to regale me with tales from 'back in the day,' as he terms it."

Already he was calming my nerves. I suspected it was a necessity for attorneys to be able to soothe with their words. "He sounds like a fun guy."

Attorney Pohoke laughed. "He's something alright. Anyway, he called last night, and I was asking if he had any tales about Shady Pines. He told me that it didn't get its name because of all the trees surrounding the property."

"No?"

"No. Apparently the original owner of the property thought it would be a fun play on words since he had a reputation for his shady dealings. Our proximity to the border and the ocean made smuggling goods a profitable business. He also managed to find himself as a person of interest for several crimes, including murder."

And just like that, all the fun feelings he'd stirred up returned to their hiding place. "Was someone murdered in the building before?" If that was common knowledge, I couldn't fathom why anyone would want to buy it.

"He didn't have those details. All I know is, the grandson inherited the property about a month ago when his grandfather died. He just wants to get rid of the eyesore and the stain on his family name."

"Makes sense to me. Well, thank you for the information."

He cleared his throat. "I hope you've been availing yourself of the right kind of information with my LexisNexis access."

Heat climbed up my neck, and I felt a flush cover my face. "I... How?"

"I can see the search history and activity."

Remorse replaced embarrassment. "I'm so sorry. I just wanted to be able to do a little investigation on my own without having to bother anyone. It was wrong. I won't use it again."

There was a pause, and I worried he was going to fire me as a client or, worse yet, end our friendship. "You've done a lot of good since you came to Danger Cove, Lilly."

"I've tried."

"And I know you took the credentials for a good reason."

"Still doesn't make it right. I hope you'll forgive me."

"You should've just asked me."

Did that mean he would've just handed over his credentials? That didn't seem likely, but I suppose it was possible. "Yes, I should have."

"Tell you what. You text or email me the next time you're going to search. As long as I feel the activity is reasonable, I won't change my password."

I vowed to myself right then and there to never make him have to do that. "Thank you. I really appreciate it. That's very generous of you."

He laughed. "Well, those of us fighting for justice have to stick together. Don't be surprised, though, if I email you to do some searches for me if I'm running short on time."

"Deal. Thank you, Mr. Pohoke for understanding and for the information."

"Have a good day, Lilly."

Feeling better about things after my conversation, I marched toward the front door ready to launch my own investigation. The lockbox for the real estate agents was locked up tight. I tried the door handle, just so I could say I did. It didn't budge either. Why couldn't it have been locked the first time Bree and I tried to enter? Would've saved me from seeing a dead body. I could go a lifetime and not see another one of those. I walked the exterior, looking for a way in. Billy had managed it at least once or twice. I reasoned if he could do it, so could I. Once I made it to the back of the building, I began to doubt my claim to match Billy's results. The feel of something crunching under my shoe made me stop.

The afternoon sun glinted off the ground. I bent down to pick up the source of the reflection. Glass shards. Looking up— correction, squinting up—I saw the broken window. Bree had been the first to notice the absence of the glass on the floor from the broken window. At the time, we hadn't given it much thought, but now it made sense.

The reason there hadn't been any evidence of the break—it had been broken from the inside.

I had no idea when this occurred, nor why, nor who had broken the window. That was a lot of big fat nothing as far as the window was concerned. My centi-senses told me this was important, but yet again, I didn't know why. Most people had spidey senses, but I had issues with spiders for many reasons— some reasonable, some not. As a result, my intuition was nicknamed after the centipede. Just to be clear, I don't like insects of any kind, but out of the options, this one flowed best as a naming convention.

Unable to draw any more conclusions from the glass other than where and how it originated, I continued around the building to look for a way in. Once the front door was in view again, I had to acknowledge defeat. I searched all around the front looking for a key or other way to enter. I moved things, tried to pry open windows, stuck my hand in nooks and crannies that kept all the heebies and jeebies dancing at high capacity. Finally after about thirty minutes, I had to concede this one to Billy. I might be smarter than a fifth grader—at least I hoped I was—but I wasn't smarter than a down-on-his-luck man. Maybe desperation made you see things others couldn't.

I arrived back at the tavern to discover Sam in the middle of several people shouting at each other. Her calming tone had started to bring the noise level down, but it was easy to see tempers were flaring. Time to provide assistance.

Stepping closer, I moved in next to Sam. "Hi, everyone. Are you the crew I secretly hired to see how my new security handled rowdy patrons?"

It was a stupid question, but it had the desired effect. Everyone stopped and looked at me, including Sam. While their gazes were quizzical, hers was humored. She put her hands on her slim hips and offered just a hint of a smile. "I knew I'd landed this job too easy. This was like a probationary test, wasn't it?"

I returned the smile and then turned to the patrons. "Sam, let me introduce you to Jessica Byers, Adam Miller, and Serena James. I like to collectively refer to them as the Shady Pines group."

Sam played right along without prompting and extended her hand to each of them. "Sam Sheraton. Nice to meet you."

Their manners kicked in, and they returned her pleasantries. Once they'd finished, I decided this was the perfect opportunity to start my investigation with a little Interrogation 101. "Look, I know things have been stressful for all of you with the auction being delayed. Why don't you take some seats at the bar, and I'll buy you a late lunch and a round of drinks?"

Furtive glances were exchanged before Adam shrugged. "I never turn down a free meal, and God knows I could use a cocktail." Serena and Jessica simply nodded and followed Adam to the bar.

Abe handed me the apron and whispered. "Are you sure you know what you're doing?"

"Don't I always?"

His response consisted of a chuckle and shake of his head as he walked away. "I'll be in the kitchen if you need anything."

Translation—I'll rescue you if you get in over your head. Returning my attention to the trio, I decided to start the liquor flowing. Maybe that would loosen their tongues a bit. "What can I get you to drink? Might I suggest our signature cocktail this month—a Dark and Stormy?"

Serena smiled. "That sounds like fun. I'll try one of those."

Jessica shrugged. "Sure why not."

Adam tossed the menu back onto the bar. "Make mine a double."

I retrieved the glasses and the rum. "Three Dark and Stormys coming up."

Once they had the drinks and had a chance to consume about half, I started with a neutral subject. "I know what brought you to Danger Cove, but I'm curious where you came from. I was born in Vegas but then lived in Danger Cove, Texas, and New York before heading cross country to end up here in Danger Cove again."

Jessica offered up intel first. "I'm from the Seattle area, but as you know, I'm hoping to relocate here to Danger Cove in the near future. I like the small-town atmosphere."

I leaned in as I handed her another drink. "Just be warned, everybody knows everybody's business here. Tough to keep secrets."

Jessica shot a glance to Adam before smiling. "I don't have anything to hide, so no worries on that front."

I couldn't swear to it, but I was pretty sure Serena rolled her eyes at Jessica's comment. But as was her normal behavior, she remained quiet. Before I could turn the attention to her, Adam pushed his glass toward me to indicate a refill. "I'm from Portland." He leaned back in the barstool as his chest puffed out a bit. "Bet you didn't know we have the highest number of strip clubs per capita of any other city."

Mandi brought a drink order up to the bar. She offered a full-wattage smile to Adam. "I bet you also know that in the old days, they used to kidnap drunks from the strip clubs and take them through tunnels under the city to the ports, where they would put them on ships headed for China to work as sailors on the ships. That's where the term *shanghaiing* comes from."

Adam turned red and crossed his arms. "Always one in every crowd."

Mandi's face fell, and her bottom lip got sucked into her mouth. I hurried to explain. "Mandi didn't mean that as an insult. She is a lover of all things trivia and enjoys sharing it with our patrons when the opportunity arises. I'm sure she thought you might be interested in the extra little detail to spice up your sharing even more next time."

"Yeah, I guess I see your point." He turned to Mandi and smiled. "I probably would've been one of those guys to get shanghaied."

Mandi opened her mouth to say something, but I worried she might inadvertently set him off again. I handed her the drinks. "Here you go, Mandi. Thanks so much."

She closed her mouth and nodded before returning to her table. "Now that our history lesson is out of the way, I don't think Serena has shared where she's from."

Serena looked like she'd rather jump into a pit of fire ants than answer my question. After a few more swallows of her drink, she murmured. "New York."

"How cool is that? I'm from a little town near Woodstock. How about you?"

"Manhattan."

"Wow! We lived in two totally different New Yorks, that's for sure." I remembered Bree's newest guest was also from New York, but with Serena's reluctance to share, I decided to save that for another day. Besides, with a population of over nineteen million in that state, it's not like it was guaranteed they'd know each other.

Freddie brought some clean glasses behind the bar. "That's cool. I'm from New York too." He grinned his special smile that typically sent women swooning. "I'm more from da Bronx though. Now that is a totally different New York than youse girls are talking about."

Serena shrugged and offered a shy smile. "I originally lived in another, less affluent area. I didn't move to Manhattan until I started working for Camilla."

I gave her another drink. "Maybe we aren't from such different places then, right, Freddie?"

He lifted the bin of dirty dishes with a toss of his head to keep his bangs out of his eyes. So adorable that one was. I still hoped he and Mandi might become more than friends someday, but only time would tell.

"Right." He turned to Serena and gave her one more of *those* smiles. "Her next drink is on me, Boss."

Serena's blush was adorable, and I think Jessica might have been a little jealous. Though with the way she'd been all secret-lover-like with Adam, you couldn't blame Freddie for not even taking a shot.

Wanting to get back to my pseudo interrogation, I asked a question that wasn't exactly what I wanted to know but hopefully would get me closer to the truth. "So if one of you gets Shady Pines, what are your plans?"

Jessica piped up first. "It's my fixer-upper project. I want to move to this area. I figured I'd rent an apartment or a small cottage to stay in while I conducted renovations."

"So a bed and breakfast?" My friend Bree wasn't here, but the question had to be asked.

She shook her head. "Not really. Portland may be home to the largest number of strip clubs per capita"—she offered a smile and wink to Adam before continuing—"but Seattle has a large unsheltered population. I want to provide somewhere for people who perhaps don't have any place else to stay. I'm still working through the details in my head, but my clientele would be much different than your friend's, I'm sure."

Adam sneered. "They're never going to give you zoning approval for a project like that. Your bleeding heart is going to bleed you dry. I've been over the numbers, but even she"—he pointed in my direction—"could figure out that's not a sustainable business model. You can't stay afloat without paying customers. Honestly…" His head shook as his lip curled. No secret he wasn't a fan of her idea.

My moral compass said Jessica's intentions were true north. Not only was she not trying to compete with Ocean View, she was trying to help the less fortunate. Adam's words hurt me more than they should and, I hoped, more than he intended. There was no way he could know what my level of education was or how I'd fared in school. Did he assume because I was the bartender that I'd reached the heights of my capabilities? Embarrassment and a hint of anger returned the heat to my face.

"Don't be a tool, Adam. You don't know anything about her or this place. They call her *Boss*. Doesn't that mean anything to you?" Jessica leapt to my defense, which embarrassed me further. I needed to find the right words here.

He shrugged as he pushed his empty glass toward me for a refill. "Means she's the shift supervisor. My friend's daughter is essentially the same at Starbucks. Big deal."

I didn't know what his problem was, but between his rudeness and outbursts, he was grating on my last nerve. I battled with myself regarding whether I should tell him where the nearest cliff he could drop himself off was or enduring his arrogance in order to learn more.

Before I decided, Serena took a deep breath and shared. "Three things you should know. First, Lilly is the majority owner of the Smugglers' Tavern, a business which has been operating solidly in the black despite the seasonal ups and downs of this area. Second, there are any number of grants and other programs that would subsidize the vision Jessica has for Shady Pines should she get the necessary approvals."

The fury vibrating off every inch of Adam's body permeated the entire room. I sent Sam a "be on standby" look which brought her moving closer to the bar. "And what's the third, you know-it-all, underachieving witch?"

Serena didn't even blink at being the recipient of Adam's condescending comment. As a matter of fact, she didn't even look at him at all. She stared forward, her gaze directed to the colored bottles decorating the back bar. "And third, the only reason you're even here is because you hated that Camilla bested you out of every deal you ever dared compete with her on. So why don't you do us all a favor and go home. Your motive for wanting the property is gone."

Major points to Serena for putting Adam in his well-deserved place. Though her desire for him to head home was in direct opposition to my new goal of proving he was the killer. He and Jack were both bested by Camilla time after time. She certainly had no problem rubbing their faces in it either. Tease the testosterone too much and you risk unleashing a beast…with a bat.

Adam stood and tossed some bills on the bar. "As far as I'm concerned, as long as you're here, Camilla's interests are being represented. I'm staying." He pulled on his jacket and gestured with a jerk of his head that Jessica should follow.

Jessica turned away from him. Apparently, she'd had enough of him for one day too. "I think I'll stay a little longer."

The dark cloud over his head raged into a full thunderstorm. I moved one step back to avoid any lightning strikes that might result. He shoved the barstool hard, bringing Sam to a position right next to him. The smile never left her face, and she didn't say a word, but the sincerity of her stance left no doubt she'd be happy to "help" him to the door should he not leave quietly. Personally, I wouldn't mess with her. But Adam had already proven he wasn't the sharpest stick at the weenie roast.

"I'm leaving." He tossed one more glance in Jessica's direction before moving toward the door.

I nodded at Sam. She'd handled him well. "Thanks, Sam."

"It's my job." Her reply was curt, and she spun on her heels and headed back to the door to resume her watchful stance. I didn't know her well enough to gauge her moods yet, but I'd bartended long enough to recognize when someone was upset. As soon as I wrapped up my little Q and A, I'd check in with her. I also happened to notice a diamond pendant at the end of her necklace. I hadn't noticed it before. It could have nothing to do with the missing diamonds, or it could mean she was wearing stolen property. That felt pretty gutsy if the latter were true. One more thing I needed to deal with and soon.

"Well," I offered, a deep breath in and out, "now that we've dealt with all of that, I wanted to tell you, Jessica, that I love your idea. If there's something we can do here at Smugglers' to help out, please let us know."

"You're assuming she'll win the auction," Serena interjected, still calm and quiet.

I shrugged and put another drink in front of her. "Not assuming anything. I just think helping those who are less fortunate is a noble cause, whether she does that at Shady Pines or someplace else. So if her idea gets approval or she has to modify it in some way to move forward, I want to do whatever I can to help."

Serena blushed and lowered her head. "I'm sorry."

I shook my head. "Don't be sorry. I can see how my statement might have been misinterpreted. I just wanted to clear the air."

"Well, you were clear in your offer of help." Jessica smiled. "I intend to take you up on it wherever I may end up around here."

"We can also coordinate with other businesses in town. There's a soup kitchen in the area too."

Jessica beamed. "Fantastic. Thank you, Lilly."

"My pleasure." I hated to ask my question on the heels of such a positive conversation, but I might never get an opportunity to talk to her like this again. "We all know how Adam felt about Camilla. Can I ask if you felt the same way?"

Jessica's smile faded. Now I felt like a tool—not a small hand tool, but one of those pointed shovels that Abe used to force the dirt into submission—for robbing her of her joy. She slowly sipped the remaining bit of her drink before her gaze met mine. "No one liked her. She was ruthless, cruel, and cunning. We all had to work our way up and earn the trust of investors to have the capital to play in the game. All Camilla had to do was ask daddy."

So, Camilla had come from money, and apparently lots of it. I glanced at Serena out of the corner of my eye, but she'd gone to work on the barbeque pork slider she'd ordered. I didn't believe for one second, though, she wasn't paying rapt attention to everything being said. She was loyal to Camilla from all that I'd been able to discern. She probably didn't appreciate all the bad talk about her former boss.

Jessica interrupted my thoughts about Serena. "So if you're asking me if any of us hated her enough to want her dead, I don't know if that alone would be enough to actually kill her, but I can only speak for myself." She pulled her bottom lip between her teeth and released it a few moments later without continuing.

Serena took another sip of her drink and then added, with a slight edge to her voice, "It's alright, Jessica. You can say it. I'm sure if Lilly looked hard enough or if the police investigation continues, they'd learn Camilla's actions didn't solely inspire hatred." She lifted her glass, "Well, if the threatening letters are to be believed."

I fought the urge to rub my temples. The suspect pool was growing by the day, and I was no closer to identifying the guilty party. Some Sherlock Holmes I was turning out to be.

CHAPTER FOURTEEN

———

After Jessica's statement, I wasn't sure where to take my mini interrogation. Instead, I decided to lighten the mood a bit. Even though both women still sported their strict and full business suit attire, it was Friday night after all. Personally, I loved being able to wear short sleeves and sundresses to work any day I wanted. I didn't think the corporate world and I would get along at all.

I removed her empty plate and placed it in the dirty dishes bin. "So, Jessica, I guess that means you're not going to sign a confession then?" I teased.

Jessica's gaze snapped to mine, but she evidently saw the humor I was trying to convey (while being maybe a little serious). The tension in her body subsided somewhat. "No, I didn't kill her, but I'm not sad she's dead."

Her admission did little to move her from the possibly guilty column on the sheet I was keeping in my head. "May I ask why? I mean, I get she was a pain." I quickly turned to Serena. "No offense."

In response, she simply shrugged. "She could be difficult."

Jessica turned to Serena, her eyes widened as though we'd just told her spinach was better than chocolate. "Difficult? That has to be the understatement of the year."

She returned her attention to me. "Do you know that"— she cast a quick glance at Serena—"witch filed a report alleging assault against me a little over a week ago?"

The question felt rhetorical as there was no way I could know, so I just shook my head as I continued to listen and wash the dishes in the bar sink. I did want to know the outcome though. "Did the police charge you?"

Jessica shrugged and leaned back in her chair. "They were 'still investigating the incident,' as they put it." She offered a bitter laugh. "Guess their star witness won't be saying much now, will she?"

While committing murder to get away with assault didn't feel like the best move in the criminal playbook, the way Jessica laughed it off was unnerving. I wondered if there was more to the story than she was sharing. Maybe the chapter that included *why* she had assaulted Camilla?

I wanted to ask more questions, but she crossed her arms over the bar to make them a pillow before resting her head. Either the weight of her confession had been more than she could take, or she'd had enough to drink. Either way it was time for her to go home. I sent a quick text to Tucker. Since there was no taxi service in Danger Cove, Tucker and I had an arrangement that on the weekend, he would provide transportation for those who needed a ride home. In exchange he received a flat fee and one free meal a week. When I'd offered the deal to him, he'd smiled and responded, "Groovy." Yeah, he was cool like that.

I signaled to Sam, who made her way to the bar. "Yes?"

"I've arranged for a ride for Jessica. He should be here in a few minutes. Would you mind making sure she gets to the truck safely?"

"Sure, but how will I know who her ride is?"

I kept forgetting she was new in town. "His name is Tucker, and he will be the only one in here with dreadlocks."

She cocked an eyebrow at my description, so I continued. "He's lanky and reminds me of the seventies."

Sam laughed. "You weren't alive in the seventies."

There was a small sense of relief at her levity. I still needed to find out what was going on with her but appreciated we could still have a pleasant conversation. "No, but the late sixties and seventies were my gram's favorite era. I spent a lot of time looking at pictures, watching old documentaries on Woodstock. You get the idea."

She nodded. "So look for someone who would look completely at home at Woodstock."

"That's the ticket. Thanks, Sam."

With a gentleness that contradicted the toughness I'd seen from her previously, Sam leaned down and spoke softly into Jessica's ear. When there was a nod in response, Sam helped her to a standing position and slipped her jacket over her shoulders. Jessica grabbed her purse and paid her bill before allowing Sam to escort her to the door.

I checked on the other patrons before returning my attention to Serena. "Do you think she killed Camilla?" I figured she'd had enough to drink that I could be direct without upsetting her.

Serena didn't answer at first. She continued to slowly sip what I knew was going to be her last beverage while continuing to stare at the back bar. I felt a pang of compassion. She had obviously been close to Camilla. She'd worked for her for…I had no idea how long. I added that to the mental list of things I needed to research. She'd also been able to deal with Camilla. Even when she was being difficult to everyone around her, Serena's demeanor had remained calm and quiet. I guess each person needed a ying to their yang. Serena had been that for Camilla, it appeared.

Finally she spoke. "I think anyone is capable of anything if pushed too hard."

It was an interesting theory, but I wasn't sure I agreed. Personally, I was more of a pacifist. Serena was in no condition to argue though, and I'd rather use my active remaining brain cells to ponder if the complaint filed against Jessica had been real or Camilla's way of causing trouble for her. Had this been a repeating pattern? As I'd suspected, Camilla had significant resources at her disposal. That kind of money could create legal trouble for her adversaries, resulting in the loss of time and money. Maybe one of them had sought revenge?

Tucker stepped inside and waved. I returned his gesture and nodded to Sam. As the two of them were helping Jessica outside, I wanted to extend the same offer to Serena. "Would you like Tucker to give you a lift somewhere? I know you're not staying at the Ocean View, but I'm sure he won't mind dropping you off."

She shook her head as she pulled cash out to pay her bill. "I'm meeting with someone, but thank you."

The clock on the wall showed it was after ten. Gram always said nothing good happened after ten at night. While I'd occasionally partaken of some good things after ten, this felt a little late for a meeting. "You sure you'll be alright? It's pretty late."

Her smile was meant to placate me, I was certain. However, she was a big girl and could have a meeting whenever and with whomever she wanted. I couldn't help it though. My protective instincts were strong.

"I'll be fine, but thank you for your kindness and for the drink."

Once she left, I waited for Sam to come back in and then motioned her over to the side bar. Not wanting to wait one more moment to find out what was going on, I asked. "Are you upset about something?"

The stoic expression on her face gave little away, but the slight twitching of her eye provided a resounding yes to my question. I'd been working on being patient and giving people time to answer questions before I jumped in again. After what felt like an eternity and a half, (hey, I was working on patience, not my dramatic tendencies), she answered.

"When you interceded earlier while I was trying to defuse the situation with those three, did you do that because you worried I wouldn't do my job? And before you answer, I know you talked to Sally."

"I was verifying employment and checking references. Standard procedure." At least that was what I'd been told.

"Are you going to fire me?"

"Did you take the diamonds?" Officer Faria had said be direct and to the point. It didn't get any more concise than that.

"No."

She sounded believable, but I sensed there was more to the story. "Do you know who did?"

"Nothing that would hold up in court." She broke eye contact as she answered.

My radar was receiving mixed signals from Sam, and I didn't like it. "You know I love theories…"

My smile was meant to put her at ease, but she crossed her arms and sighed. "And you know I don't like getting involved. Please, let this go or let me go. At this point, I'll take either choice."

Sam had given me no reason not to trust her, other than showing poor judgment by jogging around Shady Pines at night. I decided to not make any hasty decisions until I could learn more. "I'll let it go..." *For now.* "To set the record straight, the only reason I intervened earlier is because I wanted to get Adam, Jessica, and Serena to sit at the bar so I could ask them some questions."

Sam's head cocked to the side. Her arms remained crossed. "Sounds like you're getting involved in matters you shouldn't."

One hundred percent absolutely it was. "Not really. This time several people asked me to get involved."

"You have a hard time saying no?" She softened the question with just a hint of a smile. I'd take that as a sign we might be able to work through all of this.

Opting for complete honesty, I explained. "I have a hard time standing by while someone needs help."

"And that lands her into trouble more times than I can count." Tanner's deep voice made all the warm fuzzies start floating around inside me.

"Tanner! I didn't expect to see you until I got home." I moved around the bar to give him a big hug. The whole spiel about absence making the heart grow fonder? Totally true.

"Well, I was missing my girlfriend and..."

I laughed. "You were hungry and knew there'd be no food at my place."

"Except cat food and tuna, and I'm betting your new roommate won't want to share."

He continued to hold me in his strong embrace. I knew we had to separate, but just a few seconds more.

"You could've stopped by your mom's place. I'm sure she would've been happy to feed you since she too knows I typically only keep tuna in my cupboards."

"She's gone for a weekend trip with her new boyfriend." He provided us with air quotes as he said the last word. There was also a noticeable shudder. I guessed a son didn't like to think of his mom in that way, whether he liked the guy or not. "And, before you worry, Ashley is spending the night with a friend. While she may have turned over a new behavior leaf, Mom still isn't going to let a teenager be alone in the house for a whole weekend."

The sound of a clearing throat reminded me that I'd been having a conversation with Sam. I disengaged from the best hug I'd had all week and turned around as I took Tan's hand. "Sorry about that, Sam. Please let me introduce you to Tanner Montgomery, my current boyfriend." I winked at him. "And Tanner, this is Samantha Sheraton."

Seeing with his own eyes that my replacement security was female broadened Tan's already wide grin. "Nice to meet you, Sam. And just to clarify, current and future boyfriend. Took me too long to snag her to let her get away."

She shook his hand. "Nice to meet you as well."

"Hey, that's a beautiful necklace. My mom has one similar. Nice choice."

Tanner was my knight in white cotton and didn't even know it. He brought up the necklace without me having to. "It is beautiful." I agreed with what I hoped was a believable smile.

Sam's smile disappeared. "Thank you. I need to get back to my station. Are we cool, Lilly?"

Tanner shot a quick glance in my direction, concern marring his chiseled face. "Hey, I'm sorry if I upset you. Let me make it up to you. Join us for pizza night? I could bring you up to speed on Lilly's need to stick her beautiful nose in places it doesn't belong."

"Hey!" I wanted to be mad, but since he'd meshed the truth about my meddling with a compliment about my nose, I couldn't find the will to even act upset.

Sam shook her head. "I think I'm already current on that detail. I appreciate the offer, but I can't."

I worried she still hadn't forgiven my earlier interference. "Are you sure? We'd really like to have you over."

She shook her head." I'd really like to come. I just have to be at home."

"Ok, sure, I can respect that. Just know we usually get together one night over the weekend, have pizza, and just hang out."

"Maybe sometime. Thanks for the invitation." Her body language said that "sometime" would be a frosty day in Hades. She nodded to Tanner. "Nice to meet you."

Once we were alone, well as alone as you could get at a bar on a Friday night, Tanner whispered, "What was that all about?"

I maintained a hold on his hand and led him behind the bar. "I'm not sure. There's more to the Sam story than I currently know. Maybe she really couldn't come—an elderly relative or someone she has to care for? I don't know a lot about her personal history."

"Yet." Tan grinned.

I simply smiled at his comment. "You wanted something to eat, right?"

The kiss on my cheek was sweet and held a hint of promise of what was to come later tonight. Too bad he would probably be upset when he learned I planned on using the time we were all together as a research party on Camilla and those who knew her best. Translation—those who wanted her dead. I might have to sneak in some kisses and melt his heart like butter with Watson before he learned about that.

"I'll place an order directly with Tara and eat in the kitchen. I don't want to slow down your closing routine. I'll also order the pizza and have it delivered about the time we should arrive at your place."

"You're very helpful, Pretty Boy." I teased him with the nickname I'd given him when we first started dating.

"That's how we win over the pretty girls."

About an hour or so later, Tanner, Mandi, Freddie, and I had finished off half the pizza. Freddie was the first to finish. "This is the best pizza evah."

Mandi shoved him with her shoulder. "I'm going to tell Clara and Tara you said that."

"Hey! They don't make pizza." Then he stopped and paused a beat. "Do they?"

I picked up another piece. "No, but if they ever start, you better watch what you say. They're both very good with knives."

We all lifted our cups filled either with beer or wine into the air. "True that!" Freddie said.

Watson added a meow from his brand-new cat bed near the back door. Tanner had brought the bed along with some salmon-flavored wet cat food that Watson had inhaled in three bites.

Since everyone was in a good mood at the moment, I thought this was the best time to bring up my secondary agenda for the evening. "Now that your bellies are almost full…well, except for Freddie's…"

"Hey!" Freddie offered a sheepish grin, "Ok, maybe not entirely full."

"What do you need us to help you with, Lilly?" Mandi's blue eyes twinkled though I couldn't be sure if that was from her anticipation about a project or from Freddie looking very handsome in his black jeans, white shirt, and black leather jacket. He'd lost the jacket once he got inside, but the look on Mandi's face wasn't lost on me. She'd noticed.

I handed each one of them a piece of paper with a name written at the top, along with a pen. "These are the people who were either closest to Camilla or had the most motive to kill her, as far as we know, anyway. Since we have a limited amount of time before the auction to prove Jack's innocence, I thought more hands will make it go faster. If you find anything noteworthy, please write it down. Maybe seeing it all together will help us figure this puzzle out."

Mandi's adorable lips pouted when she saw the name at the top of her paper. "Serena, really? I kind of wanted to research Camilla."

"Serena shouldn't take long, but I know you'll be thorough. Don't you want to try to figure out how someone as nice as her ended up working for someone like Camilla?"

The pout turned into a small grin. "That is an interesting question. Ok, but when I'm finished, I'm jumping in on the Camilla research wagon. Deal?"

"Deal.

"Ok, so I'll take Camilla. Mandi has Serena. Freddie, I thought you'd like to dig into Adam Miller. And Tanner, my love?"

The smile on his face melted me faster than a snow cone on the pavement in July. Yup, a sugary mess, that was what he made me. "Yes?"

"Would you mind looking into Jessica Byers?"

He grabbed my hand and pulled me toward him for a kiss. Not the PDA kind of kiss he gave me at the tavern—no, this was an honest-to-goodness-foot-poppin'-make-me-forget-my-name kind of kiss. If we hadn't had company and if Jack hadn't been in jail…

"Yo', you two wanna get a room? You're embarrassing the kids. Even the cat hid his face."

The last part was enough to make me look up and across the room. Sure enough, Watson had buried his head in his paws. My laughter ruined our R-rated romantic moment. I found my composure enough to return to an upright position and face Freddie. "I don't need a room. I have a whole house."

"And guests…" Mandi added. "Guests who are providing vital research in order to ensure Jack Condor is freed."

Oh yeah, research—that was what we were going to do. "Right. Let's get started. Everyone got your phone or other electronic device with the appropriate search engines?"

"Yes, Boss." I loved it when they replied in unison. It meant we were in sync. I snuggled in next to Tanner and started Googling Camilla Cartwright.

An hour later, the yawning signaled it was time for everyone to head home. Well, everyone but Tanner. I couldn't, in good conscience, let him go home to an empty house. Yeah, that was my story, and I was sticking to it (and him)—like glue.

Mandi handed me her paper and gave me a hug. "Hope your search went better than mine. Other than when she's mentioned as Camilla's assistant, there isn't a lot about Serena's life—at least not that I could find. I do want you to know how much I appreciate all you're doing. I know you really weren't trying to get involved this time."

"Margaritas and meddling are my specialties."

Freddie's face was somber as he handed me his research. "Adam is bad news. Has a temper and"—he pointed to a starred note he'd made about a third of the way down his paper—"he plays on a softball team in Seattle."

"So he knows his way around a bat?"

Freddie nodded and then yawned again. "C'mon, Mandi. I'll give you a ride home. We'll get your bike tomorrow."

Then there were three. Tanner, Watson, and me. Watson got up from his bed, stretched, and headed toward the bedroom. Tanner scooped him up. "Oh no, little guy. Tonight, you're on guard duty. I'll keep your side of the bed warm. Promise."

"Meeooowww."

I couldn't be sure, but that didn't sound like agreement. "Tanner, he's used to sleeping in the bed with me."

Tanner set the cat down on the couch and pulled his T-shirt off. His chest muscles rippled with the movement, and I confess I forgot what my point was. "He can continue to sleep with you Sunday through Thursday nights. Friday and Saturday are mine."

My gaze managed to tear itself away from Tan's chest to Watson's angry glare. My arms slid around Tan's neck as I stepped closer. "You get five nights. He gets two. That feels more than reasonable."

Watson emitted a low growl. That was definitely not agreement. Tanner managed to remove his mouth from my neck long enough to try one last time with Watson. "I brought you a nice, soft bed. Doesn't that count for something?"

As if to prove it didn't, Watson did a couple of circles on the couch and plopped down there. He had no idea how little Tan cared where he slept, as long as it wasn't with us tonight. Tan reached down and scratched between Watson's ears before he stood, scooped me up, and carried me to the bedroom.

Absence may make the heart grow fonder, but Tanner's presence—specifically in my bedroom—made me lose track of everything else in the world. The moment his lips touched mine, murder was the farthest thing from my mind.

* * *

An hour or so later, I tiptoed into the kitchen for a bottle of water. I noticed Watson had moved from the couch to his bed. Guess he did like the gift Tan had brought him to make up for taking his side of the bed a couple nights a week. I put a treat on his plate in case he woke up before me in the morning.

The notes everyone had compiled on our suspects caught my attention. I grabbed them and headed back into the bedroom. Watson didn't even stir. Some guard cat he turned out to be. Once snuggled back in bed, I used the light from my phone to read over the notes. The info about Jessica hadn't been any surprise. The only thing really surprising about her was her choice of male companion. She had scraped her way to recognition in the real estate market. Most of her endeavors were geared toward properties that served the greater good of humanity, while Adam seemed more intent on more self-motivated reasons. Maybe the adage that opposites attract was totally true in their case. I made a note to text Vernon about the assault complaint she mentioned. I didn't think that was the kind of information I could find in LexisNexis. Well, not without alerting Attorney Pohoke. If Jessica really had assaulted Camilla, she might be more like Adam than appearances dictated. If the complaint was bogus, then there wasn't much motive other than her strong dislike of Camilla—which didn't feel like enough to me. I'd leave her on the list until the assault matter was cleared up, but she was at the bottom. I shuffled the paper to the next recap. Adam Miller, on the other hand, I firmly believed possessed the motivation to murder someone. He had a fiery temper, and I had no trouble believing he could be violent. He was not a big fan of Camilla's—not that many people were. According to his LinkedIn profile, he'd been in real estate from the start, working his way from small companies to large firms before opening his own a year ago. It also mentioned he had a side business dealing with investments in gold and other precious stones. I didn't know a lot about either of those industries, but based on the people I'd met who were involved, competitive and cutthroat seemed to be two of the main requirements for success. Maybe he hadn't meant to kill her, but his anger got the best of him?

Moving on, I looked at the notes on Serena. Mandi hadn't lied. There wasn't much here. Her online profile showed she'd started college, her field of choice business and finance. She'd even received some accolades for her work in the first three years, but she never graduated. Odd. Not that I was judging. I didn't even start college, so the fact someone made it through three years with a modicum of success impressed me. From what Mandi had determined, Serena had left college to work for Camilla about a year ago.

The curiosity kitties clawed mightily, wanting answers. I could understand that Serena was ying to Camilla's yang, but why wouldn't Camilla want her to finish college? Wouldn't that make her an even greater asset to the team?

Maybe the key was with Camilla rather than the suspects. I'd assumed the killer was someone in the real estate field since they had the most to lose at the moment. Based on the threatening letters Serena had shared about earlier, Camilla had been making enemies for a long time.

I looked at the sheet I'd written up on Camilla. Most of what I'd found had obviously been given a spin on the dance floor by a PR person. If I was going to learn anything about Camilla, I needed to go straight to the source—her family. Other than being mentioned as the source of her initial wealth, they were markedly absent from articles and images about Camilla.

I typed *Cartwright family* into the search engine on my phone. The very first result was *Cartwright Care—The very best for your loved ones.* After a few more clicks, I had a number to call from the "Contact Us" section on their website. It wouldn't get me directly to *the* Mr. and Mrs. Cartwright, but if I played my cards right and chose my words carefully, I might be able to speak with them.

My eyelids were putting on weight, and I knew it wouldn't be long until they'd win this particular battle. Before I put everything away to snuggle into Tan's embrace, I caught the three words I'd written down at the bottom of Camilla's paper. Those same three words that kept surfacing and no one cared about except me. My sigh resonated a little louder than I'd planned, bringing Tan closer. "Everything ok, Lilly?"

"You're a smart guy, right?"

The white from his smile shone brightly in the glow from my cell phone. "I've learned it depends on the day. Why? What's up?"

He was going to laugh me out of the bed when I asked this. "Do the words *skinny, punt, older* mean anything to you?"

His chuckle was embarrassing, but at least not enough to laugh me out of bed. "Nothing that comes to mind. How are they related?"

The paper and phone were placed on the nightstand so I could move into full-on snuggle mode. "I'm not sure they are, but there's something about them. Something I can't let go. Camilla had those three words written on her hand."

"Did she write them there?"

That was a very good question. "I have no idea. I've assumed she was the one to put them there, but I suppose someone else could have done that for her. Though that doesn't make any more sense than her doing it herself."

"Do you know if the words were written on there before or after she was killed?"

Ugh, why didn't I think of these questions? I rolled over so I could face him, even though it was too dark to see him. "See, you *are* smart. I didn't even think about that."

He pulled me into his warm, safe embrace. "You're too close to it. I'm an outside observer making logical observations." His soft lips anointed my forehead. "Your passion to solve the case could blind you to the details."

"I bet Sherlock Holmes never had that problem."

"You know Sherlock Holmes isn't real, right?"

"He was based on a real person." I didn't want to lose this round, though I wasn't sure why. Guess the need to be right—about something—was gaining momentum. All of my research thus far had netted me a big fat nothing.

Meow. Meow. Meow.

Scratch. Scratch. Scratch.

"Just ignore him. He'll go lay down and go back to sleep," Tanner whispered in my ear.

I tried. I really did. But Watson sounded so pitiful, I couldn't pretend he wasn't there pawing at my door and crying for me. After fifteen minutes, I gave up and got up.

"Lilly…"

The moment the door opened, I scooped Watson up into my arms. He quieted and snuggled in. I slipped back into bed, my back to Tanner's chest, and settled in once again. Watson took up his normal position at the edge of the bed. "You ok with this?" Not that I would've kicked Watson out, but I really wanted Tan to be on board.

I felt the kiss on the back of my head. "Every Sherlock Holmes needs a Watson. I'm ok with it. Now let's sleep."

In less than two minutes, both Watson and Tanner were snoring softly. Honestly, the fact males could fall asleep, on average, ten times faster than a woman…well, that widened the gender gap just shy of the Grand Canyon.

I wanted to sleep. I needed to sleep. I couldn't sleep.

Running through the checklist in my head, I decided the first order of business in the morning was to place a call to Camilla's mother, Mrs. Constance Cartwright. Maybe *she* could shed a brighter spotlight on who might want to kill her daughter.

Oh yeah, starting tomorrow I was going to Sherlock Holmes the shitzu out of this case.

CHAPTER FIFTEEN

———

I'm always amazed that I can have energy to attempt to solve the world's problems at one in the morning, but a mere six hours later, I can't muster enough to get out of bed. Normally I would sleep a little later on Saturday. This is probably because Tan typically kept me up much later than usual on Fridays, not that I minded one bit.

This time it was my mind that kept rehearsing what I was going to say to Mrs. Cartwright when I called. Wanting to get the cobwebs out of my head before I picked up the phone, I slid over Tan to avoid waking Watson. You might think that unfair of me, but the smile on Tanner's face as my body became parallel with his indicated he didn't seem to mind one bit. I gave him a quick kiss on the cheek. "Not right now, lover boy. A pot of tea is calling my name."

His pre-smile yawn told me he wouldn't put up too much of a fight this morning. One more kiss and then I was on my way to the kitchen. Once my tea was steeping and Tan's coffee was brewing, I checked the clock. It was early here, but Camilla's family was on the East Coast. I dialed the number for the corporate office. I got voicemail, but the message assured me someone would receive my information and return my call as soon as possible. I waited for the beep.

"Hello, my name is Lilly Waters. I'm the bar...I'm one of the owners of Smugglers' Tavern here in Danger Cove, Washington. I've been involved in helping with the investigation of Mr. and Mrs. Cartwright's daughter's death. If you could ask one of them to return my call at their earliest possible convenience, I would appreciate it." I left my number and then disconnected with a small sigh.

Next item on my list was to text Vernon. I sent off my list of things I'd like him to check into for me if he got a chance. I hit Send with a smile. Funny what a couple boxes of treats from the Cinnamon Sugar Bakery could get you around here. In all fairness, the pastries were amazing.

"I don't suppose you have anything for breakfast, do you?" Tanner's deep morning voice soothed over my recent activity and brought me back to the equivalent of our lazy Saturday morning routine.

"I have food for Watson, but that's only because Mandi's mom sent it. If your boss lets you come in a little later today, could you maybe pick up some staples for the house?"

He crossed the short distance to the kitchen to give me a hug and one of his breathtaking smiles. The moment was ruined as Watson threaded himself in and out of our legs in an effort to direct our attention his way. Tanner ignored him and kissed me (which helped me ignore Watson too). When he broke the kiss, he smiled. "Not only will I obtain supplies, but if you'll put some of that magic coffee of yours in a travel mug for me, I'll run to the bakery and secure breakfast for us too."

"If you keep that up, we'll have to change my nickname from Pretty Girl to Lucky Girl."

Tanner laughed. "Maybe we'll just go with Pretty Lucky Girl."

"I think that changes the meaning of the whole sentence, but will take it under consideration, as I am a pretty lucky girl too."

Once Tanner was on the road foraging for breakfast and Watson was fed, I thought about my earlier statement to Tan. If a comma was used, it would mean I was pretty *and* lucky. Without the comma, it was more a reference on my level of luck. This made me think about the words written on Camilla's hand. I pulled the picture up on my phone and used my fingers to enlarge the photo. The lighting wasn't great, but if I brightened my display to maximum and squinted hard, I would swear that there were periods or dots between each word. That made no sense at all. No comma, a comma, a dash, something…anything but a period between the words would make more sense.

Skinny.Punt.Older—what a bizarre combination of words, periods or not.

Frustrated by my lack of progress, I showered and changed without the aid of any caffeine. Probably not a good idea. When I returned for my tea, there was a missed call and a voicemail on my phone. The area code indicated my message would be from the Cartwright family. This day was shaping up to be fan-freaking-tastic. At least Tan was on his way with breakfast.

Punching in the numbers for my voicemail, I waited with pen and paper as a very formal-sounding woman left her information. "Ms. Waters, this is Constance Cartwright. While I have absolutely no idea why someone who works for a...a tavern would be involved in assisting with *my* daughter's death, I simply could not ignore the opportunity to inquire regarding your questions or information. My personal number is five-five-five, seven-two-eight, four-seven-five-two. I certainly hope you wrote that down because I will not repeat myself. And"—there was a significant pause—"should I learn you shared that number with anyone, suffice it to say there will be significant repercussions. I trust my instructions are clear."

Wow. Well, between the condescending voice and her self-important choice of words, there was no doubt that Camilla came by her disposition naturally. I saved the message, just in case I'd written her number down incorrectly, so I could listen to it again. Maybe Mrs. Cartwright never had to take her own messages, so she didn't realize they could be saved and played over and over again. If she had, she'd have known her threat to not repeat herself was both amusing and irrelevant.

Either way, I had her phone number—her very private and personal one. Yeah, I totally felt special. With a few more sips of tea and a grin, I dialed the digits. After a few rings, I hit the mother lode—well, Camilla's mother anyway.

"Constance Cartwright."

"Ms. Cartwright, this is Lilly Waters. I'm sorry I missed your call."

"Who?"

Geez, she'd already forgotten me. The shower hadn't been *that* long. "Lilly Waters. I'm helping with the investigation of your daughter's death."

"Oh. Yes. How can I help you? I've already answered that Barney Fife of a detective's questions."

I wasn't sure which member of the police department she referred to nor who Barney Fife was, but even without knowing, I knew it was an insult. Thanks to her impatient and aggravated tone, I decided to skip the *Do you know who would want to kill your daughter?* question, as I was sure that would toss me right on top of her incompetent pile. "Does the name Billy Nester mean anything to you?"

There was a very long pause—much longer than I would've liked. "May I ask what made you mention his name?"

The whole tone of her voice had changed. She'd even taken a turn toward polite. "Mr. Nester was a potential witness. He was near the scene of the crime around the time of your daughter's death." I didn't know when Billy had arrived or if he'd seen anything, but he apparently knew enough to get Jack arrested.

The thought of Jack made me wonder if he'd been released last night. Faria had said the DNA results were expected in by that time. I'd deal with that question later. Right now, I needed answers from Mrs. Cartwright.

"That…that…man…was a thorn in my daughter's side. He is a former employee of ours that got a little too friendly with Camilla at a huge party we hosted to celebrate twenty years of success with our business."

"May I ask what kind of problems?"

"Well…" She drew out the sharing with a dramatic pause. "He's always paid what I felt was an inappropriate interest in Camilla. She worked at the nursing home for a while, you understand."

I didn't, but it wasn't like that detail was mentioned on LinkedIn. She hadn't listed it on Facebook either. I'd wanted my investigation to be as thorough as possible. My online research also hadn't revealed from her more recent activity who might have wanted to kill her. Or if there was anyone she'd met in the last year or so who *didn't* want to kill her. "No, ma'am. I didn't realize that. What position did she hold?"

"She filled many positions during her time with us."

Translation—they couldn't find a place that either she could do the job or make her happy. I couldn't imagine her being in charge of patient care. That thought was terrifying. "A woman of many talents."

Her fake amusement shared with me what I was certain she wouldn't voice. "Yes, well, after the incident at the party, we found her a home as the head of acquisitions. She'd been dabbling in real estate for years. That's where her true passion rested."

"Always good to find a job where we can truly be ourselves." Even if our true selves annoyed everyone in a five-hundred-feet radius. "You mentioned that Billy paid inappropriate attention to Camilla? Can you be more specific?"

She huffed. "I'm not sure any of this is relevant. He just always seemed to be where she was, and his presence exacerbated whatever challenges she was experiencing in her current role. Honestly, his obsession with her was unwelcome, unwanted, and unhealthy."

I couldn't disagree with her even if I'd wanted to. It appeared Billy had been obsessed. There wasn't a big leap between obsession and murder. I'd seen that countless times on the television shows. They had to get their ideas from somewhere, right?

"I take it whatever happened at the party was the inciting incident that led to his termination?"

"Yes." The shudder in her voice made even the one-syllable word have impact.

"What did he do?"

"He plied her with enough alcohol to not only make her behave inappropriately, but she was a complete embarrassment to the entire family on what was to be a jewel in our crown of achievement. I can only assume his intention was to get her drunk enough to accept his advances."

Talk about your December-May romance. And hey, I was a you-love-who-you-love kind of gal. But this was different. Camilla didn't return his affection. As such, I couldn't even imagine how sharp her tongue would have been as she shunned him time and time again. Love must make you do some crazy things. "After the incident at the party, Billy was terminated, and Camilla was moved into acquisitions?"

"Yes. I gave her what she'd always wanted—a way out. Unlike the rest of the family, she hated being involved in the day-to-day operations. Now her sister, Candace. She is our pride and joy. I know the nursing homes will flourish for years under her direction."

I let her bask in the glory of her *other* daughter for a moment. Finally, she met me back in the moment. "After Mr. Nester was terminated, he disappeared and hasn't been seen or heard from since. Not until you mentioned his name." There was another pause. "Are you saying that man was near my daughter before she died?"

The anger and former tone had returned. I was still trying to process that the Billy I'd met could be capable of the activities she claimed. "He has been seen in the area, yes. No one has seen him in the last twenty-four hours though." The fact that Billy had provided testimony that got Jack arrested and then hadn't been seen again weighed heavily on my mind.

"Fantastic. An incompetent, small-town police force that has allowed him to escape."

Before she went too far off the deep end, there was another question burning in my brain hot enough to roast the marshmallows Mandi and I finished off a couple nights ago. "Mrs. Cartwright, may I ask one more question?"

"Only if you promise to help track down that man and bring him to justice. People like him shouldn't be allowed to wander free! My daughter was murdered, Ms. Waters. You must hold him accountable for his crimes."

Her anger was understandable. "I'll do what I can. You have my word."

"Your word means nothing to me, as I have no idea the level of your commitment to the truth or my daughter."

In all fairness, I liked the truth far more than I liked her daughter, but no sense in pointing that out. "My grandmother taught me to always be truthful. I would never disrespect her memory by being anything but honest with you."

My words mollified her. "Alright, ask your question."

"Do you know why Serena left college a few months before graduation to become your daughter's personal assistant?" I hastily added, "Not that I don't think working for your daughter wasn't a lofty pursuit." I tried to use words that might appeal to her.

The laughter that came through the phone indicated I most likely failed in that arena. "You apparently did not know my daughter well."

"No, ma'am, I did not." Not that I wanted to either.

"My daughter shunned the family business despite the affluence and status it provided her. Rather than learning our business like her sister, Candace, she chose to demand a part of her inheritance as seed money for her real estate adventure. Her goal was fast cash and easy money. She didn't care who she hurt to close the deal. Though I don't—didn't—approve, her tactics were obviously successful. My guess is Serena succumbed to the promise of wealth beyond her dreams."

Serena hadn't struck me as highly materialistic, but I didn't know her any better than I'd known Camilla—or Billy apparently. "With all due respect, Mrs. Cartwright, from what I do know, Serena has been working for your daughter for about a year now and appears to be her personal assistant rather than partner in joint wealth-seeking adventures."

"Perhaps the girl lacked the aptitude to achieve anything more. You have heard of the Peter Principle, haven't you?"

I had not. "Thank you for your time, Mrs. Cartwright."

"You will keep me informed." It was a statement, not a question.

"I'll do what I can. Thank you." I disconnected before she could humiliate me any further with her condescending tone or spewing principles I'd never heard of. Maybe Abe could tell me. Or Freddie. Or Mandi. Or Tanner. Yeah, pretty much everyone I knew would know more about this than I did. The thought made my stomach turn upside down and rail against the idea of food.

"Breakfast is served." Tanner's cheery voice filled the room and lifted my spirits the tiniest of bits.

"Thanks." I offered a kiss on the cheek to show my gratitude, even if I was no longer hungry.

"Hey, what's wrong?"

"Mrs. Cartwright returned my call." I finished my tea and filled him in on the conversation, leaving out the parts that played into my current inferiority complex. See, I did know some big words.

Tan ate his breakfast and got ready for work as he listened.

I googled Candace Cartwright. No one had mentioned a sister, but I hadn't asked. If Camilla was the black sheep of the family, Candace was the golden child, from her biography on the Cartwright Care website. As COO (chief operating officer), she had guided the business to a highly profitable venture while still maintaining a high quality of care. Impressive.

I clicked on a video of an interview from a highfalutin charity event. The interviewer had managed to secure a spot on the red carpet. She'd asked Candace to comment on the latest escapade of her younger sister. Candace had politely declined to comment and shared about how wonderful the charity they were all supporting had done in the past year under her guidance. The interviewer glossed over those details and returned the topic to Camilla. After a few more deflections, Candace walked away.

The pattern repeated on a few more videos. It was obvious there was not a lot of love lost between these two sisters. It didn't do anything other than feed my curiosity about the Cartwright family. Seemed to me that Serena would've been better off aligning herself with Candace rather than Camilla, but what did I know. Apparently not nearly enough.

As Tanner drove us to work, I tried not to think about how Billy might have played me, how I still didn't understand why Serena would leave college to work for someone who had only made her wealth by stepping on other people, and where I would end up eventually, without a college education. That last thought was totally self-serving, but I was feeling a little—ok, a lot—insecure right now.

"Do you want to tell me what's really bothering you?"

"No."

Tanner gave me a sideways glance and opened his mouth to say something but must've decided against it. His mouth closed into a thin, concerned line. I would tell him—eventually. I just needed time to process. Right now my feelings resembled a pity party rather than a legitimate, actionable character flaw. I managed a reasonable smile. "I promise it will be alright. I just need some time."

He lifted our intertwined fingers to his lips, easing them into soft satin as he kissed the back of my hand. "I know you'll tell me when you're ready."

I winked. "Right after I share with Watson."

Tan laughed. "I can see my concerns about not having competition from your new security were misplaced. I should have been more worried about what was going on at home."

This time it was my turn to kiss his hand. "I have enough love for both of you. He's just home more."

"Can't argue with that."

Tan and I were the first to arrive at the tavern, which was surprising given I'd been delayed with my phone call. With only an hour to go before opening, there was no time to waste.

"Sorry we're late, Boss—" Tara started.

"—Mom isn't feeling well, and we needed to make sure she had everything she needed," Clara finished.

My twin chefs operated as one unit not only in the kitchen but also in conversation. Tara was technically the head chef. Because they were connected on a level that far surpassed the BFF wavelength that Mandi and I shared, they always knew what the other was thinking and worked as one. "No worries. I hope she feels better soon. You don't think it's contagious, do you?"

They both shook their heads. "No, but we'll use extra—"
"—sanitizer and bleach today to be sure."

"Thanks, ladies. Now that you're in the kitchen, I'm going to head out front and help Tan get things set up there. I wonder what's keeping Mandi and Freddie."

Both sets of shoulders shrugged as they slipped on their gloves and grabbed the hairnets. At least I wasn't the only one in the dark. "Let me know if you hear anything."

When I exited the kitchen, Abe was sitting at the bar, nursing a cup of coffee from the Cinnamon Sugar Bakery. "Rough night last night, Abe?" I tried to keep the humor out of my voice. Since I was normally surrounded by twentysomethings, the fact that the sixtysomething was the one with a hangover tickled me.

"I offer a two-word explanation for my state this morning."

I started slicing fruit and prepping the bar. "Oh, I can't wait to hear this."

"Agnes. Tequila."

The knife was placed carefully on the bar before I gave in to a fit of laughter. Hey, something was always funny until you lost an eye…or a finger. I was dangerous enough with a knife without adding shaking. "How could you not have known about Agnes's love for top shelf tequila?"

He waved away my question. "Oh, I knew about it. What I forgot"—he lifted his head and smiled—"was how low my tolerance had become for the sinister spirit."

I patted him gently on the shoulder. "If Mandi and Freddie make it in, you can hang out in the greenhouse until the pain subsides."

"Don't mollycoddle me, Mother. I'll be fine as soon as the caffeine kicks in."

Oy vey. First it was the Peter and his principle, and now it was Molly and her coddling. Who were these people? "Don't what you?"

"It means to treat someone indulgently or protectively. I think it originated long before my generation, so yours has probably never heard of it."

"There's a lot I haven't heard of apparently," I grumbled as I took out my frustration on the lemon.

"Sorry. I'm not following."

"Who is Peter and what is his principle?" There, I'd admitted I was clueless. Couldn't say it made me feel any better.

Abe's smile was tender. "You mean the Peter Principle?"

A sigh escaped before I could stop it. "Yes, that's the one."

"It means that a person rises to their level of incompetence."

My pity party took a break as I absorbed this new information. Mrs. Cartwright believed Serena hadn't become successful because she lacked the ability to do so. Well, the ability to do so under Camilla's guidance anyway.

About that time Mandi and Freddie burst through the door, chatting nonstop. I waited for them to breathe. "Glad you two could join us today." I softened my words with a smile. They were never late, and I had no intention of getting cranky with them the first time they were.

"Sorry, Boss. We were studying and lost track of the time," Freddie offered as he grabbed a stack of wrapped silverware and started putting it on the tables.

"You both have the same class?"

Ironically, both Mandi and Freddie blushed at my question. And here I thought Clara and Tara were the only ones who were twinsies. Mandi was uncharacteristically quiet and suddenly focused on all her opening tasks. Finally, Freddie spoke. "Nah, we're just being study buddies, ya know."

Mandi's complexion now matched the color of her hair. This was a teasable offense, but I'd save it for when we were alone. She was embarrassed enough. "What are you studying, Freddie?"

He brought a rack of clean glasses to the bar. "It's this cool class about websites and apps that are used for multi purposes. I mentioned it earlier, remember?"

I hoped there wasn't some person's name attached to the concept. Otherwise, I was calling in sick today. "What do you mean 'multi purposes'?"

Freddie's dark eyes twinkled. "For good and evil."

That explanation was clear as mud. "Well, I'm glad you're here."

"Don't worry, Boss. We'll get set up, but once things slow down, I'll show you just like I promised. There's a totally cool project I'm working on. You'll love it."

I wasn't sure that I would, but his excitement was hard to ignore. The least I could do was take a few minutes to see the project. "Sounds great."

We'd been open a little over an hour and gearing up for the lunch rush, when Bree walked in the door. From the look on her face, I couldn't tell if she was happy, angry, or something entirely different. I adopted a proceed with-caution-approach. "Hey, Bree. You're in early." Usually she stopped in closer to closing time.

She plopped down on the stool. "Jack Condor has been released."

CHAPTER SIXTEEN

———

At least I now understood the expression on Bree's face. My feelings were mixed as well. I put a Dark and Stormy in front of her without prompting. "I'm guessing the DNA results came back showing it wasn't him?"

Bree shrugged. "I have no idea. He stopped by to tell me the good news. I'm happy for him, but…"

"But he presented the most likely suspect," Mandi finished.

"Not according to my research," Freddie added as he made his way to the kitchen with a bin of dirty dishes.

"Who does he think did it?" Bree stopped nursing her drink and perked up at the news.

"Adam Miller."

Bree returned her attention to me when I supplied the name. "Do you support his theory?"

"No."

"You have someone else in mind then?" Bree's green gaze pierced into my brain, looking for answers.

"I don't want to believe anyone capable of such a thing." Even to someone like Camilla…

She huffed and downed a few more swallows of her drink before arching an eyebrow. "Right, but we both know people *are* capable."

Sad but true. "Fine. If I had to pick from the possible list of suspects right now, I'd say Billy Nester had means, motive, and opportunity. I'm still not convinced he did it, but he is the most likely."

Billy was the prime suspect, but I couldn't accept my gut instincts about him were wrong. They'd not let me down so far, but I couldn't dismiss what I'd learned about him this morning. Add to that what I already knew, and the odds weren't in his favor.

Bree nodded and returned attention to her drink. I decided I needed a little fresh air. Tara had a BLT set aside for me in a container. Because my breaks were unpredictable and typically short, I'd learned to appreciate the sandwich even if the bacon was cold. Freshly brewed iced tea and my sandwich along with a gentle breeze as the sun peeked through the trees. I took a seat on my favorite bench and inhaled a long, fresh breath. Yes, this was nice.

"Lilly?" The whispered voice erased any calm I'd managed to find.

I'd come to recognize the whispered voice, as each time he said my name, my blood pressure spiked a few points. "Billy?"

I caught a glimpse of his dark jacket in the thick of bushes off to the left. "Was wondering if I might stop by tonight for some more food? I'll be moving along soon, but…"

The thought of meeting Billy at night did not sit well. The thought of him moving on and possibly getting away with murder was not acceptable. I hadn't even taken a bite of my sandwich. Forcing calm to my jittering nerves, I stood and took a few steps toward him. "Here, take this. I can get another. If you let me know what you like, I can bring some out to you each afternoon."

Two birds. One stone—er, one Billy. He'd come by in the daytime, and I hoped in the end, the promise of regular food would make him stick around until all of this could be sorted out.

"You're very kind."

My blush heated my face as I knew my motives for helping were only partially pure. I supposed that was better than one hundred percent unpure, right? "Just paying it forward for those who have helped me in the past."

Billy sat next to me and chewed his sandwich slowly. Finally he responded. "I try to do that too."

Not the story Mrs. Cartwright was telling, but I also had no idea what percent her motives added up to. "How did you end up out here, Billy? Are you originally from this area?"

He finished half the sandwich and then closed the lid. Saving some for later—I understood that concept too. He stood, and the old gray eyes gazed into mine. "I appreciate your help, but where I'm from and why I'm here...well, that ain't none of your business."

He didn't know much about me if he thought that would stop me from—well, anything. I wanted to see if he'd open up at all about the Cartwright family. "I know you used to work for the Cartwrights. There's been enough talk about Camilla. I was wondering if you could tell me anything about Candace?"

The container was opened up again, and he pulled out the remaining half of the sandwich and took another bite. "Ms. Candy is good people. She runs a tight ship, but she's always the same. A real cool cucumber. Only one thing gets under her skin."

"What's that?"

"Not what—who. Camilla." He shook his head and offered a small smile. "Good Lawd she drove her big sister crazy. Not only did she not join her in the family business, Candace believed Camilla was doing everything in her power to disgrace the family name. Talk about cat fighting. Whew-ee. I saw a big one right before Camilla headed out West. She told Ms. Candy this one would be the biggest deal yet."

It was also the same time Billy got fired, but we'd not mention it. "I don't have any siblings, but I can see why that would be upsetting. You were a fan of Camilla's though, right?"

His face registered shock and maybe disgust. "There you go, asking questions that ain't none of your business."

Billy was one hundred percent correct—it wasn't any of my business, but I still wanted to know. I decided to stand up and move a little closer to the back door. I leaned against the wall and shrugged in a noncommittal way to convey disinterest. "I'm naturally curious."

Billy moved closer into my personal space, forcing me to work hard not to squirm under the intensity of his glare. "You know what they say curiosity did to the cat, don't you?"

Fear mixed with anger and boiled into a dangerous mix. Fortunately for Billy, my spicy side—sarcasm and sassiness—always won out. I managed a smile despite the cauldron of emotion. "I only remember the satisfaction bringing it back."

The menace in his expression morphed into merriment. "Yeah, I guess you're right about that. Just be mindful of your manners."

An *Or what?* hovered right on the tip of my tongue, ready to jump me off the safety ledge I'd managed to crawl back onto. Instead I saluted, "Sir, yes sir."

He grabbed the container and headed back into the bushes. The moment he was gone from sight, the wall served its purpose of holding me up as I sank heavily against it. The adrenaline surge faded, leaving a shaking in my body I couldn't subdue.

"Lilly? You alright?" Tanner's concerned voice eased the trembling.

"Yes, just upset about this whole Camilla situation. Normally, I'd have at least some clue at this point who did it." I turned and looked at him with a pained expression. "There are far too many suspects to keep up with."

The warmth of his arms surrounding me melted the remaining chill. "Just breathe, take a step back, and consider who had the most to gain from her death. Didn't Ms. Ashby mention that last year when you were trying to get to the bottom of your last mystery?"

I nodded into his chest. "Yes, she said that things aren't always what they seem and by paying attention to all the details, pieces start to come together." Reluctantly lifting my head, I made my confession. "I just feel so…inadequate right now. Everyone around me is taking steps to better themselves by going to college. What if I've Peter Principled out?"

Tan's grin encouraged rather than mocked. "Lilly Raine Waters, I've known you for about three years now. In that time you went from living above a garage with no idea where your next paycheck would come from to a part owner of a successful restaurant and owner of your own home. You are leaving Peter and his principle in the dust at the present moment."

His words made sense but didn't stop the unease that had settled low in my stomach. "It's not the present I'm worried about. It's the future."

Tan stepped back and lifted my chin to ensure he had my attention. "If that's the way you feel, my beautiful girlfriend, then do something about it."

"I'm just not sure what or how. Free time isn't something I have a lot of these days."

He shrugged. "If it's important enough to you, I know you'll find a way to make it happen." The rogue smile appeared as he pulled me closer. I was confident it was to make sure I couldn't hit him as he said whatever he was going to say next. "You are by far the most stubborn person I've ever met."

Yup, there it was—a smackable offense, even if it was entirely true. Despite the insult, his words encouraged me. I was resilient. I would figure it out. I just needed to decide what "it" was. In the meantime, I'd back-burner that and set about taking a second look at all the suspects.

"I'm going to take that as a compliment."

Tan squeezed me tighter and then kissed me on the forehead. "It was meant as one."

We separated and started back inside. Tan stopped and pointed to some ants over on the concrete. They were working together to pull a piece of bread off to wherever their anthill was, and for the record, I did not want to know the location. I just wanted to be sure it was far away from the tavern. "I don't like bugs, but I like that they're working together."

"Teamwork makes the dream work." Tan grinned.

I released his hand and looked over my shoulder as I made my way back inside. "You come up with that all by yourself?"

His laughter put a smile on my face. My stomach was empty, but my confidence meter had started the important crawl toward full. Back behind the bar, I waved to Abe to let him know Tan was on his way back to his post. He made his way over to me. "Nice lunch?"

My stomach rumbled in answer making Abe chuckle. "I see you tried to sustain yourself on love rather than bacon."

I didn't want to lie to Abe, but I didn't want to tell him about my run-in with Billy either. "Isn't love the be-all and end-all for everything?"

"Based on the rumbling in your tummy, I'm going to have to say no."

"Are you this motherly with Agnes?" I winked as I popped an orange slice into my mouth. Vitamin C for the win.

"My relationship with Ms. Thermopolis is not up for discussion." He tried to sound serious, but the sparkle in his sapphire gaze gave him away.

"Then neither are my lunch activities with Mr. Montgomery."

Abe laughed and nodded. "Touché, my dear."

"Might I ask you to actually tend to the paying customers, or is that beyond your abilities?" Mr. Impatient sitting at the end of the bar was apparently getting hangry. Tanner's sister, Ashley, had taught me that expression—a cross between hungry and angry.

And just like that, the confidence meter hit the slippery slope downward. I turned toward the haughty Eastern accent. Having spent time in New York for many years, I recognized it immediately. I plastered a smile on my face and turned toward the patron. "I'm sorry for your wait, sir. What can I get started for you?"

He lifted a pair of glasses on a handle in front of his beady black eyes. They resembled marbles, unemotional and devoid of the sparkle I witnessed in Abe's and Tan's gazes. The scrutiny he gave the menu made me think he was reading a manifesto rather than the meat selections of the day. After what had to be an eternity and a half, he lowered the plastic-coated paper. "Have you nothing but sliced, cooked beef or fowl that has been coated and deep fried?"

I had no idea who this big, burly pompous asteroid was, but no one was going to talk about *my* tavern or the food that Tara and Clara prepared with such disdain. From the looks of the buttons straining to keep his shirt together, he hadn't been *too* picky about his food. "With all due respect, sir, my chefs are among the finest in this area, and they carefully select the meats and how to prepare them on a daily basis. Our offerings lean toward bar food because, well, we are a bar." I left out the sarcastic addition of mentioning that he might have missed the big sign on the way in. I wanted to straighten him out, not be rude. "If you prefer a more refined selection, you might want to check out the Lobster Pot."

"Mr. Winchester, how nice of you to stop in. I trust you're enjoying your stay here in Danger Cove." Mandi recalled him perfectly from when she'd checked him in at the Ocean View B&B. Her tone came off far less aggravated than mine.

"Good God, woman. Are you the only one in this town who works? Your work ethic is to be commended."

His words sounded more like a backhanded slam of Mandi rather than a compliment. The arrogant tone of this man worked its way under my skin and generated an irritation twice what Camilla had managed to do in the short time I'd interacted with her. I had to take a few deep breaths to keep my customer service at the level required. "Might I recommend the lobster bisque with a freshly made multigrain roll?"

The beady black of his eyes lightened a bit at my suggestion. "I doubt you'll manage to make it as well as they do back home, but I'm willing to give it a try, as the bed and breakfast I'm staying at believes breakfast consists solely of dough and sugar. I doubt her kitchen has ever been used."

There might be a grain of truth in those words, but I'd never admit it to him. "At least let us try. If you aren't satisfied, your meal is complimentary."

Mandi rolled her eyes as she stepped away. I guessed he managed to get under her skin as well. "Would you like something to drink while you wait?"

"It's soup. How long can it take?" And just like that, he managed to reignite the irritation.

My teeth formed an ivory barrier against the sharp retort standing ready at the tip of my tongue. Instead I decided to ignore the bait. He might be trying to play the part of a wealthy blue blood, but his manners showed a distinct lack of class. My guess was he loved a fight. He wasn't getting one from me today. When I didn't answer what I considered to be his rhetorical question, he picked up the drink menu, scanned it, and then returned it to the holder. "I'll have a Cosmopolitan."

This had to be a test. The laughter bubbling in my empty gut begged to be let out. The idea of this grouchy man ordering a pink drink deserved at least a giggle. I swear if I could find a way to snap a picture, it would bring me hours of enjoyment later. "Sure thing. House vodka or do you have a preference?"

He ordered a premium vodka, of course. I took extra care to make sure it was perfect, as I didn't want to hear him complain again. Clara brought his soup and bread out right as I put his drink in front of him. While he enjoyed his soup, I decided it was time I got to know him and what he was doing here in Danger Cove. Well, what he was doing besides aggravating everyone he came in contact with since arrival.

I let him enjoy a couple bites. The look of contentment on his face assured me that even if he did complain about something—and I knew he would—it would be a complete fabrication. "You're visiting from New York?"

The spoon clacked onto the bowl. He wiped his mouth before gracing me with an annoyed look. "I fail to see either how you know that or how it is any of your business."

He might like to aggravate, but my sassy side was a force to be reckoned with—just ask Tan. "I know because you are now in Small Town, USA, and not much happens here that everyone doesn't know about sooner or later. It's my business ..." I grinned. "Well, because you're in Small Town, USA."

"I contend it is not your business, but in the interest of being able to return to my soup before it's cold..."

I put my elbows on the bar and leaned forward, doing my best to keep my humor contained. "That must mean you're enjoying it."

"The soup is acceptable, perhaps even a small measure above that. I am from the New York area. My area of expertise resides in the finer things in life. People contact me to assess the value of their goods."

"So you're an appraiser?"

"Young lady, the service I provide is far beyond that of a mere appraiser. Now please, return to your bartending duties and allow me to finish my meal in peace."

Infuriating. Irritating. Infantile. Those three words described the services he provided if you asked me—which no one had. It wasn't much, but more than we knew before. I'd met enough tourists either visiting or passing through to know there was a specific purpose for his time in Danger Cove. I just didn't know what it was.

Yet.

Mercifully, other customers needed my attention, so I left Mr. Winchester to finish his bisque in peace. When he raised his hand to indicate he was ready for the bill, I breathed a silent prayer of relief. I know I'd baited him in order to learn some things about him, but he didn't play nice in the interview sandbox. I was ready for him to take his toys and go home. I handed him his check. In exchange, he provided me with a credit card. I swiped the card and waited.

Declined.

Ugh. The last thing I wanted was another confrontation with this man, especially regarding a twenty-dollar tab. Before I could make a decision on how to handle this situation, his impatience surfaced.

"Is your equipment incompetent?"

I fought the urge to argue with this pompous putz that equipment couldn't be incompetent...only people. Instead, I handed him the card. "No, sir. It appears your card has been declined. Would you like me to try again, or do you have an alternate form of payment you'd like to use?"

Ruby would have been proud of the restraint I'd just shown. I waited as his face blotched in various shades of red, a nice mix of embarrassment and anger. He reached into his wallet, retrieved some cash, and tossed it on the bar in front of me. "Don't expect to see me in here again." He huffed as he headed out the door.

Subtracting his bill from the cash he left resulted in me pocketing an eight-cent tip. Big spender this one was. He struck me as the kind of person who liked to pretend he was something he wasn't. At least I wouldn't have to worry about him trying to pay with a bad credit card again. There could've been a simple reason the card was declined. I remember that happening once when I was younger when we were traveling. The bank did it to make sure we hadn't been a victim of fraud. I preferred to think Mr. Winchester's was because he'd been incompetent and forgot to pay his bill.

I shot a quick text to Bree to let her know there was a possibility his card would be declined when he tried to pay for his room. We looked out for each other around here. That was the plus side of everyone knowing your business in a small town—they also made every effort to help protect your business as well.

She texted me back a *Thanks* and also shared with me that Candace Cartwright had checked in. I immediately shot a text back. *No way!*

Yes way. She had business in Seattle. Wanted to stop in to see the place where her sister was killed. Morbid, eh?

For sure. Let me know if you learn anything.

Always. You do the same.

The door opened, and Detective Marshall, my least favorite member of the Danger Cove police force, stalked in. The look on his face told me this wasn't a late-lunch social call. "Good afternoon. Can I get something started for you?"

"Ms. Waters, I'm going to need you to come with me."

That was never a good sign.

* * *

Thirty minutes later I found myself sitting in the interrogation room at the Danger Cove Police Department. Oh, they didn't call it that. Instead, they referred to it as the interview room. You and I both know the way they asked the questions— at least of me—was about the farthest from an actual interview— at least any that I've been on—that you can get.

Sadly, this was not the first time I'd been "escorted" into this room. I recognized immediately that it hadn't changed one bit since my initial visit. The dim room desperately needed a coat of fresh paint. The lighting had to be a throwback to the lantern days when a yellow glow cast about the room. Maybe they thought people would confess just to get out of this place. They could be right. Each time I was here, I would pledge community service by painting the room a brighter color and replacing the light bulbs. Each time, Detective Marshall would ignore my generous offer.

The smell of pizza wafted into the room, making my stomach rumble. After donating my lunch to Billy and being forced to leave the tavern before my dinnertime, the absence of food made its presence known. "Did you at least bring me a slice?"

Detective Marshall tossed his notebook down on the metal table with a thud before plopping himself down onto the folding chair opposite mine. The creaking noise made me worry the chair might give out under his weight. "What are you talking about, Miss Waters? I haven't had pizza in a couple of days."

Warning klaxons reverberated in my brain. Not only had Pizza Guy *not* had his comfort food in forty-eight hours, but he'd consumed enough pizza in his life that the scent permeated his entire being. He could be a poster child for a heart attack in waiting. Wanting to start off things on the right foot, I leaned forward and tried to convey sincere concern. "Why don't you go grab a bite. I can come back."

His expression hardened. "Nice try. You may be released once you've answered all my questions completely and honestly."

I sighed. Rarely did I answer his questions that way— which was probably why he specified. In the interest of getting this over as soon as possible, I nodded. "I always try to do that."

Something between a snort and a laugh emitted from his rotund face. "I'm still waiting for you to succeed. Let's get started."

"Sure." I shrugged and tried to look relaxed.

I lost sight of the ballpoint pen in his large hand but could see him writing my name, the date, and the time at the top of the legal pad. Since I hadn't done anything illegal and had kept my snooping to myself—mostly—I vowed to make this interview short and sweet by answering his questions just like he wanted. I'd also not ask for my attorney…yet.

"Ok, let's get started. What were you doing at Shady Pines Motel on Monday evening between the hours of five and six?"

Oh, right. I had done something technically illegal. Though trespassing ranked as a minor offense where murder was concerned. Because of the specificity of his questions, I decided there was no point in denying it. They'd probably found my fingerprints, or Bree may have had to implicate me when she was questioned a few days ago. Either way, I'd go with honest and do my best not to share the complete story. If he knew I'd found the body...

"Bree asked me to go with her to check out the property before the auction. For the official record, I didn't want to go, as that place is disturbing, but friends help friends, right?"

The knitted eyebrows and stern glare in response to my question led me to believe he didn't agree with me on this point. After another moment or so of uncomfortable silence, I continued. "The door was unlocked when we arrived. We assumed that meant one of the real estate agents for the auction was already inside."

He nodded. Since he wanted honest and complete, I continued. "We looked around but didn't see anyone." I left out the "at first" part. "After exploring, we left. That's when I called the police department to report the unlocked door."

The glare intensified, but he didn't say anything for several moments. Finally he put the pen down. "Stand up and remove your jacket."

This was new. "What?"

The vein in his neck started throbbing. "Stand up. Remove your jacket. What part of that is unclear?"

"Should I call my attorney?" I didn't want to cause the vein to burst. The walls needed a facelift, but red would not be a good color. I also didn't like where this was headed.

"Did you kill Ms. Cartwright?"

"No!" This time it was my face that flushed. How could he even think that? I might bend the rules from time to time, even stick my nose in where it didn't belong, but that was as far as my rap sheet progressed. "You know me. How could you even suggest that?" Rare tears gathered in the corners of my eyes. He could accuse me of lying, of withholding the truth, of undying curiosity and I would have taken it. But this...

My words softened his expression a bit, and he expelled a slow breath. I was sure he was getting a lot of pressure from the Cartwright family to wrap this up quickly.

"I have to pursue all leads. You were there around the time of her death. We need to eliminate you as a suspect. In order to do that, I need you to remove your jacket so I can see your arms." His gaze pleaded with me to comply without further argument.

I stood and removed my jacket. I wasn't sure what I expected, but him taking my hands and lifting my arms so he could study my forearms wasn't among them. The shocked expression on his face caught me off guard. I realized he was looking at the scratches Watson had graced me with the night we first met. I smiled. "Oh, those are from my cat. My barking dog doorbell startled him, and he used my arms and chest as a launching pad."

Detective Marshall didn't smile. Instead he dropped my hands and rubbed his face. "I think you should call your attorney now."

CHAPTER SEVENTEEN

———

The next few moments of my life were spent in stunned silence. After swallowing hard several times, I managed to locate my voice somewhere in the pit of my stomach. "Why?"

Marshall gestured to the chair, and I sat without argument. "I shouldn't be telling you this, and"—his gaze refocused on mine, the intensity of which stole my breath—"my telling you doesn't change the fact you should call your lawyer."

I nodded. The one word I'd managed a moment ago no longer even an option.

"We found skin under the victim's fingernails."

This I knew from my conversation with Officer Faria, but I remained quiet to let Detective Marshall finish sharing. It was so rare he did, I didn't want to mess it up.

"We believe her attacker came from behind. It's reasonable to believe she struggled and scratched her assailant."

"Chloroform."

Any goodwill he'd tried to extend toward me vanished with my spoken word. "You better explain yourself right now. How do you know she was chloroformed?"

"We should probably call Attorney Pohoke now."

The folding chair violently scraped against the linoleum floor as he abruptly stood. The angry red hue of his face scared me almost as much as Shady Pines at night. "I'll call him, and then, Miss Waters, you have some explaining to do." The words emerged in a measured beat from tight lips.

While I waited for him to return, I absently rubbed the scratches on my arm. I'd almost forgotten they were there. Alarm spread through my body as I realized my charm bracelet wasn't on my wrist. My mind scrambled to remember if I'd taken it off or not. Fear clutched my heart as I realized how much I'd stuck my hand in all kinds of nooks and crevices in an effort to find a key or way in the last time I was at Shady Pines. That *had* to be where it was. Which meant…

I'd have to go back. Tonight. Ugh.

Of course, that depended on if they let me out of here. I knew I didn't kill Camilla. Smack the smug, condescending look off her face, maybe, but murder was not in my arsenal. It was just a matter of how long it would take Mr. Pohoke to clear all of this up.

The tears tried to find their way to the surface, but I pushed them back. My bracelet, complete with the two matching charms from my grandparents, represented my most valuable possession. Not because of monetary worth, but sentimental significance. The two charms had finally been reunited a little over a year ago, and I didn't care if I had to descend the depths of hell to get it back.

By the time Detective Marshall returned with my lawyer, my emotions were under control. I had a mission—well, two missions. First, clear my name. Second, find my bracelet. I nodded at both men as they took their respective seats.

Attorney Pohoke took my hand. "Lilly, do you and I need a moment alone to speak first?"

I shook my head. "No, but I need you here to make sure my words aren't taken out of context." My gaze snapped to the detective's. "No disrespect intended."

The shocked expression on his face would have amused me if the reason for my being here wasn't so serious. He wasn't used to me being compliant. "None taken. Why don't you start from the beginning?"

I recounted for him everything that happened from the moment Bree and I entered the motel to finding Camilla's body. I shared about the sweet smell which prompted me to think immediately of chloroform.

"How do you know what chloroform smells like?" Detective Marshall asked.

I shrugged. "I guess I don't know for sure. Not like I would whip some up in my kitchen." My attempt at humor fell flat with both men. I sighed. "I watched a lot of crime shows growing up. They always described it as an oddly sweet smell. At first I thought it was fancy perfume, but as you shared more about what you believe happened, I think that makes more sense."

When I finished, Attorney Pohoke took over. "I assume if Ms. Waters submits a DNA sample for comparison, you will release her pending the test results?"

Detective Marshall leaned back in the chair, creating a dangerous-sounding creak in the flimsy piece of furniture. "Given her forthright statement here today and her lack of a serious criminal record."

"Hey, I don't have a criminal record at all. Being curious isn't a crime."

"Don't get me started, Miss Waters, or I'll be happy to provide you accommodations while we wait for the DNA to come back."

The heavy sigh escaping my mouth couldn't be stopped. "Fine."

"Since this is your first offense at trespassing, agree to pay a five-hundred-dollar fine, and I'll waive any further charges or required court appearance."

My mouth opened, but my lawyer's hand on my arm snapped it shut. His kind eyes, disappearing hair, and almost translucent skin made it impossible for me to contradict his wishes. I was paying for his advice after all.

"Ms. Waters will be happy to pay the fine as long as it does not appear anywhere as a matter of record."

Detective Marshall rubbed his temples and then exhaled slowly. "Deal. I'll figure out the paperwork and get it over to you."

His smile warmed my heart. "Thank you. Now may I suggest we get that DNA sample so my client can return to work. I'm sure there are many thirsty citizens of Danger Cove awaiting her return."

It was almost time for the dinner rush by the time I made it back to the tavern. Thankfully, Mr. Pohoke had given me a ride. "Thank you so much. I appreciate your coming over on such short notice."

He smiled and patted my shoulder. "No worries, dear. Thankfully, it's been a little slow in Danger Cove lately."

"You can always count on me to liven things up for you." I smiled and hoped he found this attempt at humor more entertaining. That would be much better than him thinking I was not only a password-stealing pain but something much worse.

He chuckled. "Without a doubt. Now, if you're ok, I'm going to go home to the missus."

"Please bring her in for a date sometime soon. My treat. It's the least I can do. Well, that and pay the bill when you send it."

"We might do just that. Enjoy your evening."

The moment I walked in the door, Tan pulled me into a hug. "What the heck happened?"

For his concern, he received a quick peck on the cheek. "I'll explain later, but everything is fine. Just a misunderstanding."

His gorgeous face contorted into a "that's doubtful" expression, but he let it go. "Abe's been doing his best to cover at the bar. Agnes has helped him with the more complex cocktails. It's been amusing to watch the two of them. They make a great couple."

"Agnes has been helping? How?" The thought of Agnes Thermopolis having free access to her favorite brand of tequila—the most expensive we stocked—worried me. Not because she couldn't pay. Her lottery winnings assured her of being financially solvent the rest of her life. I worried more about her getting a little too tipsy and providing far more entertainment than the patrons had been accustomed to. Her love of tequila and the company of handsome men had brought her to Smugglers' Tavern many times, either to celebrate or commiserate the status of her relationships.

Tanner laughed. "Don't worry. She's behaving. I think Abe is a good influence on her. She's just letting him know what different cocktails are made up of and how to prepare them."

You had to love teamwork. "Everything running smoothly during my unexpected absence?"

He returned my earlier kiss on the cheek. "It's been busy, but we had it under control. Sam stopped by earlier for a salad to go. She certainly drew the attention of some of our patrons."

The smile on his face as he shared got my attention. "How so?"

"Business suit, hair styled, and heels that added a good three or more inches to her height. Even Tucker was speechless. She was gone five minutes before he managed to respond to her question of how he was doing today. Too bad she wasn't here to hear his response of 'groovy.'"

Personally, I'd never seen Sam in anything but jogging attire and the standard black jeans, white shirt, and Converse tennis shoes she wore to work each day. "Do you think she was going on an interview?"

He kissed me on the forehead. "I'm sure it's nothing to worry about. Don't borrow trouble from tomorrow, ok?"

Nodding, I made my way to the bar, trying to follow his advice. "Hi, Agnes. Hi, Abe. You guys are the best for stepping in while I had to be out. Abe, if you don't mind hanging in there for a few more, I'm going to check on things in the kitchen, and then I'll give you two a much-deserved break."

"No worries, dearie. I've had a blast. Plus"—Agnes blushed, a perfect match to her red hair—"I enjoyed being here with Abe."

Before I could comment, Abe shot me a look that suggested I do the unexpected and not offer any reply. I winked at him and then smiled at Agnes. "I'm so glad. Again, thank you both."

Tara and Clara stopped what they were doing when I stepped into the kitchen. "Everything ok, Boss?" This time their question came across in unison. They must've really been worried.

"Everything's fine." At least I hoped it would be. I *knew* I hadn't killed Camilla, but that didn't translate to everything being ok.

"You've had some calls," Tara offered.

"They sounded important," Clara finished.

Heading to the office, I saw I had three missed calls on my cell from Bree, one from my mother, and messages left on my office phone. Those would have to wait. I shot a text to my mom letting her know work was busy and I would give her a call as soon as I could. Next, I dialed Bree. She answered on the first ring.

"I have been worried sick about you. Freddie said Pizza Guy took you downtown to the big house."

My eyes rolled even though she couldn't see me. "The big house? More like the little interrogation room."

"Was it because of me?" Her voice lacked some of its normal confidence.

"Yeah, but it's not one hundred percent your fault."

"Oh, I'm so sorry, Lilly. I'll happily take partial blame. You *did* agree to come with me. You shouldn't be so susceptible to peer pressure at your age."

There was the Bree I knew and loved. "I'll work on that. Did you call to check on me, or was there something else?"

"Of course there was something else. You know Mr. Blowhard who's staying here?"

"If you're referring to the one and only David Charles Winchester, then yes."

Bree chuckled. "Well, as he's the Fourth, there have to be at least three others of him, which is a terrifying thought, by the way."

Valid point. "Ok, the one and only we've met."

"Yes, that's the one. Well, I overheard him on the phone."

I gasped to feign indignance. "You were eavesdropping?"

"I'll have you know it's not eavesdropping when they are talking loud enough for anyone dusting right outside their door to hear."

"You were dusting?" That would be as surprising as her cooking.

"Never mind that. Do you want to hear what I heard?"

I could imagine her standing with her hand on her hip as she gave me a dirty look through the phone. "Yes, please."

"He's planning to head to Canada when his visit here is done. He was noticeably irritated that the auction had been delayed. He told whoever he was talking to that if delivery didn't come by the end of the weekend, the deal was off."

"Any idea who he was talking to?"

"It was a phone conversation, not on speaker, that I was listening to through a solid wooden door. You should be impressed I even knew he was talking. I did hear him tell whoever was on the opposite end of the call that Candace Cartwright had shown up and there could be problems."

"Interesting." Winchester wasn't a fan of Candace. Billy had allegedly been a fan of Camilla's, but his response to my question made me think the elder Cartwright woman might not have fully understood what was going on.

"Life is never boring around here. I still want points for my creative housekeeping."

I chuckled. "You're right. Thank you for dusting just at the right time and sharing what you learned with me."

We disconnected, and I dialed Jack Condor's number. It took him several rings before he answered. "What do you want?"

"Jail time must've hardened you, Jack. Usually you at least pretend to be polite."

"Oh, hey, Lilly. Sorry about that. I've been getting nonstop calls from newspapers and other media outlets wanting to do an interview. I swear if that jerk journalist Duncan Pickles calls me one more time asking for an exclusive…"

"I thought you liked that kind of thing."

A loud harrumph echoed through the phone. "Not when all they want to talk about is that witch Camilla. Even in death, she's still getting more attention than me."

It was hard for me to feel sympathetic, and I was too tired to even try to fake it. "I'm calling in a favor."

"I don't owe you any favors."

"Did I or did I not help you when you were being held on suspicion of murder?"

"The DNA freed me, not your investigation."

"Still, I was one of the few people who believed you didn't do it even though the evidence pointed directly at you. I might remind you that until the DNA reveals who did it, you're still a suspect."

The silence stretched longer than I wanted it to, but finally he sighed. "Fine, what do you want? But not because I owe you. The way I reckon, you're gonna owe me one."

This man was unbelievable, but I needed to get this done. "I need the real estate agent code to get in the lockbox to open the door for Shady Pine."

"You're kidding, right?"

My patience was done. "I'm not kidding. I've been sucked into this whole Shady Pines mess, and now my bracelet is missing. The only place it could be is there. I intend to go there after work, find it, and never step foot in that dreadful place again. Now give me the code."

I grabbed a pen and wrote the number down he provided. "Thanks, Jack."

"Be careful, Lilly. Something's going on at that place. Something more than a real estate transaction."

"I know, Jack. I know. I just don't know what it is." Why couldn't I put this puzzle together?

Freddie peeked his head into the office, his dark bangs falling carelessly across his eyes. "Hey, Boss. Ok if I use your office to work on that project I was telling you about during my break? I'll be close if you need help."

Guess whatever product he put in his hair in the morning had lost its grip by the evening. I often battled with that myself.

"Sure, Freddie. I just finished a few calls and need to get out there to relieve Abe."

"And Agnes, though I think she's having a ball." He grinned.

"She enjoys being at the bar as much as I do." Agnes and I had been through a lot, and a good portion of it had been at the bar.

"True that." Freddie moved into the office and now held his laptop as he waited for me to vacate the area.

I stood, letting my hands slide over the mahogany finish. "Here you go, Freddie."

He moved in and set up his laptop. Pride rushed through me as I considered how far he'd come. From being homeless to an employed college student. He was taking advantage of every opportunity life had given him. "I'll give you some privacy."

"Wait!" He grinned and motioned me around to the side of the desk. "You said you'd let me show you."

He was right. I had. "Ok, show me this really cool thing." I smiled as I remembered him sharing that detail with me earlier. "Quickly though, before Agnes takes over completely."

Freddie used his fingers to push his hair away from his eyes, revealing excitement swirling in the brown orbs. He moved his hands over the keyboard, typing in a web address. "Check this out."

Returning to his side, I leaned down so I could watch what he was doing on the screen. He'd typed in *what3words* and hit Enter. A few more keystrokes and a map was displayed on the screen. "What am I looking at?"

"This site is the best way to reference locations worldwide."

My lack of understanding and feelings of inadequacy started to surface again. "Don't we have house numbers and street names to do that?"

He nodded. "Yeah, but roads and highways get torn down, rebuilt, renamed, so it can make it hard to keep track, right?"

"Right."

"And what about places that don't have roads?"

I shrugged. "Why would you be going to a place that doesn't have a road or address?"

The grin on his face widened into a wicked smile. "Because sometimes you don't want people to know where you are."

A memory of Freddie telling me about his class studying innocent websites used for nefarious purposes surfaced. "Ok, I'm with you. Show me more." There might have been just a hint of excitement in my voice at the thought of learning something new along with him.

"This site basically breaks the entire world up into three-by-three-meter squares. Each square is designated by a unique series of three words." He pointed to an area on the screen. "Part of Smugglers' Tavern is located in the ports.tests.lime grid."

Seeing the words on the screen brought my entire focus to the screen. "Can you type in any three words to see the location?"

"Sure. What three words do you want me to enter?"

The world around me faded away until there was only me, the screen, and Freddie. "*Skinny. Punt. Older.*"

Freddie gave me an odd stare—either at my having three words at the ready or the odd combination of words I gave him. After a brief moment, he lowered his head and typed in the words. The air caught in my throat, holding steady to see if that combination returned anything relevant. Anything I could connect to Camilla—to her murder.

His hands paused for a few moments before looking up at me. I couldn't take it another moment longer. "What is it or...I mean, where is it?"

He enlarged the screen to zoom in on the spot identified. His finger pointed to a red marker on the screen. "That, Boss Lady, is located inside Shady Pines."

CHAPTER EIGHTEEN

———

It was difficult to remain calm, as something—though I still wasn't sure what—had clicked into place. "You were right, Freddie. This is way cool. I'm going to let you return to your assignment. I need to get back out there." My thoughts tilt-a-whirled my brain as I considered this piece of the puzzle.

"Boss? Lilly?" Freddie's urgent voice stopped the ride for a moment.

"Yes?"

"That's it? Just thanks, Freddie. Do your homework."

My blue gaze locked with his brown. I didn't want to involve him, but he knew me well enough to know there was a lot more going on. "You're too smart for your own good."

He smiled. "Yeah, I know. So what's going on? What are you going to do? What are *we* going to do?"

"I'm not sure yet. Your website helped me at least understand, in part, why those words were written on Camilla's hand."

"For real?"

I nodded. "For real. I assume it directed her to a location inside Shady Pines where something or someone was waiting for her. That part I still have to figure out. Until I do and know how to handle that information, we're not going to say a word to anyone outside our little family about this. Capiche?" The last thing I needed was for anyone to interfere with the plan, such as it was, forming in my head. I'd been behind the eight ball this entire game, and it was high time to be proactive in the strategy.

He pulled at his ear as his head lowered. His protective instincts were almost as strong as Tan's. Ugh—Tan. He could and would definitely interfere with my plan. I'd have to figure out how to do whatever I was going to do without telling him. It wasn't how I wanted to roll in our relationship, but history had taught me he would tie me to a chair and spoon feed me until they either caught the killer or he believed I'd step back and let someone else handle it.

"Ok, Boss. But I've got your back if you need me."

"I appreciate that, Freddie. Let's keep this just between you and me until I figure out a plan." The unspoken command there was to not tell Tanner.

His bangs ruffled in the breeze from his exhale. "Not for nuttin', but remember we are a great team, and we want to help as much as you do."

No point in disagreeing. "I know, Freddie. Thanks for hanging with me on this one. Ok, I really gotta go. See you after your break."

Back at the bar, Abe looked relieved that he didn't have to make drinks anymore. "Thanks, Abe. Why don't you take your dinner break? You and Agnes grab some food, my treat. The temperature is nice outside. You can sit in the beer garden. Be all romantic." I winked with the last words.

"I can drink tequila in the beer garden, correct?" Agnes leveled a mock glare at me.

"Of course, Agnes. I would never try to deprive you of your tequila."

She laughed. "Especially not after I've been so helpful. C'mon, Abe, wine and dine me."

He washed his hands and tossed his apron before circling the bar to extend an arm to escort her. "It would be my pleasure, m'lady."

Agnes took his arm and tossed her red curls as she looked back at me with a wink. "He may be a few minutes late returning from dinner." Abe blushed as Agnes cackled.

Talk about opposites attracting.

Mandi brought an order up to the bar. Her harried expression indicated it had been a busy night. I took a moment to look around the establishment. Every booth and most tables were occupied. I noticed that Jessica and Adam were hanging out in the booth in the back corner. "I called Ashley to come in and help. Hope that was ok."

"Totally ok. Sorry I wasn't here to take care of that." I made the drinks she needed and gestured for her to meet me down by the service area.

"What's up?" she whispered.

"You up for some adventure tonight after work?" My BFF loved getting into trouble with me. Well, most days anyway. Sometimes the trouble quotient was too high for either of us, but thankfully we'd always managed to get out of it without a scratch—mostly.

"Oh. Em. Gee. Yes! It's been too long. Where are we going?" The energy returned to her tired frame and amped up the sapphire of her eyes.

"It's a surprise, and..." I moved in closer as I put the drinks on her tray. "It's a secret adventure. You cool with that?"

Her rosy bottom lip got pulled in between her teeth as she weighed her options. I wanted to sway her decision in my favor. "Please? It wouldn't be the same without my bestie."

The lip was released, and she nodded. "Cool."

"Great. We'll meet at your apartment after we close. Think you can get the keys to the car?" Neither one of us owned a vehicle. It wasn't really necessary, as Danger Cove was small. We either rode our bikes or shared a ride on my motorized scooter. If we needed to go anyplace farther, Tan chauffeured.

"I'm sure I can. Mom and Dad said they were staying in tonight." She noticed Ashley come through the kitchen door. "I'm going to deliver these drinks and then give her some tables. Talk to you later."

I waved to Ashley and mouthed a thank-you to her for coming in on a weekend. Since she'd picked up some college classes, her availability was much more limited. She waved and nodded to me, but her face lit up when she saw her big brother. Now that he worked in Seattle through the week, they didn't get to see much of each other.

The next person through the door was my favorite Danger Cove police officer, Richie Faria. I smiled and waved him over. "Good evening, Detective. What can I get started for you tonight?"

Richie blushed. I knew of his aspirations to be a detective someday, so when it was just me and him, I referred to him by that title. He told me it made him uncomfortable, but he always smiled and blushed, so I kept doing it. I know I looked forward to the day he became a detective. Maybe when that happened, I'd see less of Pizza Guy.

"Evening, Lilly. Just getting a turkey burger and sweet potato fries to go. I'm on patrol tonight."

"Sucks having to work on a Saturday night, doesn't it?" I put a soda in front of him for while he waited. "Cookies for dessert?" Hey, if you had to work on the weekend, you deserved a treat, right?

He grinned. "That will definitely help the night be better. Thank you." His smile faded. "Unless you're giving me them in exchange for a favor or information?"

I shook my head. "Not this time. This is a just-because and a thank-you for keeping the streets of Danger Cove safe."

"Thanks, Lilly." He took a few sips of his drink and then pointed to the scratches on my arm. "Those really from a cat? I didn't know you had one."

I retrieved my phone from my jean pocket and pulled up one of the hundred photos of Watson I'd snapped since he came to live with me a few nights ago. I showed a few of the cutest ones to Faria.

"Aww, he's a cutie."

My parental pride purred like a momma cat. "He's smart, funny, and adorable."

Richie pointed to my arms again. "And in need of declawing."

"Nah, I just need a new doorbell. Anyway, these marks did land me in trouble. I'm sure you know I'm awaiting DNA results to prove I'm telling the truth about not killing Camilla. I'm a little hurt that everyone who's been to the motel hasn't been hauled in to be checked for scratches."

He rubbed his head, his expression abashed. "Yeah, sorry about that. I'm sure you'll be cleared by end of business on Monday."

I shrugged. "It's just paperwork. I know I didn't kill her. Nothing more than a case of being at the wrong place at the wrong time."

Clara brought his food out. "Here you go. Enjoy."

Richie opened the bag and inhaled. The smile on his face was totally worth keeping the chocolate chip cookies on hand. "Thanks, Clara."

She waved and headed back to the kitchen. He put his jacket on and grabbed his wallet to pay the bill. "When you think about it, I'd say you were at the wrong place at the right time. A little earlier and maybe you would've seen who killed her."

"That would've been better, right?" Though we were usually on the same page, this time his logic left me confused.

He shook his head. "If you'd been there earlier and witnessed the crime, we might be investigating two deaths instead of just one." The somber tone of his voice hit the intended target.

"You're right. I hadn't thought of it that way."

He smiled. "Always good to look at a situation from all sides." He lifted the bag. "Thanks again, Lilly. Stay safe."

"You too."

I considered how fortunate I'd been *not* to have witnessed Camilla's death. Not only because that would've made me a witness and subject to silencing by the killer, but also because stumbling on a dead body after the fact was bad enough. Watching someone take another life… Shudders skittered down my spine. That was not something I ever wanted or wished on anyone.

Commotion from the area near the corridor to the restrooms jerked me out of my morbid thoughts. Adam and Jessica were yelling at each other. Of course the police had just left, I started around the bar, but Tan waved me off. Oh yeah, I should let my handsome security man handle this. Plus, I remembered Sam getting upset when I intervened when she was handling a dispute. I'd just keep my little butt right here serving drinks.

Adam slid out of the booth, followed closely by Jessica. He grabbed her forearm, generating a noticeable grimace on her face. "You have got to stop. This is crazy. Enough is enough. I've tried reasoning with you. I'm done."

Jessica jerked her arm away and pushed Adam violently. Tan's solid frame stopped his free fall. "You're hurting me!

We're not married, this is not the fifties, and for the love of all that is holy in the world, I do not take orders from you!"

Adam's skin flushed as his hands clenched into tight fists. From this distance, I couldn't be sure, but it looked like his nostrils flared like a bull seeing red. He lunged toward Jessica, but Tan's hold on him prevented him from even getting close. Tan turned them so he was between the two, which left his back to Jessica and prevented him from seeing her advance, arms flailing.

"Tanner! Behind you!" It was the best I could do from the distance that separated us. Freddie had heard the commotion and emerged from the kitchen, but he wouldn't be in time either.

Tanner turned and lifted his arm to defend against the flail while holding Adam with the other. Jessica was totally fighting like a girl. By that I mean she had both arms working in a windmill motion, her hands slapping anything that entered the radius of her reach. Once Freddie had a grip on Adam, Tanner turned his full attention to Jessica. A swift duck and move maneuver ended with Jessica in a headlock.

She twisted and turned, but when that didn't free her, she screamed, "Let me go!" She continued to struggle, but he maintained his hold. After a few more seconds of effort, she quieted. Tears covered her red face. "Please, let me go. I'm sorry."

Tanner turned to look at Adam. He appeared calmer as well. I'd learned over the years that people were either microwaves or Crock-Pots. A microwave person was quick to respond, heating up quickly with an intensity that could boil a situation over in about a minute. Once the Stop button was pressed or the door was opened, though, there was nothing left but a small bit of residual heat.

A Crock-Pot person, on the other hand, would take a long time to heat up, but once they got there, they stayed hot for a long time and took hours to cool down completely. I'd go out on a limb and say that both Adam and Jessica were microwaves.

"I'm sorry. He pushed every single button I own and wouldn't let up." Jessica shot a disapproving look in Adam's direction.

Adam just shook his head. He reached into his wallet and handed Freddie some bills. "That should cover our tab, plus a generous tip to make up for the commotion." He looked around to the curious gazes watching their outburst. "I'm sorry, everyone. Please forgive our disturbing your meals."

Once Adam exited the building, Jessica pulled herself free from Tan's grasp, not that he was trying to hold her any longer. She stormed out of the tavern without a word. Tan followed. I was certain it was to make sure she actually left. Now that the excitement had died down, everyone returned to their meals as though nothing had happened.

Tanner came to the bar a few minutes later. "Can I get something to drink and some ibuprofen, please? She was quite the fighter."

My gaze was drawn to some red marks on his arms. Jessica had definitely put up a fight. Hopefully, not enough to leave any bruises. "Let's get you back to the kitchen. We'll grab you some iced coffee and pain reliever."

"Ok, Boss." His smile warmed me to the very tips of my toes. Once I'd made him his drink, we went into the office so I could get the medicine from my purse. While I was there, I decided to go ahead and reapply the ointment to my arms.

"Guess you need that with you at all times thanks to your new roomie."

I finished my first aid and returned everything to my purse. "Yeah, he's not a fan of my doorbell. Going to have to get that changed."

I reached out and gently touched one of the reddened areas on Tan's arms. "Seeing Jessica try to free herself earlier made me think of something."

His hand covered mine as his lips curled into a smile. "Oh? How strong your man was?"

I chuckled. "That too. This was more in relation to what might have gone down when Camilla was murdered."

"Tell me."

"Detective Marshall believes Camilla's attacker grabbed her from behind and that she fought to get free. I'm also ninety-nine percent sure she was chloroformed in an effort to subdue her."

"Is that why you were at the police station earlier—to give a statement?"

"I'm a suspect."

He sat up straight, the smile all but disappeared. "What? Why?"

I held my arm up. "The scratches. You were fortunate that Jessica didn't use her nails, but Camilla obviously did." A small detail occurred to me about the order of events. If chloroform had been used to subdue Camilla, the bat hadn't been used first. I wasn't sure if it mattered, but it wouldn't make sense for Jack to have knocked Camilla out with the bat and *then* have used the chloroform. Talk about overkill.

Tanner turned to face me and took my hands, kissing the back of each one. "You don't think Jessica was the one, do you?"

My shoulders shrugged of their own accord. It had been a standard response for most questions in this case. I just didn't know. "I have no idea. She's obviously familiar with the basic technique."

"She was in long sleeves tonight too," Tanner observed.

"And when Adam grabbed her forearm, she was obviously in pain."

Tanner leaned back in the chair and expelled a long breath. "That could be the reason, I suppose, but Adam is strong. Depending on how firmly he had hold of her arm, it might have caused pain for anyone."

He was right, but I liked my theory better. "True, but play along with me for a bit. It's the closest I've come to a lead or suspect in this whole mess."

"You mean this mess you assured me you weren't going to get involved in?"

A slow smile spread across my face. "You know I can't help trying to figure things out. Plus, it's different now that they have sort of placed me on the top of their suspect list. This is self-preservation—creating an alternate theory of events."

He laughed. "You're watching too many crime shows again."

"Can I help it I binge watch *Law and Order* on my day off?" I produced a dramatic sigh. "Especially since my boyfriend is off molding young minds every Monday."

Tan grinned and shrugged. "It's a tough job, but someone's gotta do it."

My lips found his and tried to convey all the emotions I had a hard time expressing. "You do it better than anyone I know. Those young minds are lucky to have you, and I'm fortunate to have you in my life too…even if it's only on the weekends."

He pulled me closer, and I tried to ignore the fact I could be getting ointment all over his clothes. As the kiss deepened, I realized I didn't care. That was what washing machines were for, right? The loss was immediate when he pulled away, but the warm smile he offered helped lessen the intensity. "Maybe someday down the road, we'll find a place halfway so we can be together every day and night?"

It sounded nice. It truly did. I just couldn't see leaving Danger Cove. I'd moved around my whole life, and for the first time since Gram died, I knew this was where I was meant to be. Gazing into his sparkling, warm blue eyes, it made me think that maybe there might be some compromise to consider. I returned his smile. "Maybe."

"You ok, big bro?" Ashley burst right into our Hallmark moment. She had a knack for that. Probably something little sisters were known for. As an only child, I couldn't say for sure.

He held up his hands to show the already fading marks. "I think I'll live."

She grinned. "Too far from your heart to kill you."

"You know it."

Ashley hesitated for just a moment, which was totally unlike her. I was sure the thought of something happening to her big brother was not a happy one. For the record, I was right there with her on that one. Ashley moved closer and gave him a quick hug. "Glad you're home. I've missed you."

Tan, in response, looked up from the embrace, the unspoken question in his gaze. I nodded. He loved his little sis and had been a father figure to her for the last few years since their father passed. They needed some time together. "Why don't you and I hang out tonight?"

Ashley separated from him and cast a glance in my direction. "You sure? I know this is usually the time you spend with Lilly."

He punched her arm. "I like being with you too. Lilly's cool with it."

She cast me a doubtful glance. Though I would miss our quality time, I knew they needed some sibling time. And truth be told, it worked out for my secret Operation Bracelet Retrieval plan too. "I'm cool. You guys have fun. Mandi and I will entertain each other. Next weekend, maybe the three of us can grab some food and watch a movie together."

Ashley nodded and shrugged. "If I'm not too busy. I do have a life, you know."

If I was that difficult as a teenager, someone should have smacked me more. I decided to let it slide. We'd made some good strides in our relationship—no sense tossing in trouble tonight. I smiled at Tan. "Now that's settled, we should probably get back to work."

Ashley nodded and headed back to the dining area. "Catch ya after our shift, Tan. Glad you're ok."

The moment she vacated the office, he caught me in a steal-my-breath kiss. I almost forgot about my duplicitous reason for my generosity. Almost… I rationalized I would've done the same thing even if I weren't going to Shady Pines after work to find my bracelet.

A shiver cruised up and down my spine as I breathed a silent prayer that was all I found.

CHAPTER NINETEEN

A full moon hung high in the black, silk sky, casting an unnatural glow over Shady Pines. For the record, that upped the sinister factor by at least ten. I inhaled deeply to summon the courage necessary to get through the next thirty minutes. Mandi was sitting next to me in the front seat of her mother's car. I turned to see how she was reacting to the sight before her. "You ok?"

"Define ok."

"You're ok enough not to bolt on me—that's how I define it." If she turned tail and ran, I couldn't blame her. The auction was tomorrow, so this was my last chance to find my bracelet. Otherwise, this would be the last place I'd want to be tonight too.

She grabbed my hand and squeezed. "No man—or woman—left behind, right?"

Her comment reminded me of the time we'd gone searching in a cemetery after dark. We'd promised then we'd stick together no matter what. As a result, we'd found what we were looking for. The memory gave me courage to face the monstrosity in front of me. "Right. So let's do this so we can get home in time for pizza."

"And play with Watson," Mandi added with a smile.

Thoughts of snuggling with my cat and watching him devour his wet cat food filled me with positive energy. "Yes, we'll spoil him rotten when we get back to the house."

"Sounds like a plan. Maybe you can tell me what we're looking for now?"

Oh yeah, I'd not mentioned that part yet. "My bracelet is missing. The only place I can think that it might have come off my wrist is here when I was trying to find a way in before."

She nodded. "We have to find that. I know how important that is to you. Where do you want to start?" Mandi's voice sounded strong and sure. Yet another reason why she was my bestie.

"As much as I hate it, I spent a lot of time outside trying to find a way in the last time I was here. We should probably check the perimeter."

She laughed. "As frightening as that sounds, it still sounds better than going inside."

"True that."

We started to get out of the car, when she put her hand on my forearm. "Wait."

I twisted in the seat to face her. "You haven't changed your mind already, have you?" I prayed she hadn't. I really, really didn't want to do this alone.

Her red hair moved as she shook her head. "I think we should park the car in that old driveway we passed a minute or so go. The trees lining it should keep the vehicle from view."

I'd been hiding near that old house the other night when I'd seen Sam and Adam. It was a good plan. If someone else was lurking around, I didn't want them to know we were doing the same. "Smart and brave. This is why you're totally my person." I gave her a quick hug before settling into the seat and returning to the spot she mentioned.

Mandi nodded. "Besties always!"

We grabbed everything we needed before I locked the door and slid the keys into my front pocket. The walk to Shady Pines was made in silence. Once there, we started at the front door and worked our way left to search the building. Flashlights and pepper spray at the ready. My boyfriend had been an Eagle Scout, and I'd picked up some good habits from him. Always be prepared—that was my motto now. Well, one of them anyway.

I aimed my flashlight high while Mandi kept hers low. I also directed the light into all the nooks and crannies I'd put my hand in before looking for a way in. The number of beady insect eyes that scrambled in response threatened my resolve. Only

Mandi's presence by my side gave me the courage to keep on keepin' on.

We'd made it about three-fourths of the way around when I noticed something different traversing in the sky. I lowered my flashlight and had Mandi do the same. I pointed to the place in the sky I saw the blinking lights. "Do you see that?"

She blinked a couple of times to focus her eyes in the darkness. "The red and white lights in the sky?"

"Yes?"

"What is it?" She whispered even though I was pretty sure there wasn't another soul in the area—at least I hoped not.

"I'm not sure. Too low and small to be a plane."

She chuckled. "You think?"

"Now's not the time to be sassy." True, I'd opened the door for her, but she didn't have to skip through with such enthusiasm.

"There's rarely a time one shouldn't be sassy. You taught me that."

When the girl was right, she was right. "Ok, I deserved that. But seriously, what do you think it is?"

The lights ventured closer to where we were. "I think it's one of those drones. The cost of it defines its range." Translation: someone could be close by.

I'd heard Freddie and Tan talking about drones and had seen them in videos on the internet, but that's as far as it had gone. The thought of someone being able to remotely surveil or whatever else in God's name those things did frightened me. Technology and I were only friends as far as my laptop and smartphone were concerned. Everything else reminded me of *Star Trek*, *Star Wars*, or some other futuristic type world. "What would it be doing here?"

My question made her look away from the drone to give me a look. "You can't seriously expect me to know that."

"And here I thought you knew everything," I teased.

"I know everything that should be known. This is an unknown."

"You have an answer for everything, don't you?"

"Yup." She chuckled.

The humming sound closing in refocused our attention. A moment later the drone disappeared into the motel. I nudged Mandi. "That's the window that was broken from the inside—the room Camilla was murdered in."

"Shut the front door."

"Yup." We quieted as we heard a thud, and then the hum of the drone returned as it exited the window and headed north before disappearing into the inky sky.

"Did you hear what I heard?" Mandi whispered.

"I did."

"We're going to check it out, aren't we?"

Mandi knew me so well. "We have to look inside anyway."

She sighed. "Ok, let's finish the perimeter and get this over with. You know anything that is being delivered in the darkness of night by a drone can't be good, right?"

I knew. "Hey, Mandi?"

"Yeah?"

"Two things."

"Only two?" She gave me a nervous laugh.

"First, Freddie was able to figure out what the three words on Camilla's hand meant."

"He's pretty smart." I could almost hear the pride in her voice.

"He is. I'll save the details for later, but just know that they represent a three-by-three-meter square that put her in the room that the drone just dropped something off in."

There was a pause as she processed the information I gave her. Finally, she spoke. "Then let's double time this. When we get inside, as much as I hate to suggest it..."

"We should divide and conquer so we can be as quick as possible?"

"You read my mind."

"It's that wavelength we got going on." I grinned despite the looming danger.

"Then you'll know I'm planning on searching for your bracelet while you check out whatever is in that room."

I gave her a quick hug, and a bout of nervous laughter escaped. "Yeah, I figured that's the way you'd want the workload assigned." This was turning out to be more dangerous than I'd anticipated—and I'd factored pretty high in my planning. No way would I send Mandi in that room instead of me. Though, I might wish she was going with me. Guess someone needed to be able to run for help or call the police if needed.

We finished checking the outside of the building and found ourselves standing at the front door. My fingers only trembled slightly as I keyed in the code Jack had provided. The door creaked loudly in the silence of the night. If I thought the outside was ominous, the interior of the motel, with the beams of light streaming in through dingy windows, sent new shivers spreading from my spine to the tips of my toes and fingers.

"I'll start looking for your bracelet." Mandi whispered even lower than she had outside.

I grabbed her arm and pulled her close. "Not yet. I want to make sure Billy isn't in here. I'm not sure how he fits into all of this, but I'd rather sneak up on him than the other way around."

Mandi's expression contorted to confusion. "You know something I don't, right?"

"I did some checking, and even if I hadn't, his story about just passing through and being down on his luck doesn't add up. Maybe if it hadn't been at the same time there was going to be an auction and then a murder. Too many coincidences for comfort, if you ask me."

After a few heartbeats, she nodded "Ok. Where should we check for him?"

I gestured to the door leading to the two corridors. We started with the room he'd been in when we first found him. It was empty. Other than disturbed dust, there was no evidence someone had been squatting on the premises. We moved to the end of the hall and checked each room before moving to the other corridor and repeating the process. Nothing. "Guess he found a new place to sleep."

"Hope he's ok," Mandi offered in a quiet voice.

Despite knowing his history, I couldn't argue. "Me too."

"Let's do what we came here to do and get the heck out of here."

Mandi took off to search the rest of the downstairs for my bracelet while I tiptoed up the stairs toward the room where all of this started. My pulse increased a few beats per measure (Dad would be proud I thought of it that way) with each step down the hallway. What if the person who'd killed Camilla was already in the room to retrieve the cargo the drone had dropped? They certainly wouldn't be happy to see me—another witness.

That thought tripled the beating of my heart to a steady boom echoing in my chest. If it sounded as loud to others as it did to me, I'd already lost any element of surprise.

Breathe, Lilly. Think. Be logical.

No more than fifteen minutes had elapsed since the drone had come and gone. *If* someone was waiting, they would've grabbed it and left, right? No one would stick around in this menacing motel for one second longer than necessary.

I retrieved my phone from my back pocket and pulled up the website Freddie saved in my phone. I typed in the three words and waited for the GPS to work its magic. A few moments later, the data confirmed what I already knew.

The coordinates led directly to the room where Camilla had been killed—the room that perhaps held important clues to why she had been killed. This realization lessened my confidence about going inside. I took an extra few moments to give myself a pep talk. That along with my pepper spray clasped in my sweaty palm would have to be enough.

With one final attempt to expel the growing fear with a long breath, I left the relative safety of the hall and stepped into the room. My gaze scanned the area as quickly as possible while still making sure I didn't miss anything. Namely, an unwelcome person.

Empty.

Well, not entirely. There just inside the broken window was a small brown pouch. The light from the moon provided a spotlight around it, as if knowing it was the star in this scene. I licked my lips, praying whatever it was provided answers.

Now that the target was in sight, I made the strides necessary to cross the room. Leaning down, I picked up the leather bag and opened it. Moving closer to the window to take advantage of the moonlight, I jostled the bag until some of the contents spilled into my open hand.

"Those are diamonds!" Mandi whispered loud enough to set off every nerve ending in my body and cause a few of the precious stones to fall out of my hand.

"Good Lord, woman, you scared me." We both bent down to retrieve the gems.

"Sorry."

"Better it was you than someone else." I moved the diamonds around in my hand, feeling the number and weight of them. "Any idea how much these are worth?"

Mandi ran a couple fingers over them. You couldn't blame her. Diamonds were a girl's best friend. "I'm sorry to say, I don't. I'll try to find out. But I can tell you one thing..."

I stopped staring at the diamonds long enough to look up at my friend. "What's that?"

She picked up one and held it in the light. Truthfully, I'd seen prettier diamonds, but that didn't mean these weren't valuable. They looked dull, and there were some that were different colors than I would expect. "These are diamonds in the rough. If someone possessed the knowledge and tools to polish and cut them, this small bag would be worth a fortune."

Mandi placed the diamond back in my palm. "A fortune worth killing for."

CHAPTER TWENTY

———

"I knew it!" Not even this creepy motel could diminish my joy at this moment.

"Knew you've lost your mind?" Mandi whispered. "And lower your voice. I should remind you that we have no idea when the person who those diamonds belong to will come to collect."

She gestured for me to put the diamonds back in the bag. I complied, but it wouldn't stop me from sharing. "I've known in my gut that this was always about more than this lousy piece of real estate. Honestly, I don't know the first thing about real estate investment or running a motel, but even I could see this was a money trap." My chest puffed out. "Take that, Peter Principle."

Now that the diamonds were secured, Mandi looked up to the ceiling—typically a sign she was thinking deeply about something. "What now?"

Her gaze returned to mine. "First, why are you fussing about that principle? And second, Camilla didn't strike me as a bargain shopper."

"Of course, she wasn't a bargain shopper! She had more money than I could probably imagine."

"So why go to all this trouble to secure uncut diamonds?"

Ugh! Just when I thought I was making some headway into this puzzle, another piece jumps in screaming *Fit me in! Fit me in!* I took her hand and started toward the door. "I don't know why. One problem at a time, ok? We need to figure out what to do with these diamonds and then get out of here. Problem solving should only be conducted in a well-lit room."

We'd made it almost to the end of the hall where the stairs were, when we heard the door open downstairs. Using our clasped hands, I pulled Mandi into an empty room. My eyes had adjusted to the darkness, so I scanned the room for a hiding place. The only viable option was the closet. I wasn't claustrophobic, but the thought of sharing the small space with Mandi and the untold number of insects did not settle well in my stomach.

Mandi sensed my dilemma and took the decision away as she forced me into the small space. I focused on slow, quiet breaths—in and out—while immersing myself in pleasant thoughts of Watson to stop from imagining what might be occurring in the darkness around me.

In one hand, I had a death grip on the diamonds. In the other, pepper spray. I couldn't see, but Mandi was a smart girl, and I'd bet my next week's paycheck on the fact she had her pepper spray primed and ready too. I reasoned if we were discovered, we'd blind them with an overdose of pepper and then run like crazy to get away. The merits of the plan were thin, but it was all I had.

We waited and waited, but no one came. Odd, but I wasn't going to complain. "I haven't heard anything for a while. Do you think we should try to get back to the car?" Mandi whispered next to my ear.

"Yeah. Let's get the heck out of here." The creak of the closet door resounded loudly in the empty room, and we both froze and held our breaths. My heart pulsed a powerful beat inside the large vein in my neck. I feared it might burst and create an even louder sound.

Still nothing.

We moved quietly down the stairs and, once outside, took off like we were in the gold medal race of the hundred-yard dash. Don't let anyone kid you—fear is a powerful motivator. You add in adrenaline, and you're a high-powered rocket with premium jet fuel.

At the car, we didn't even stop to catch our breath. I unlocked the doors, and we slid inside. I gave a cursory thought to my still-missing bracelet, but I'd have to conquer that problem another time. It made me sad, but under the circumstances, I didn't see many options. The engine purred to life, and a moment later we were on the main road heading back to Danger Cove. I chanced a look at Mandi, and she was grinning from ear to ear. I couldn't help it—I started laughing. We'd done it. We'd escaped unscathed from another close call. I'd been so preoccupied, I hadn't even stopped to make sure I didn't bring any unwanted guests with me from the closet. Mandi's laughter joined mine in the car. "That was crazy!"

I shot her a quick look. One day we wouldn't be so lucky—but today wasn't the day. Once the rush release was finished and the laughter subsided, I checked my mirrors to make sure no one had followed us. "We should go somewhere and think about what to do next."

Mandi nodded and pointed to the bag now resting on the seat between us. "Especially since we just technically stole those diamonds."

This night was going from bad to worse. With the scare of being caught, I'd dashed right out of Shady Pines with the diamonds still clutched in my sweaty palms. I wasn't sure what else we could've done with them—maybe hide them? If these were stolen, we'd just committed the same crime. Great. Not even my worthy attorney could get me out of this one. I needed some time to think.

The Waters Memorial Park was just ahead. It would be a good place to collect our thoughts and figure out the next steps. I turned into the parking lot and pulled into a spot under a streetlamp. Once the engine was turned off, Mandi unbuckled and turned to me. "I'm pretty sure what we need to do next is obvious."

And just like that, the wavelength got distorted. Maybe that was a side effect of all the nerves firing at one time. "It's not obvious at all. You realize what we've got here, don't you?"

She nodded. "Besides stolen property?

Don't be a drama queen." I huffed. She was right, without a doubt. I just didn't want to let go of the first advantage I'd got since this whole mess started.

"Takes one to know one." She grinned. "But you know I'm right this time."

No way was I going down that fast. "Let's continue this debate at my house. I can't just turn these over to Detective Marshall without getting myself arrested. We need a plan. Let's stop by the pizza place to see if they have anything left we can grab and take with us. We can ask Watson to be the tiebreaker."

She smiled, but added, "As long as you understand that the police have to be notified. This is way out of our league."

I sighed. "You're right, but I want to see if there are any angles we can work first before we tell them. This case has had me at least three steps behind the entire time. These"—I held up the bag of diamonds—"are the first real bit of progress I've had."

Twenty minutes later, we pulled into my drive. My stomach grumbled in response to the smell of sausage, cheese, veggies, and perfectly seasoned pizza sauce wafting out of the box and into the range of my nose. The porch light illuminated the front door with a nice ambient glow.

"Lilly, what is that on your front door?" Mandi's voice was a combination of caution and curiosity.

I handed her the pizza and removed the envelope that had been nailed to the door. Without even knowing what was inside, I knew it wasn't good. When someone nailed a message to your door, it wasn't normally to say they'd just dropped by to say hi and borrow a cup of sugar. I could hear Watson meowing loudly from the other side of the door. That did nothing to ease my anxiety.

My hands shook as I ripped the envelope open. There in meticulous print was a message:

We have your boyfriend's sister. We propose an exchange. The diamonds for Ashley Montgomery. Bring them to the motel.

As if to prove they meant what they said, one of the blueberry earrings that I'd been teasing Ashley about was also included in the envelope. Though I tended to be skeptical from time to time, I wouldn't have doubted their claim even if they hadn't included the memento.

"I thought Ashley was hanging out with Tan tonight?" Mandi's voice pitched into full-blown worry mode. I recognized it immediately because I was right there with her.

"She was supposed to be!" I grabbed my phone and dialed Tan.

"Hey, Lilly. To what do I owe this surprise? Figured you and Mandi would be knee deep in ice cream and rom coms by now."

"And I thought you were hanging out with your sister tonight."

"We are."

"She's with you?" Normally I didn't rapid fire him with questions, but that was what happened in worry mode.

"Not at the moment. I dropped her off at the house so she could finish up some homework. She was jonesing for a cheesesteak sandwich from Not for Nuttin', so I told her I'd pick some up for us before we hang."

My silence must have spoken volumes, as it only took Tan a few seconds to follow up his answer. "Lilly? Is something wrong with Ashley?"

"They've taken her." My voice trembled as I delivered the bad news.

"Who has taken her? Taken her where? Lilly, what's going on?!" Yup, he'd now joined Mandi and me in full-blown worry town. At this rate, there was going to be overpopulation in less than an hour.

"I don't know. The bad guys. I..."

"The ones who killed Camilla?"

"I don't know."

"Why did they take her?" I heard the squeal of the brakes and the tires through the Bluetooth connection on his end. If I had to guess, he'd done a U-turn and was headed back to Danger Cove.

This question I didn't want to answer. I knew why, but he wasn't going to like it. "I'm going to get her back. Please drive carefully."

"Answer my question, Lilly!" I heard a few forced breaths before he continued. "Just wait for me to get back. We'll go find her together."

"I can't, Tan. I'm sorry. I can't risk something happening to her. I promise I had no idea my actions, accidental or not, would come back on her. Mandi and I found something—something they want. I'm going to give it to them and get Ashley back. Please trust me."

"This has nothing to do with trust—this has to do with me wanting to protect two of the people I..."

"I love you. Please drive safely. You know how to find me." With those words, I cut the connection and put my phone on silent. He'd be mad, but I had to believe he'd forgive me. Thanks to an app we both had on our phones, he could track me—well, at least the GPS signal on my phone—and know exactly where we would be. I lovingly referred to it as the stalker app, but at a time like this, I was grateful for the technology.

My next call was to Officer Faria. I quickly highlighted the situation for him. "Can you bring reinforcements but keep them on the DL? I don't want to do anything to jeopardize Ashley's safety."

"Lilly, I'm in the next county over. Got a call about a terrible accident. I'll make sure you get backup and be there as soon as I can." He paused for a moment. "Lilly, I need you to wait on the backup. Understand?"

"I understand." Didn't mean for one second that I was going to wait. By the time help arrived, it might be too late. I wasn't going to jeopardize Ashley's life sitting around waiting.

"Ok, good. Thank you for that. Before you go, I need you to tell me what DL is so I make sure I keep it there— wherever that is."

If the situation weren't so serious, I would've gotten a giggle from his question. Since it was serious—life and death serious—I just filled in the information. "Downlow. It means keep them quiet. Once I get her out, you can charge in like the cavalry."

"Or if I decide in my professional opinion, before you bring her out, that you need extra assistance..." His tone brokered no room for argument.

"I can live with that." And I truly hoped that I did— live—to tell this tale at some point in the future, along with Ashley.

"Hey, Lilly?"

"Yes?" I really didn't have time to talk, but he was a man of few words, so I tried to pay attention when he chose to share things with me.

"The DNA came back."

If possible, my heartbeat increased from a tap to a stomp. I was certain *The Lord of the Dance* was hosting an encore performance under my rib cage. "And?"

"It wasn't a match to anyone we have in the system, but we were able to confirm it is female DNA."

The killer was a woman. Guess that eliminated Billy Nester and Adam Miller. Of course, that also moved me closer to the center of Detective Marshall's target. Since I knew I didn't do it, that put Jessica at the top of the suspect list. I admit I was surprised. She had a temper. We'd witnessed that earlier, but I still didn't think she had it in her. I remembered her alcohol confession about the pending assault charges. Maybe that was the motive. Securing funding to open an establishment to help the needy would be difficult with a criminal record. Maybe she hadn't thought this all the way through. *Or maybe she'd been lying about that all along.*

Given the missing diamonds from Sam's last position, I couldn't discount her entirely either. She did arrive in Danger Cove at about the right time. Could she be involved in this in some way? My head hurt from all the potential deception from these two women.

"You still there?" Faria's voice disturbed my thought pattern.

"I'm still here, but I have to go. See you soon."

"Be careful, wait for backup, and don't be a hero."

I laughed. "Who? Me? Never!" Ok, perhaps occasionally I liked to swoop in and save the day. This time I'd settle for saving Ashley.

We disconnected, and I unlocked the front door. "Mandi, can you get Watson some food and give him some loving while I secure the necessary supplies?"

My phone buzzed with a text. It was from Vernon. The message read: *Camilla allegedly assaulted by Jessica in bathroom at charity event. No witnesses. Rumors say C was jealous that J was being recognized for her contribution. Hope this helps. V.*

That still didn't answer whether Jessica actually did assault Camilla or not. Still didn't seem like a motive for murder, unless Jessica thought the charges—especially if false—could threaten her plans or ruin her reputation. One step forward, two steps back.

Right now, my focus had to be on Ashley. I grabbed the Mace and changed into black jeans, black sweatshirt, and tennis shoes. If we had to run and hide, I wanted to be able to blend in as much as possible. Briefly, I considered finding some face paint I'd used last Halloween to make my face black as well, but then dismissed it. I assumed I'd be face-to-face with someone who would make the exchange. No sense looking like I was on one of those zero-dark-thirty ops you see in the movies.

This was a simple exchange. Plus, there was always the chance I could get a confession out of the woman—aka Jessica—if she was the one who killed Camilla. At this point, I truly didn't know. I made sure my recording app was up and ready on my phone so it would only require a quick press of my finger to trigger the device.

I picked up Watson before we headed out and gave him some TLC under the chin and behind the ears. In addition to some powerful purring, Watson rubbed his head under my chin. He stopped long enough to stare directly into my eyes. The black slits surrounded by the yellow-green orbs and dotted with brown flecks had a concerned look to them. It was almost as if he sensed I was about to head into danger.

"I wish you could come with us, but I don't want anything to happen to you. I'll put out some extra food just in case…we're late getting back." No need to unnecessarily worry my little Watson.

"Lilly." Mandi's quiet voice broke into our little love fest. "We should probably get going."

With one last hug and kiss to Watson, I put him down and headed out. Once in the car, I turned to Mandi. "When we get there, I'm going to go inside and make the exchange. You slip over into the driver seat and be ready to go when I get back with Ashley or if things go sideways."

She grabbed my hand. "That's not how this goes. We are always together. We should be together!" The intensity of her voice almost made me change my mind.

Almost.

"Normally, I would agree. This is different. I have no idea who or what will be waiting for me inside or what will happen after I give them the diamonds. I need you to be my eyes and ears outside so we know which way they head or"—I squeezed her hand tighter—"to find the backup and bring in reinforcements if needed. Ok?"

She chewed on her bottom lip for a few moments before nodding. "Ok."

The drive to Shady Pines was made in silence. My phone continued to light up with calls from Tan, but I couldn't deal with that right now. He would only try to talk me out of this. I'd gotten us all into this mess. I needed to get us out. Even though it was mostly my strong desire to get my bracelet back that had prompted my unexpected discovery of the diamonds, it didn't matter.

This was my fault, and I needed to fix it. Ashley was in danger, and I still didn't have my bracelet. Emotion surged and lodged in my throat. This was not how this night was supposed to go down. Mandi, Watson, and I should be consuming massive amounts of calories and fat while feeding our internal romantic. Tan and Ashley should be bonding over an alien movie and Philly cheesesteak sandwiches. This was about as far from that as possible.

The moon had slithered behind dark clouds bathing the motel in shades of gray and black. Yeah, that wasn't creepy at all. A crack of thunder resounded in the distance. "Well, isn't that perfect. A storm's a brewin' to make this night even more ominous."

Mandi offered a nervous giggle. "Guess it is a dark and stormy night."

I flashed her an amused look. "I'm sure Abe will be happy to hear that."

Our smiles faded. Abe would be as unhappy with our escapade as Tan. Oh well. It was too late to turn back now. "Once I get out, pull the car back to a distance where you can still see but aren't close enough so that you could be dragged into whatever happens."

"Lilly…"

The warning in Mandi's voice tugged at my conscience, but I couldn't listen. "Please. I need to know you're safe and that you've got my back."

"Even if I'm way back?"

I nodded. "Even then."

"What about the police? They'll be here soon, right?"

Though I bent the truth occasionally, I could never lie to my best friend in the whole world. "Richie is sending backup since he's over in another county." I offered a small smile. "That's what we get for living in Small Town, USA. Anyway, they will be here as soon as they can." Something else had been gnawing at the back of my brain. I turned to Mandi. "Since you'll have some downtime…"

"Not funny, Lilly!"

I smiled to ease the tension. "Can you see if you can learn anything else about Winchester? Call Vernon if you need to. Maybe he can find something that Google or LinkedIn doesn't have. His arrival seems almost as suspect as…" I stopped myself from saying Sam's arrival.

"As what?"

"Nothing. The timing feels too convenient with everything that's going on. Worth checking out, right?"

"Guess that's better than sitting here worrying about you."

We exchanged a brief hug before we both got out of the car. She came around to the driver's side while I slipped the Mace into my front pocket. In one hand was the diamonds, in the other my cell phone.

"Be careful."

"Aren't I always?" I asked with a small smile. Not wanting to hear the sassy answer I knew was forming behind her pretty white teeth, I headed toward the front door. Before going inside, I turned and waited until she'd pulled away. My gut told me it was the right thing to do, even if whatever part of my body that housed my fear factor shouted loud and clear that I was an idiot.

My hand slipped on the doorknob the first time I tried to open it. This was new—my anxiety manifesting itself in moisture. I wiped them on my jeans and tried again. Success!

The door creaked, announcing my entrance into the room. So much for being stealthy. My gaze scanned the room, hoping to see Ashley standing there with an annoyed look on her face.

Without the benefit of the moon, my eyes had trouble adjusting to the darkness. Guess the small amount of time I'd spent outside wasn't enough for them to adapt. The details of the room were awash with an inky blackness. I couldn't really make out anything even though I had a familiarity with it thanks to my previous visits.

Not wanting to be a target any more than I already was, I stepped backward until I encountered the wall away from a window, allowing me to fade into the shadows. I managed to swallow the rock-sized lump in my throat and then exhaled slowly to force a calm in my voice I certainly wasn't feeling. "I'm here. I have your diamonds. Where's Ashley?"

A shuffling noise to the right, near the doorway to the corridor housing the room we found Billy in the other night caught my attention. A form stepped out of the darkness and closer to the window. A crack of lightning joined the brewing storm and illuminated the silhouette enough for me to recognize the figure.

David Charles Winchester the Fourth.

CHAPTER TWENTY-ONE

———

I'm not going to lie. I was caught completely off guard. I might have suspected he was involved somehow, but this was much more *involvement* than I'd anticipated. He was certainly not who I was expecting. After Faria's call, I was not expecting a *he* at all. My mind whirled to make sense of all of it. His mind, however, was singularly focused.

"You have the diamonds?"

I nodded, still unable to speak.

"Give them to me."

"Where's Ashley?" There. I'd found my voice when it mattered most.

"Give me the diamonds, and then you'll get that brat." He sneered as he started to advance on my position.

A small glint of humor cast itself upon my worry-filled brain. Ashley had a way of finding the trigger points on people and pushing them until you thought you might explode. Don't even get me started on how she'd terrorized me when we first met. I evaded his first lunge at me. I might not be in top physical shape, but I had Mr. Blowhard here beat by a landslide.

"You insufferable little wench."

His growl amused me further.

We played tag a minute or so more before I reiterated my position. "Tell me where Ashley is, and I'll give you these lackluster diamonds." Yeah, that was right, Mr. Winchester. I'd studied the goods.

He stopped chasing me, though *chase* would have been too generous—we'd basically been playing evade and try to capture. He was on the losing side. He huffed and puffed a few moments before a feral grin broke out on his face. "They will be perfection when I'm through with them—worth more than someone of your standing would appreciate or be able to afford. I'm a master at cutting stones to extract their maximum brilliance and, of course, price. Your friend, however, is running out of time while you play these games with me."

His choice of words removed any sassy retort I might have been conjuring up. They also explained the heavy suitcases that Mandi had mentioned. They must have been filled with the tools necessary for cutting the diamonds. Instead of reveling in at least one mystery being resolved, images of Ashley buried somewhere, unable to breathe, filtered into my mind. I blamed a recent crime show I'd viewed on generating that particular image. I really needed to find better things to watch after work.

I took the necessary steps to close the distance between us and handed him the bag of diamonds. Fun and games were over. I hadn't considered he might not have Ashley with him here to make a fair exchange. "Where is she?"

He grabbed the pouch and moved toward the door. "She's in this building. You better hurry." He waddled toward the door and then stopped. "Oh, and you should think twice about going to the police about this. I have friends in very low places nearby. I get one whiff of trouble from your friends at the police force, and you'll have more than one little brat to worry about. Am I clear?"

I nodded and hoped that would be enough for him. I could only hope Mandi would be able to figure out where he was headed so we could let Faria know when he got here. He might have not been the one to kill Camilla—or at least not acted alone—but his threats would only buy him a little time, not a get-out-of-jail-free pass. Once I rescued Ashley, and I most definitely was going to rescue her, I'd make him pay for causing so much trouble.

I started up the stairs, assuming he would want her as far away from us as possible to give him time to escape if I'd played nice in the first place.

"Ashley! Ashley! Where are you?" I screamed as loud as I could in the empty corridor and then did my best to silence the Indy 500 of nerves and adrenaline speeding through my body.

From the end of the hall, I heard muffled cries. That was enough for me. I urged my legs to give me one hundred and fifty percent despite the lack of oxygen. Once in the last room, I tried again. My prayer was that her muffled cries would serve as a homing beacon over the drum line in my ears. "Ashley, let me know where you are."

This time the muffling was much closer. Only a few feet away I guessed. I quickly moved into the next room and used the flashlight on my phone to search the area. I noticed the closet door was ajar. I threw back the door and lowered to my knees. Ashley's hands and feet were tied, and she'd been laid down on her side. That, by itself, wouldn't have stopped her, but the duct tape covering her mouth and most of her nose ensured she only received enough air to keep her alive for a short time. Guilt ripped into me as I tore the duct tape from her nose and mouth.

"Ouch! That hurt!" Ashley cried as she gulped in her first full breaths of air.

I went to work on her hands and feet. "I'm so sorry, Ashley. That bastard…"

The moment her hands were free, she rubbed her face where the tape had been, but I heard a small giggle. I refocused from the knot around her ankle to her face. "Are you laughing?"

She nodded and pushed me away from her feet. She went to work on the knot herself. "You cursed."

"I…" Her chuckling forced a small smile. "That's right. I did. I'll ask forgiveness later. Right now we have a bad guy to catch." I stood and helped her to her feet. She immediately pulled me into a hug.

"Thanks, Lilly. You saved my life. I'm not sure how much longer I would've lasted."

Any relief and mirth I'd experienced slid down my leg and retreated into the dark closet she'd been held hostage in. "That's my fault too. All of this is my fault."

She grabbed my hand and started pulling me in the direction of the stairs. "You saved me. In the end, that's what matters."

I wasn't sure I agreed with her, but there'd be plenty of time for self-recrimination and guilt assigning later. "Mandi's waiting outside, and I'm sure your brother will be storming the castle any moment."

My words stopped Ashley cold, forcing me to run into her and almost knocking both of us down. She shook her head and whispered, "This is all *my* fault. If I hadn't asked him to go on a food run, he would've been there to help protect me in the first place. So stupid."

I grabbed her shoulders with my hands and shook gently. Her gaze snapped to mine. "There's no way you could have known Mr. Blowhard would be lying in wait to snag you. We'll argue over fault later. Right now let's get you home."

"No way! We're going to go get them."

"Ashley..." Before I could argue with her, something in her word choice gave me pause. "What do you mean *them*?"

"He had an accomplice—a woman."

Now we were getting somewhere. "Did you see her? Do you know who it was?"

She shook her head. "No. I was in the backseat of his rental car. I could only see the back of the person. She was dressed all in black and wore a ball cap."

I didn't want to argue with Ashley, but I needed a little more information to believe her version of events. "How do you know it was a woman?"

Not wanting to lose too much time, I guided her outside so we could pursue this dynamic duo of diamonds and death. I searched for the car, fully expecting Mandi to be pulling up for our dramatic getaway. Instead, a small sliver of light moved toward us. I pushed Ashley behind me. "Who's there?"

"It's me." Mandi moved out of the shadows to join us in the front.

"Why aren't you in the car?"

"Can I answer your question first?" Ashley's impatience was legendary. A near brush with death hadn't changed that a bit, might have even heightened it.

"Ashley, I'm so glad you're safe!" Mandi pulled her into a hug. "What question are you going to answer?"

"How I know Windbag Winchester's accomplice is a female."

Mandi nodded. "She's totally a female. Men don't carry purses. I was hiding in the bushes and saw her meet up with Winchester when he came out."

Ashley threw her hands up in exasperation. "Sure, Mandi, steal the kidnapped girl's thunder. That's what *I* was going to tell Lilly. Geez, not even being in the center of the action lets me be the center of attention."

She found herself embraced in another hug. "Oh, I'm sorry. Sometimes my mouth gets running in high gear, and it just won't stop. I mean, I talk a lot already, especially when it comes to trivial matters. Not that this is trivial. I think fear and adrenaline makes it worse."

Mandi stopped when she realized Ashley was chuckling. "You made your point. No big deal—except I get to pick the food and movie on Monday."

"You will totally be the center of attention, promise. But now…"

"Now we go catch a killer." The fierceness in Mandi's voice and her choice of words gave me pause.

It was reasonable to assume this woman was a killer. It was also reasonable to assume, based on the possibility that Ashley was deprived of air and could've died if I hadn't found her in time, that Winchester was certainly comfortable with the path toward taking a life. "As much as I want to catch this person, we don't even know where they are. Any ideas?"

Ashley leaned against the front door and gestured with her thumb back to the motel. "This is the most ideal place for a covert meeting of bad guys I could think of."

For once, I agreed with her. "True, but they obviously left. Mandi, did you see anything?"

"No. I got out of the car and hid in the bushes to give me a better chance to hear things while still staying hidden. Whatever they did say was very brief, then they went their separate ways."

"We've got nothing then. I'll call Faria to let him know Ashley is safe and secure, then we'll all go home."

"That's no fun," Ashley whined, but offered no further objection.

We walked to where Mandi had parked the car. I jumped in the front seat while Ashley slid into the back. "Since we can't go after them, at least tell me who you think the killer is." Ashley leaned forward and switched her gaze between Mandi and me.

Mandi flashed me a quick look before answering. "Lilly is convinced it's Jessica."

Ignoring her question, I pulled the phone from my back pocket and sent a text to Tan: *Ashley is safe. See you soon.*

Mandi caught the words on my screen. Because she knew me so well, she caught the meaning in my look. I wasn't ready to give up on this just yet, but I also wasn't going to endanger Ashley. To be honest, I had no idea *what* I was going to do, just that I had to do something.

"Ooohh, she has a temper. Tan told me all about her. Is she your only suspect?" You could almost hear the adrenaline pumping through Ashley as she asked her question. I felt sorry for Tan having to deal with her, but I guessed he would enjoy every moment of it, knowing she was still alive to give us all grief.

"She's the only viable one I can think of." I sighed. "She had motive, means, and opportunity. She's also female. DNA under Camilla's fingernails confirms the attacker was a woman."

"What about her sister? Tan also told me Camilla and Candace weren't that close. Maybe she hated her enough to kill her?" Ashley had leaned back and was staring out the window. "I can't imagine hating anyone that much, but people have killed for less."

Before I could send a "don't say anything" look to Mandi, she jumped right into Ashley's theory. "I don't know much about their relationship, but she has been in the area on business. We don't know when she arrived, so it's possible she could have been in the area the night Camilla was killed."

Ashley jumped forward again. "Exactly. Oh man, can you just imagine what a field day the tabloids will have with this? Sister kills black sheep of the family in a fit of rage. I couldn't tell for sure, but I'm almost certain the woman with Winchester was carrying a designer purse. The gold letters glinted from the beam of the headlight. Reminded me of pictures I have in my wish book."

"A wish book?" Yeah, I had no idea what this was or even if I should know about it.

"It's no big deal. I just cut out pictures from a magazine and paste them into a blank journal. Things I like, things I want to have someday...you know."

She sounded embarrassed, and that wasn't my intention. "I think that's really cool. Maybe you could show me sometime? I'll start one for myself. Could be fun."

Mandi chimed in, "Me too."

"Yeah, maybe." She wouldn't be Ashley if she got excited about an idea I had come up with. Her not turning it down with a snarky remark and giving me a maybe was about as close as I could get to agreement. I'd never had a sibling, but I liked to pretend Ashley made up for that by giving me the grief a sister would. I was totally ok with that.

We pulled up in front of the Montgomery house. Tan's Mustang was in the drive. He'd been pacing the porch, but as soon as the car was in park, he was opening our door. "Thank God you all are alright!"

Ashley was pulled into a fierce big-brother hug. The moment I stepped out of the car, he pulled me in, making it a group hug. He looked up and smiled at Mandi. "Get in here and make it official."

Mandi grinned and put her arms around the group as well. This was nice. He smelled really good too. I'd learned his secret about how he kept his T-shirt so white (a spare in his locker at work), but his ability to smell like a breath of fresh ocean no matter what time of day or what activity he'd just finished still mystified me. I was pretty sure I smelled like I'd bathed in a big batch of Triple P: perspiration, panic, perfume.

Once he'd bear-hugged us completely, he finally let go of everyone but Ashley. "Let's not tell Mom about this, ok?" He smiled.

Ashley nodded. "Deal."

"We are going to call the police though. The fact that this could happen in Danger Cove..."

"No!" My voice was a little louder than I intended.

Tan put his hands on his hips as his eyebrows raised. "And why wouldn't we?"

I licked my lips. "Because Winchester threatened me and those I love with some bad guys he apparently has connections with if I did. Officer Faria already promised to send backup. We need to let him know Ashley is safe. As for the reinforcements, we need to keep them away for just a bit."

His head shook as he ran his fingers through the golden blond hair. "Until?"

"Until I can figure out our next steps. I need you to trust me. Give me just a little time to deal with a few things, and then we'll tell them all we know and make Winchester pay for what he did to Ashley."

Tan grabbed his sister's hand and ushered Ashley inside and then shut the door. Her grumbling could be heard through the solid wooden panel. He pulled me into a hug. "I don't like this, but I don't like the idea of you or anyone in our little 'family' being in danger again either. Thank you for saving her."

My head shook. "It was my fault to begin with, but can we save the lecture for tomorrow?"

Large, warm hands spanned and covered both of my cheeks, lifting my face until my lips were touching his. Warmth, love, and gratitude spread through me like honey making me forget my guilt—at least for the moment. "You can be reckless, but I don't believe for one second you intentionally did anything that would put my sister in harm's way."

He was right about that. "Never."

"Please keep me posted on what's going on. I can't leave Ashley by herself, or I'd be right there with you." One more brief touch of his lips to mine.

"I love you."

He smiled, his toothpaste white teeth gleaming in the porch light. "I love you too."

Tanner offered Mandi a brotherly hug, and then we were headed back to my house.

"You two are so cute," Mandi teased.

"So are you and Freddie." That's right. Two could play at her game.

She blushed enough I could see it in the blue and green lights from the dash. "We're just friends."

"Mmhmm. You keep telling yourself that."

Mandi's phone buzzed with an incoming call. She answered the call and put it on speaker. "Hey, Vernon."

"I'd ask why you were asking about this Winchester fella, but I'm sure Lilly put you up to it."

"Guilty as charged," I said with a smile, even though he couldn't see me.

"Well, stay away from him. He's bad news."

He needed to tell us something we didn't know. "Can you tell us why? The staying-away advice is about thirty minutes too late."

Vernon's sigh said it all. "There haven't been any arrests, but he's been mentioned in several shady business dealings that have gone south and ended in violence. There's a criminal organization behind all of it, but I need more time with my sources to figure out who's behind all the shell companies. Word on the street, though, is he's been down on his luck and looking for new opportunities…whatever that means for a career criminal. Just stay away from him, ya hear?"

"We hear," Mandi and I answered together.

"Thanks, Vernon. Let us know if you find anything else out. We'll do our best to avoid him."

"Don't play around with this, Lilly. Do better than your best usually is when it comes to avoiding trouble. This is a police matter." With that final instruction, he cut the connection.

With this new information, not only did I take Winchester's threat even more serious than I had before, I also sent a prayer of thanks to heaven that he'd not seriously harmed Ashley or me during our time with him.

We pulled into my drive in silence. This time no notes were nailed to my front door. Instead, leaning against the railing of my porch was Billy Nester. I glanced at Mandi before palming my pepper spray. I had no idea why he was here, but I wanted as much of an advantage as possible.

"Billy, what brings you to my neck of the woods this late at night?"

"I have information that may help you find where they've taken the diamonds."

CHAPTER TWENTY-TWO

———

Against my better judgment, I let Billy into my home. I can't explain why, other than my gut told me he wasn't as bad a guy as Constance Cartwright wanted me to believe. Maybe he'd just fallen in love—obsessive, all-consuming love—with the wrong woman. Sadder things had happened. Also, I was afraid to ask him how he knew about the diamonds. That could spell bad news, as he might be using me and Mandi to help him recover them. Ugh, this was all maddening.

I scooped up Watson when we entered the kitchen. "Hey, big guy, did you miss me?"

"Meow," he responded as he butted his head up against my cheek.

I flashed Mandi a smile. "That means yes."

She chuckled. "I didn't realize you spoke cat."

Billy pulled out a chair at the table and made himself at home. "No, she's right. A cat gives you lovin' by butting their head against you. Means he really likes you."

Billy either needed to provide me some information or leave to allow me to plan my way out of the mess I was in. "I suspect he likes me because I feed him. Speaking of food, I'd offer you something, Billy, but I haven't had a chance to go to the grocery store, and I have no idea what happened to the pizza we got earlier." Seriously, what had happened to it?

Billy blushed and rubbed his head. "I might've found it on your front yard when I got here. Reckoned you wouldn't eat it after it was on the ground. Sorry…"

Pizza mystery solved. "It's ok. I'm not really hungry anyway."

This last bout with danger had diminished some of my desire to get the bad guys—this one in particular. Don't get me wrong. Crime should pay. But as it's been pointed out to me time and time again, it's not my job. The only reason I cared at the moment, though, was because of what these particular set of bad guys had done to Ashley.

Once Watson had been fed, I turned my attention to Billy. "Did you see who Winchester was with?"

He shook his head. "No, I was hiding in the woods. Her back was to me."

"How do you know where they are?" I was too tired to play twenty questions, but here I was, fishing for information. Darn curiosity kitties.

"I don't exactly."

"Billy! Just tell me."

He rubbed his face, the weathered hands speaking of a life of hard work and very little pampering. "The man only said three words to the woman. Three words that didn't make any sense, but she nodded and headed off in the opposite direction." He hung his head. "I'm sorry. That wasn't much help. I don't even know why I'm here."

I put my hand on his shoulder. "Those three words could lead us exactly to them. Don't ask how, as I'm too tired to explain. What exactly did he say?"

Billy relayed the three words to me. I nodded as I typed them into my phone. "You're here because you want to help."

He shook his head. "Every time I try to help, it only causes problems."

"What do you mean?" Mandi asked before I could suggest we table the discussion until after we caught the bad guys. While Mandi tried to pry the information out of Billy, I texted the three words he'd provided to Freddie and asked him to return an address to me. I could probably do it on my phone, but Freddie's laptop had a bigger screen and was easier to maneuver.

"I tried to help Ms. Candace out, but I ended up getting myself fired."

Wait. This was news. "What did you do to help Candace Cartwright out?"

He smiled as his eyes closed. "Ms. Candace is a right fine woman. She looks after all those people. Makes sure they have the best care—took good care of my momma before she passed."

I didn't want to split hairs with Billy—especially since he was bald—but Candace was the COO—she didn't provide the actual care. However, I understood what he was saying. The Cartwrights created an environment that provided top-notch care. "What did you try to do to help her?"

His fists pounded on the table, startling both Mandi and me and earning him a glare from Watson, as it paused the inhalation of his food. "That fool sister of hers always causing trouble. I did my best to get her in trouble. Thought maybe if she caused enough problems, they'd cut her out or off—something. Let Ms. Cartwright do her job without worry."

Maybe we had it wrong and Billy had a crush on a different sister. Still meant he could've killed Camilla to get her out of Candace's hair. Wasn't farfetched at all, really. Well, except for the DNA evidence. Ugh, I kept coming up emptier than Agnes's tequila bottle on a Saturday night.

"Don't you think a scandal would've hurt the nursing home business and the family?" Mandi asked.

"Nah, I wasn't aimin' for a scandal, just enough to get that vile woman away from being the center of attention."

"It worked too, didn't it? After the fiasco at the party, Camilla was moved into a position that would keep her out of the day-to-day business. She was a pain, but, Billy, what if something even worse had happened? A public relations nightmare could have made families start wondering about the care their loved ones were getting. They could've taken them out and placed them in a home where maybe they wouldn't have received the type of care they needed." His intentions might have been honorable, but his methods were questionable.

"You sound just like Ms. Camilla's assistant, Serena, now." He huffed.

"You know Serena?" I asked just as my front door busted open. It was Tanner, and if the set of his jaw was any indication, he was determined. I just wasn't sure about what.

"Hey, Tanner. I didn't think you were going to let Ashley out of your sight."

"She's with a friend. Do you know where they are?" His tone brokered no room for any lighthearted banter.

My phone buzzed with an incoming text message. A quick glance revealed it was Freddie with the address. I held my phone up. "We just received it. Why?"

"We're going after that son of a biscuit-eating bulldog. No one messes with my family and gets away with it."

This Tanner was Caveman Tanner on steroids. Not gonna lie—it was kinda hot. Yeah, those thoughts would have to wait too. He cut me a look with a raised eyebrow.

"You were going anyway, weren't you? Well, now we'll all go together."

I shrugged. "Technically, we were undecided, but you support me every time I want to rush headlong into danger. I'm happy to return the favor."

He nodded. "You have the go bags?"

Mandi and I picked up the backpacks resting at our feet and lifted them for his viewing pleasure. "Stocked and ready to go. You trained us well."

A small smile was the first crack in his expression since he'd arrived. "Mandi will drive. I call shotgun. Lilly, you keep watch out the back."

No objections from me. I kind of liked the fact he was taking charge. My guess was he hadn't got past the first stage of the plan. The "let's get 'em" part was the easiest stage. It might be a little sad that I even knew about the details of making such a plan. "You got it." I debated whether or not to text Faria with where we would be so he and the backup he sent could find us. Vernon's warnings *did* include letting the police handle it. This was a risk I was going to have to take and pray it wasn't a mistake to go against Winchester's threats. "I'll text Faria to let him know where we are. Maybe he will finish up with that accident or redirect the backup in time to help with our capture."

Billy stood up. "I'm comin' too. Having additional muscle can't hurt none."

"Sure, come on. You'll need to stay out of sight unless we call for help though, alright? We don't want to complicate whatever already major mess we're going to be walking into."

He nodded his head. I hoped that meant he'd actually follow those words of instruction. With one last stroke of Watson's fur, we headed out the door armed only with our phones, Mace, Tanner's desire for payback, and some geriatric muscle. Oh yeah, this plan was doomed.

Mandi killed the headlights about a quarter mile before arrival at our location and relied only on the smaller, less bright running lights to guide us. I made a mental note to squeeze in a nail appointment on my day off, as they would have to see if they could repair the fact I'd gnawed every last one of my fingernails down to the quick in that quarter of a mile.

Once we were about a hundred yards from the location, she pulled off onto the side of the road, and all illumination was extinguished. Using a set of binoculars from my go bag, I tried to determine what kind of situation we were walking into. "Two cars. One room off to the side lit up brightly. Rest of the house is dark."

"Whose house is that? I mean, if it's Winchester, he's staying at Ocean View," Mandi said as she dug into her bag until she produced her binoculars and put them to her face for a closer look.

"I think it's one of Glover Rentals. The owner, Blake Glover, has some property out here, if I remember correctly. Mom and I looked at some when we had to move out of the house at Craggy Estates after Dad died," Tan answered, before asking a question of his own. "Two people?"

"Unable to confirm," Mandi answered. "But reasonable to assume."

"So what's your plan?" I asked, hoping to make Tan stop and reconsider all of this, at least until Faria arrived with some official support for storming the gates. Winchester's words of warning still loomed like a dark cloud over my head. I hoped none of his *friends* were nearby, ready to assist him if needed.

His beautiful mouth had just opened to ply me with what I was certain was the best plan ever—he was my man after all— when another car pulled up, and a woman got out. We were still too far away for me to be able to tell who it was, with the lack of lighting from our direction.

"That's Ms. Cartwright!" Billy whispered loudly, even though I was certain we were too far away for her to have heard us regardless.

"Which one?" I asked rather than try to guess. Did I mention how tired I was? Guessing took a lot of energy, and I'd already expended my quota for the day.

"The good one." Billy smiled, the affection for the *good* Cartwright evident on his face.

Drawing on what I knew about the Cartwrights, I hazarded a guess. "Candace?"

"Yes."

The woman we now believed to be Candace Cartwright made her way to the front door and knocked. Someone answered and invited her in. From what we could see of the shadows, they avoided the room that was currently lit. Thankfully, there were a lot of windows all around the house. When another dimmer light appeared to the right, I assumed that meant someone had gone to the back of the house.

"My plan is simple," Tan started.

"I like the idea of simple. Offers up less chance for it to go horribly wrong." Trust me. I knew a thing or four about things going horribly wrong. Of course, Tan's idea of simple and mine might be two very different things. I'd have to reserve judgment until a few details were provided.

"I go up to the front door and knock. When whoever opens it, I head directly for that windbag, weasel Winchester. I'll then proceed to beat the crap out of him for abducting and almost killing my sister. By the time Faria arrives, Winchester will be more than happy to confess. If for no other reason than to make me stop using him as a punching bag."

"Sounds like a great plan to me," Billy joined in as a testosterone twin.

My next words would need to be chosen carefully. I leaned forward and slid my hands over the seat and Tan's shoulders and pulled him into a pseudo hug. "You know how much I love it when you go all macho caveman, and I would love nothing more than to see you kick the shitzu out of that jerk."

"But…" Tan filled in the necessary word for me.

"But we need to achieve the proverbial two birds with one stone goal."

I could feel the deep rise and fall of his chest even though his sigh was quiet in the still of the night. "Meaning?"

"Meaning, I'm pretty sure one of the people in there is Camilla's killer."

He shook his head. "There's no way to prove that. Not without the DNA."

"Or a confession."

He chuckled. "You think she's just going to open up and admit to you she killed Camilla and then let you walk out scot-free? My plan is simple. Yours is delusional."

My arms squeezed him a little tighter. "What if we combined our plans?" The modulation in my voice captured not only Tan's attention but the other people in the car as well.

"What do you have in mind, Lilly?"

Mandi's eagerness told me she had about as good judgment as I did. The guys might be oozing bravado, but Mandi and I had both our feet squarely in Reality Town.

I gave Tan a quick kiss on the cheek before releasing him. I retrieved my phone from its spot on the seat next to me. "Mandi, can you pull up Glover Rentals' website on your phone?"

She nodded and got her thumbs moving over the screen. "Got it. What do you want me to look up?"

I gave her the address where our persons of interest were located. "Type that in and see if a layout of the house is available. I know he has floor plans for some of the rentals, as people occasionally like to see that before they rent."

A few more taps of her fingers on the phone and she held it up for my inspection. "Got it."

We looked at the layout, and the plan began to form in my mind. I pointed to the screen as I shared, "Here's what I'm thinking. Mandi and I will figure out how to get in through this door in the back. We can then hide out in this closet next to the dining room area and listen to learn what Candace and the mystery woman are talking about. I'll keep an open phone line to Tanner, and Mandi will record the conversation on her phone."

"Why the open phone line to me?" Tanner asked.

"In case we need a distraction. You can enact your part of the plan."

The gleam in his eyes as he thought about punching Winchester should have frightened me, but it had quite the opposite effect. *Focus, Lilly.* "But what if you don't need a distraction?" He pouted.

"I promise to do everything I can to let you get some payback."

Tan cracked his knuckles, which forced Mandi to allow a small giggle to escape. "The goal is to get anyone to say something to implicate themselves. We'll have it on a recording, and Faria can use that to arrest people."

My macho man nodded. "I'm game with giving it a try, but how are you and Mandi going to get in? Not like you can just knock on the door."

"I think I can help with that," Billy piped up from the seat next to me. I'd almost forgotten he was here.

"What you got, Billy? I'm all ears."

He grinned. "Ever wonder how I got into Shady Pines in the first place?"

The question had occurred to me when I'd tried to find a way in. "I did actually. Don't tell me you can walk through walls. If so, we need to talk long-term strategy here."

Billy chuckled. "Nothing quite so fancy. I'm pretty good at picking locks." He reached into his pocket. "Got my own set. From an uncle, a gag gift that has served me well over the years."

One side of me wanted to take Billy to the bar, buy him some drinks and a hot meal, and hear his whole story. The other side of me said that would take too long and the bad guy and girl would get away. Another time perhaps. "Never thought I'd be happy to know a picklock." I took a moment to look at each person in the car before taking a deep breath and exhaling. "Ok, let's do this."

Tan waited in the car while Billy, Mandi, and I made our way along the wooded area to circle around to the back of the house. In order to keep myself from sharing all the ways this could be my worst plan ever—and believe me, that was saying something, as I'd had some doozies in the past—I reviewed all of my conversations with Billy in my head. It was my way of triple checking myself to make sure he wasn't really a part of all this and was about to double cross us.

Something else that bothered me—besides the thought of tree-dwelling bugs falling on me as we slinked by them in the dead of night—was how or why Jessica fit into all of this. She had told me she'd rented a place around here rather than staying at Ocean View. Could this be her place? Had she known about the diamonds all along? Is that why she killed Camilla? If that was the case, I was going to need to make an appointment to get the sensor in my gut checked. I totally bought into her whole helping-people story. Forget the Peter Principle—I was a total sucker.

We were a few feet away from the door when something Billy had told me previously stepped into the spotlight of my memories. "Hey, Billy?"

"Yep," he answered as he decided on which pick to use.

"Earlier, before Tanner came in, you mentioned that Serena had given you pretty much the same advice I'd just given you. I didn't realize you two were that close."

The look on his face couldn't easily be identified. It could have been an *I've been caught in a lie* face or a *Do we really need to talk about this now?* "We weren't close. You sure do ask a lot of questions." He raised his hand to stop my defense of my actions. "I'll 'splain later, but we knew each other from the nursing home."

Guess that made sense, both the waiting until later and them knowing each other from the nursing home. Depending on how involved Serena had been in the day-to-day stuff of Camilla's life, she might have been with her at the nursing home while Billy worked there. "Ok, but later."

He sighed but nodded before signaling us to wait there while he picked the lock. He put his ear to the door and listened. Good idea. Probably smart to do your best to make sure no one was hanging out in the area when you were coming in uninvited.

While he worked his magic, I dialed Tanner. He answered on the first ring. "Ok," I whispered, "this is our open line."

"Hey, Lilly, can I ask you a question?"

Now I understood how Billy felt. "Can it wait? We're about to illegally break and enter into a Glover rental property with the hopes of apprehending a diamond thief and potential murderer." Geez, when I said it out loud, it sounded even more insane than I'd originally planned.

"Is this how it always feels when you're closing in on the bad guy?"

The fact I'd "closed in" on a bad person enough to even be asked that question made me wonder if I should reevaluate the choices I made. "This is the first time I've technically closed in on someone. Normally, it's just my dumb luck that gets me face-to-face with the evildoer." I couldn't help but grin at the fact that it was true. Usually, it was a case of the wrong place at the wrong time that landed me standing (or tied up) in front of them. Yeah, welcome to my world.

This was the first time I knew the identity of the bad guy. The part that really bothered me though? Who was the bad girl?

CHAPTER TWENTY-THREE

———

I slid my phone into my jacket pocket and tiptoed inside the back door of the house. Once Mandi and I were inside, Billy closed the door behind us. We'd decided he would stay back in the bushes behind the house (I knew he felt at home there) in case the plan went completely haywire. Tan would provide support from the front and Billy from the back. We stepped inside the hall closet and closed the door, leaving only a small crack. I made myself a promise. If I got out of this mess alive, I'd never step inside a closet again except to retrieve clothes or shoes. Felt like a small price to pay.

Once my heart rate settled back into a high-normal rhythm, I listened to the voices coming from the other room. The little voice inside my head prayed I'd recognize something familiar from her tone or other identifying trait when someone spoke. If she spoke a confession, well, that would be the nicest thing she could ever do for me and our little plan.

"Your aunt has taken a turn for the worse. You need to come see her soon. She misses you."

Logically, I assumed that was Candace's voice. Whoever the other woman was must have an aunt who was a patient in one of their nursing homes.

"I'm going to try, but I'm not sure what I'll be doing next with everything that's happened." The other woman spoke in a loud whisper, making identification challenging.

Ugh, I really wanted to be closer. I could barely hear. And what they were saying didn't make any sense. If the other woman was Camilla's killer... Mandi's heavy breathing right next to me wasn't helping either. I turned my head so I could whisper next to Mandi's ear. "You need to control your breathing. In and out, slowly and quietly."

She flashed me an annoyed glare that was evident even in the tiny sliver of light provided by the crack at the door. "I'm trying. Not even trivia is taking my mind off the insanity of this."

I ignored her and tried to focus again on what was being said. We'd need to work on our eavesdropping skills later. I grabbed her hand and squeezed to try to reassure her.

"We'll need to talk about the financial arrangements once you're back in town. With Camilla gone, I'm afraid the perk she offered you can't be extended for more than thirty days."

There was a loud noise, like something was slammed onto a table. Mandi and I both jumped and then froze as our activity caused something in the closet to bump against the wall. Mandi's heavy breathing returned, and my heart rate kicked into double time, initiating a thundering deep within my chest.

"Did you hear that?" Candace asked.

"What I hear is that after all I did for you and your family, you're willing to turn my family out on the street." Now that she was speaking a little louder, I started to work out in my mind where I'd heard the voice before. And I knew I'd heard it before.

I turned to Mandi to ask her if she thought it was the same person I did, when I noticed the look on her face. She wasn't looking at me. She wasn't looking at the door. She was looking about halfway up the small crack in the door. Her gaze was fixed on the biggest black spider I'd ever laid eyes on.

Rather than scream, I scrambled backward to get away from the monster arachnid, every nightmare I'd ever had about the eight-legged creature flashing across the screen of my mind. The movement jostled and disconnected him from his thin thread and landed him right on my bare forearm.

This time I couldn't stop my verbal gasp. "Spider!" All rational thought fled save the need to dislodge the hairy beast. Fear had magnified him to ten times his normal size—at least. I shoved open the door to escape, my hands rubbing my arms in an effort to knock it away. I stumbled forward and ran straight into the woman whose voice I'd been trying to place.

"Serena?!" Now wasn't the best time to be excited about the discovery of the mystery woman. The spider had sent my plan from shaky ground to full-on earthquake mode.

Everything switched from high speed to slow motion the moment I said her name. My mind tried to process and put together exactly what was going on so I could come up with an explanation for why my BFF and I were hiding in the closet of her rental place.

Note to self, factor avoiding bugs into any future plans to catch bad guys. Scratch that...factor avoiding bugs into any future plans. Period.

Without saying a word, Serena moved for her purse. I couldn't fathom why until she pulled a gun out of the designer handbag. I was willing to bet a month's profits she didn't have a permit for that. I also knew better than to even ask. She pointed the gun in the direction of everyone else in the room and gestured for us to all sit down at the table. Mandi and I quickly obeyed. Candace remained frozen to her spot on the floor, like a statue, with her mouth agape.

A moment later, Candace found her voice. "What in God's name are you doing, Serena? Who are these people, and why are they in the house you are renting?" Her tall frame, platinum blonde hair, and striking green eyes all added to her bewildered presence as she'd straightened her spine. Of course, I couldn't fathom why she chose to ask ridiculous questions that could get her shot.

"I suggest you sit down and shut up." Serena smiled before adding, "Guess that means I'm telling you what to do. How about that for a change?"

Candace might not have understood everything about what was going on, but she was smart enough to realize the woman holding the gun was "she who must be obeyed" at this moment. I wasn't nearly as well educated as this particular Cartwright, but I'd figured that out within about a half a second. Street smarts for the win.

Once seated, Candace lifted her hands in the traditional surrender motion. "I'm sitting. Now can you please explain what's going on?"

Serena's wild-eyed expression helped me decide—for once—that I'd keep my mouth shut and let Candace do the talking. I did venture a glance in Mandi's direction. Our gazes connected, and I glanced down to her jacket pocket, where I knew her phone rested. Offering her a quizzical look, I hoped she understood that I was asking if her phone was recording. A slight nod answered my question. God bless BFF wavelength.

Now that we'd established that, I also prayed the connection between my phone and Tan's ear was still viable despite my bug-avoidance antics. I could use a Caveman Superhero rescue anytime now. I'd even settle for a distraction to give us a chance to bolt out the back. Officer Faria or the backup *had* to be on their way by now. Right?

After pacing the length of the room a few times, Serena finally turned in our direction. I preferred the pacing, as the gun was pointed at other targets. She directed her anger toward Candace. "For almost a year now, I've been cleaning up after your sister. Making apologies for her, taking the brunt of her narcissistic behavior, and watching her treat other people, including me, with the utmost of disdain and disrespect."

Candace wisely kept her mouth shut. She'd been dealing with Camilla's behavior her entire life. When she didn't respond, Serena continued. "I did it for two reasons. One, the discounted price for the care of my aunt. She's the only family I have left, and your family's nursing homes are among the best in the country. She deserves nothing less than the best."

"What's wrong with your aunt?" Mandi's curiosity was sometimes worse than mine. Rare, but this was a prime example. I'd hoped Serena was so focused on Candace that she'd forget about Mandi and me.

Serena pulled the last chair from the table and moved it about six feet away. Still close enough to be reasonably accurate, even if she were a horrible shot. Though she relaxed in the seat, the gun was still pointed squarely in our direction. Fan-freakin'-tastic.

"My aunt developed early onset Alzheimer's. She needed care that I couldn't give her. All of the nursing homes in my part of New York were just..." She visibly shuddered, causing the gun to shake in her hand. Not good.

I'd been taught there was nothing more frightening than a nervous woman with a gun. Though I usually agreed with that assessment, I might contend that an angry woman with a gun beat that or at least came in at a photo finish for second.

"I'm so sorry," Mandi offered. "That had to be a horrible feeling. What did you do?"

There was a small hint of relief on Serena's face...almost like she felt someone finally understood what she'd been going through. "I couldn't afford any of the nicer places for her until I finished college. Sadly, my aunt didn't have that kind of time. So I decided to apply for a position in finance at Cartwright Corp. I didn't have my degree yet, but my record and achievements were impressive. I'd hoped there would be a discounted rate for family members of employees or that with that kind of bump in my salary, I could afford the monthly fee."

Not wanting to make Mandi take all the heat, I leaned forward a little and tried to ease Serena off the danger ledge. "You must love your aunt very much. I felt the same way about my gram. I would've sacrificed anything to make sure she had everything she needed in those last days."

Serena stood and pointed the gun right at me. Dark, expressionless eyes transformed into hard, angry orbs shooting directly at me. It didn't take a super sleuth to know my tactic had failed. Hoped Mandi appreciated me figuratively and possibly literally taking this bullet for her. This brought taking one for the team to a whole new level. My plan had gone sideways in every possible way. Maybe we should've stuck to Tan's idea.

"Why does everyone always have to make this all about *them*?! I thought you were different." The calm, cool Serena I'd come to know and appreciate was nowhere near this room.

I followed Candace's earlier example and raised my hands in surrender. "I'm sorry. I didn't mean it like that. Just wanted you to know you weren't alone."

"But I am alone. Don't you get it? I didn't get the job I wanted."

Mandi jumped back into the fray. Her voice must be more calming than mine. Besides, the more she talked, the better chance we had for help to arrive. "But you did get a job, right?"

Serena paced the length of the room a few times. I chanced a look at Candace, but she was focused on whatever the woman with the gun was going to do next. "Camilla hired someone else, even though I was perfectly qualified. Instead she offered me what she said was an even better position—her assistant."

Mandi nodded. "Definitely not what you signed up for. But at least that got the care for your aunt, right?"

Candace decided to join the party again. "Right. We offered the employee discount even though Camilla's ventures had taken her outside the realm of the nursing home."

Serena shot Candace a smug look. "Oh, you have no idea how far outside that arena she was playing."

"What do you mean? She was a real estate investor, a very good one if the reports are to be believed." Candace seemed genuinely perplexed.

To be honest, so was I. Personally, my confusion was focused on Tan. Why hadn't he stormed the gate? Did he not realize she had a gun? Did he think we were all having tea and cookies back here? A worse thought to consider—had my tap dance to avoid the spider caused my phone to disconnect? Even so, wouldn't that have been a *things have gone terribly wrong so come help* sign? Ugh! If he wasn't going to rescue us right now, then I might as well try to get some answers.

"Camilla was getting bored with real estate, wasn't she? I mean, according to Mommy Dearest, she could never stand still for very long. Always looking for the next great thing. Was she tired of the easy wins she had against Jack, Jessica, and Adam?" I was sure there were more people, but those were the ones I knew.

Serena threw her head back and emitted a scary hyena laugh. "I knew you were a smart one." She pulled a chair up and plopped her crazy butt right down in front of me. I'd wanted information, not up close and personal with a gun.

She leaned even closer. "Probably too smart for your own good. Why don't you tell me more about what you think happened."

I swallowed the ball of fear that had lodged itself soundly in my throat. "Well, since there are uncut diamonds that were dropped in the dead of night to an abandoned motel, I assume an illegal aspect factored in somewhere."

Serena stood up so abruptly, she knocked the chair over. The sound brought Winchester from the other room. "What in blazes is going on in here?! I'm trying to work." It was at that moment he noticed Mandi and me. "I thought I told you two to mind your own business."

Technically, he'd told me not to call the police. Of course, I hadn't followed those instructions to the letter either. Surely Tan had called the police and directed them to our new location by now. "We were looking for Serena. How could we know you'd be here? How are you involved in this anyway?"

Winchester leaned against the door and offered a smug smile. Before he could respond, Mandi piped up. "You're cutting the diamonds, aren't you?"

He wagged his finger at her. "Smart, yet stupid." He looked at Serena, all humor disappearing from his expression. "You know you're going to have to clean up this mess."

She shook her head. "There's no need for that. You and I will be long gone. Your *friends* arranged for everything, correct?"

He harrumphed. "As long as you hold up your part of the bargain, they will." The expression on his face seemed to indicate he didn't believe she would keep her end of the deal…whatever that was. He turned and stepped out the door. I assumed he was getting back to work.

"So I'm guessing BARAG is the front for some criminal syndicate?" I wanted to get this information recorded and then plan some kind of escape since Tanner, my knight in white cotton, hadn't made an appearance yet. "What is your part of the bargain?"

Candace piped up and interrupted my little line of questioning. "Who cares about some crime syndicate. I want to know what happened to my sister!"

Serena turned and took menacing steps toward Candace. "Your sister was small minded and could never see the big picture. She only cared about the thrill of the deal—none of the details! I…I was the one who took care of everything else while she claimed *all* the glory and all the profits. I stumbled on this little side deal she'd cooked up…one she tried to hide from me! Did she think I was an idiot?!!"

Everyone in the room that didn't have a gun believed that to be a rhetorical question, as none of us, myself included, answered. Serena got right in Candace's face. "I found evidence that she'd reached out to procure uncut blood diamonds."

Candace's face morphed into a look of horror. "She wouldn't! That goes against everything our family stands for!"

"She would, and she did." Serena laughed. "Well, she tried. Like everything else, she didn't think past getting the diamonds. That was all that mattered to her. Not the money…no, of course not! She already had more than she could ever need. I, on the other hand, had vision to see opportunities where she did not."

Candace shook her head, the disbelief continuing. "She wouldn't do that. She liked to be the center of attention—that was her major fault."

Serena's face flushed red with anger. "She betrayed me! After everything…*everything* I did. All those details she forgot that were necessary to close real estate deals, smooth ruffled feathers to avoid defamation lawsuits, research to find dirt on people to use against them. All the dirty work! Then that witch finally decided to get her hands dirty—and she couldn't even do that right!"

A few details started clicking into place from what Serena had shared. "She wanted to hide the location of where the diamonds would be delivered. That's why she wrote it on her hand rather than somewhere else."

Serena's attention riveted to me. "Like that would stop me. She was so self-absorbed, she didn't even notice me…she never noticed me!"

This was it—the moment we'd been waiting for. I just needed her to state it for my official record. "So you followed her to the hotel, and then what? You got in an argument? Did you plan to kill her? Did you somehow convince Jack to help you?" I needed to know once and for all if he was involved. I'd also like Serena to spill the truth. If I was going to die, I needed it to mean something. Even if Serena let us live, I held little hope that Winchester would. Honestly, my hope was she'd confess and moments later we'd be rescued.

"You killed my sister!" Candace foiled my little plan with her outburst. Unless Serena followed that up with, "Yes, I did!" then my attempt at securing a confession had just fallen flat.

Her outburst captured everyone's attention, which gave her time to use the long legs God gave her to close the short distance to Serena and tackle her better than a Super Bowl defensive MVP. The impact knocked Serena to the ground, sending her gun sliding across the floor. There was little doubt the noise would bring Winchester back into the room. I chanced a quick look to Mandi, and we both knew in an instant we needed to help. Though how we should help would send us into a quandary if we stopped for even a second and thought about it.

I handed my phone to Mandi. "Call Tanner." With one final, deep breath, I made my way to the gun, deciding for the moment to ignore the women wrestling on the floor.

A moment later I had the gun, but before I could do anything with it, strong hands grabbed my wrists in an effort to wrestle the weapon from my grasp. Winchester! This man had aggravated every nerve from the moment I'd met him. If I didn't do something quickly to ease his grip on me, any advantage I might have gained would be gone. My self-defense lessons scrambled to the forefront of my brain, causing me to take a step closer to the man and lifting my knee to connect solidly with his family jewels.

The tactic worked, and his grip lessened enough for me to jerk my hands away. Unfortunately, in the flurry of activity along with the moisture coating my hand, the gun went flying and landed right next to Candace. She spotted it and pushed hard against Serena, giving Candace the time needed to grab it and scramble to her feet.

Candace wasted no time in pointing the barrel directly at Serena's chest. "As I was saying, you killed my sister." She put an exclamation point on the end of her statement by pulling the hammer back on the gun. I couldn't be sure, but she seemed fairly comfortable with a firearm.

"You wanted her dead too," Serena offered with more conviction than I would've been able to muster with a gun pointed at me.

The sound of another gun cocking brought everyone's attention to the door. Standing behind Candace was Windbag Winchester. He had recovered enough from my attack and had his gun pointed in the direction of the two women. That helped explain Serena's boldness a bit more. *Her* backup was not only here but was prepared too!

Serena crossed her arms. "Took you long enough. Let's pack up and get out of here. You can finish the diamonds after we arrive at our new location."

Winchester chuckled. "You should've vetted your help a little better. I believe I'll take it solo from here. Thanks for pulling me out of the gutter, but I tire of doing someone else's bidding for a small pittance. It's time I took control of my destiny and cashed in on my hard work. No more slumming it with the hired help for me."

"You…you…ingrate!" Serena screamed and then barreled toward him. The move surprised Candace enough that she got out of the way. I didn't blame her. I wouldn't want to stand between those two maniacs either. Winchester was caught off guard enough that he wasn't able to fire the gun. Instead he graced us with a loud "oof" as he hit the floor and his gun came loose.

In all the ruckus, I heard a loud sound coming from the front of the house. I prayed it was *our* rescue team. I bolted toward the gun and willed my sweat-slicked hands would hold it securely.

Just as I grabbed the weapon, I heard "This is the police!" and then a blur of long dark hair and a white shirt followed by a scream from Serena as her body hurled through the air and landed on the other side of me. I looked up to see Sam and Officer Faria. He looked disappointed and a little miffed that Sam had made it to the scuffle and subdued the bad guys…well, guy and girl.

Sam smiled. "Even though I didn't receive an official SOS, I thought this might be a time you needed my help, Boss Lady. Hope I wasn't too late."

I slumped into one of the chairs we'd been forced to sit in earlier. A small chuckle escaped as the adrenaline eased the pressure it had been holding over my heart. "Just in time, Sam. Just in time."

CHAPTER TWENTY-FOUR

———

Faria handcuffed Serena and Winchester before securing the handguns. I gladly gave mine up without any hesitation. He cut Sam a small glare before stating, "For those who followed my instructions and waited outside, we're all clear," which immediately brought Tanner rushing into the room and to my side.

He pulled me into one of his giant bear hugs. "I was so worried about you!"

I didn't want to seem ungrateful, but him showing up late for this particular date almost got me and Mandi killed. "What took you so long?" I lifted my head from his chest to give him a kiss. "Not that I'm not grateful you eventually showed up, but Sam and Faria get credit for saving the day."

Sam grinned. "Who do you think called me? It took me a few minutes to get here since I'd just started my jogging route. I arrived just before Officer Faria."

Why she would choose a route that ran by Shady Pines made no sense to me, but I'd save that question for another day. "I can understand that, but what about our plan?"

"That plan had so many holes, it could form a pro golf course. Let's see..." Faria held up his fingers and pointed to each one as he counted off the major problems. "Not calling the police sooner, not waiting for the police to arrive, illegal breaking and entering, not securing the premises before entering, relying on civilians as your backup...shall I go on? We would have breached sooner, but we needed to survey the premises to learn where everyone was located." His plan was far more cautious than mine had been. Guess that was why he wore the uniform. "Hey! It was better than Tanner's initial plan, which basically was a bust-in-and-beat-'em-up kind of deal. At least ours..." I gestured to Mandi to hand me her phone, which she did. A couple swipes on the device and Serena's voice came through loud and clear as she ranted away about her relationship with Camilla.

Faria frowned. "That might help with motive, but it's not exactly a confession. I'll take a copy of it anyway."

Mandi sighed. Usually we were better at getting confessions. "Of course. Sorry we couldn't get you the proof we needed. Is it at least enough to clear Jack Condor of any wrongdoing?"

Faria shook his head. "Not yet. He could still be involved somehow, and since Miss Serena didn't confess to being there..."

I noticed Serena sport a small smile. I moved in front of her. "I know you think you had a perfect plan, but I'm betting you'll change that belief once they fingerprint you and match it to prints found in the motel along with DNA proof."

Her smile vanished. "What DNA proof?"

My turn to smile. "It took a little longer than they show you on television for the chloroform to knock Camilla out, didn't it? She fought for her life." I lifted my arms up and pointed to the scratches. "I'm betting you have some scratches on your arms too. See, the reason I know the scratches are important is because the police tested my DNA. They wanted to see if it was a match for what they found under Camilla's fingernails. They didn't have a match in the system, but they could tell the attacker was a woman." I pointed to the cotton sweater she was wearing. "You've been wearing long sleeves or jackets since that night. I'm guessing you didn't want to explain or bring unwanted attention from the police. You also didn't have a new amazing cat named Watson to give you a reason for the scratches, did you? Your perfect plan wasn't so perfect. You should've found a female to be your scapegoat."

Serena's face fell. My guess was she hadn't originally intended on framing Jack, but when he showed up that first night Camilla was at the tavern, it was too good to pass up.

Faria spoke into the radio clipped on his shirt. "Someone wake up a judge and call Glover Rentals. We need to search this place top to bottom for additional evidence and secure everything we've found here."

While Faria and his men were reading rights and bagging evidence, I returned to my spot closer to Tanner. "We know why Serena's plan didn't work so well. What happened to ours?

Tanner laughed. "About the time the giant bug joined in. The last thing I heard was your quiet scream voice, 'Spider!'"

I punched him. He totally deserved it. "Knowing how I feel about bugs, and he was giant and hairy by the way, why didn't you come to my rescue then?"

"Because I know my girlfriend. If anyone could talk their way out of that, it was you. I went to get Billy so we could try to peek in the windows and assess the situation."

For the record, having a gun pointed at me—in my humble opinion—was a situation that didn't require much assessment. "Where is Billy?"

"That's where the plan took another turn on the toilet twister," Tan explained.

"Eeww." Mandi said what I was thinking, even if it felt incredibly accurate.

"He bailed?" That man was a real piece of work.

Tanner shrugged. "I guess he got nervous about all the breaking and entering and who knows what else. He apparently took off without bothering to mention that little detail to me."

It didn't surprise me. I might have done the same thing if I were in his shoes. "What took the police so long?"

"Once I realized Billy was gone, I called Faria to give him our updated location. I also called Sam for backup. Because I had no idea when anyone would arrive, and as caveman as you like to think I am, I didn't want to run in blind with no backup and get us all killed."

I pulled him into another hug and whispered in his ear, "Smart thinking, Pretty Boy."

He blushed at my use of the nickname. I was pretty sure he'd give me grief for it later, but I felt the occasion warranted extra affection. "What happens next?"

Faria spoke into his radio, asking for the status of the warrant and additional backup to process all the evidence. The crackled voice responded an ETA of less than five minutes. Winchester's inner rage colored his skin to a bright red hue, while Serena had returned to her stoic self. The only evidence of her distress was the tears silently trickling down her face.

I turned to Candace. "You ok?"

She plopped into the chair in a very improper manner. "I have no idea. It will take me a while to process all of this."

"What happens to Serena's aunt now?" At my question, Serena's chin snapped up as she locked her gaze on to Candace.

Silence hung heavy in the room as we waited for Candace to process an answer. She lifted her head, her eyes clear and some of the earlier focus present. "I've been cleaning up my sister's messes for as long as I can remember. I'm hoping this will be the final time." She moved to stand in front of Serena. "You and I both know your aunt doesn't have long. I can't, in good conscience, disrupt her life now. I'll make sure she's cared for."

Serena's tears broke through as she sobbed. "Thank you. I'm so sorry. So sorry…"

Normally I wasn't highly sentimental except when it came to my gram—God rest her soul. This act of generosity showed me another side of the privilege the Cartwrights seemingly flaunted at every turn. Maybe Candace was the golden child. It helped me understand why Billy liked her so much.

Detective Marshall broke into our moment. "Well color me surprised. Another huge mess, and Ms. Waters is right in the middle. You can't seem to stay out of trouble, can you?"

Gee, how I'd missed this big lug. Not! Before I could give him my standard, sassy response, Tanner leapt to my defense. "It was my fault this time, Detective. She just came along for the ride." He grinned like one of the young schoolboys he taught. "Love makes you do crazy things."

He huffed. "Love shmove. You just gave her a good excuse to get right in the middle of the fray." He turned his attention to me. "I suppose you have a signed confession to turn over to me. That's usually the result of your shenanigans."

Awww, he said the nicest things. "Not this time. Sorry."

My words caught him off guard. "What? But…"

I couldn't leave him dangling out there on that ledge. "I think we helped with motive, and the scratches on her arm along with DNA proof should place her at the scene. Besides"—I caught Serena's gaze—"I think she might be willing to share what she knows about the crime syndicate to help her cause?"

Serena nodded. She was good with details. No doubt she had done her research on this organization and would have enough to perhaps garner her some leniency.

He sighed. "The paperwork on all of this is going to be a nightmare, but all part of the job, I suppose. Ok, Faria, let's get these perps out of here and processed so I can catch a few winks before my shift begins in…" He looked at his watch. "Ugh! Four hours."

Since I knew Pizza Guy would be disappointed if I didn't do something to aggravate him, I held up my hand. "Wait one moment please. There's one more thing I need to do."

All eyes in the room turned to me. I walked over to stand in front of Winchester. His hands immediately went to his groin area, and he visibly flinched. I smiled but kept my knee still. I patted him on the cheek and smiled. "Tsk, tsk. You may play dirty, Mr. Winchester, but I don't. You should be very thankful that you'll be behind bars where Ashley can't get to you. I don't think she'd be quite as nice as I am. Right, Tan?"

Tan was grinning from ear to ear. "Definitely right!"

Once the Danger Cove Dispensers of Justice left with Serena and a hobbling Winchester, I returned to Tan's embrace. "Will you tell Ashley I did my best to avenge her?"

He laughed. "No."

"But!" How rude.

Tanner pulled me into another big hug. "You can tell her yourself. She'll get a kick out of how you warned him about her."

A yawn from Mandi ended the after-hours festivities. "Guess we should get to bed. I don't think our boss will let us come in late tomorrow," Mandi teased.

"Never," I agreed with a tired smile. "Thanks again, Sam."

"Hey, when my fellow security officer sends an SOS, I have no choice but to answer. Glad I could help save the day. I just have one question."

That felt fair after she'd participated in a grand rescue. "Sure."

"Is it always like this?"

Both Tanner and Mandi answered in unison. "Yes!"

Sam chuckled. "Great. Guess I'm in for an adventure."

The weather outside reared its ugly head as thunder and lightning echoed agreement with Sam's statement. I pulled her into a quick hug. "Well, that's what happens…" I looked to Mandi, expecting her to finish.

She nodded and smiled. "On a dark and stormy night."

EPILOGUE

———

Mornings are not my favorite time of day. This morning the only thing that made me get out of bed was the responsibility I owed to Watson, Smugglers' Tavern, and my Danger Cove community. They would expect us to be open and ready for business when they got out of church or finished their morning chores. They might also have slept in and decided to have a lazy Sunday and have someone else serve up their lunch or dinner. Either way, I needed to be ready.

Watson snuggled in and protested with a meow as I stretched in an effort to wake my body enough to grab the necessary shower. A couple of well-placed scratches under his chin had him doing the same stretch routine. "C'mon, Watson. Let's get your breakfast and my tea, then we'll face today. Tomorrow, though, we're sleeping in."

"Meow."

My phone buzzed with an incoming call. Officer Faria. I hoped this was good news. "Good morning. To what do I owe the pleasure of such an early morning call from you?"

"Morning, Lilly. Sorry for the time, but wanted to catch you before you went into work." He yawned as he ended his sentence.

"Sounds like you've been burning the midnight oil."

He chuckled. "Something like that. I can't go into a lot of details but wanted you to know that Winchester is going away for a long time for the part he played in Ashley's abduction, threats with a deadly weapon, and possession of conflict diamonds."

"Good to hear. I'll be sure to let Ashley and Tanner know. I'm sure she'll feel better knowing he's behind bars."

"You should know..."

The way he said it made me think I wasn't going to like whatever he thought I should know. "What?"

"He's offering to turn in information he has on the low-level ranks of the crime organization behind BARAG in exchange for a lesser sentence. Apparently, they have what he called a transportation network that uses low-level thugs like himself to transport all sorts of illegal or ill-gotten goods using drones or other means to transport them."

Guess that explained how the diamonds were transported fairly easily and largely undetectable. "He referred to himself as a low-level thug?" Didn't sound like the Winchester I knew.

Richie laughed. "I might have assigned that title to him."

That was more like it. "He deserves that title for sure. So how is that knowledge going to bring down a whole syndicate?"

"He turns on the little fish..."

I sighed. "They turn on the big fish." Sometimes our justice system didn't feel so just when bad guys got a break because of *badder* guys. "I don't like it, but I get it. What about Serena?"

"Feds swooped in to talk to her. Above my paygrade. Sorry."

"Ok, I understand. Thanks for sharing what you could."

I shot a quick text to Vernon to see if he could discover anything. I had no idea how high his contacts went, but it was worth a shot.

An hour later I unlocked the door to the tavern and started on all the paperwork. My heart saddened, as I missed the sound of my bracelet clinking against my desk as I moved about. I'd asked Faria to double-check as they processed everything. He promised to text if they found it.

"Hey, why the glum face?" Abe's cheery face lifted my spirits a bit. "I heard you survived the night and the bad guy and gal are behind bars."

"How in the world did you hear that? It was like one in the morning when it all went down." Maybe he'd been taking lessons from Vernon about cultivating police contacts.

The blush on his face told me more than any words he could speak. "Oh wait. I bet Agnes has a police scanner at her house. She used to work at the station—it wouldn't surprise me if she did. Were you hanging out at her place late last night?" The red hue deepened, and all the pieces clicked in my sleep-deprived brain. "You spent the night! You ol' dog, you."

His bony finger pointed in my direction, but the smile on his face and the way his eyes sparkled diminished any effect it might have. "Not a word, young lady. Not a word."

"Let's make a deal." My smile wouldn't be deterred. I was so happy two of my dear friends had found a little happiness with each other.

"Your terms?"

"I really want to continue my education, but school isn't in the cards for me at the moment with all the responsibilities I have here. I was thinking of signing up for an online business class. Would you be willing to tutor me if I need help? I just want to make sure I am up to speed on what I need for the tavern to be a success."

He closed the distance and pulled me into a hug. "Of course. I will be honored to help. I already think you're one of the smartest people I know. The desire to continue to learn is one of the greatest gifts we have as humans."

My heart swelled with both his agreement to help and his praise. Abe had been like a grandfather to me since we met. We'd always looked out for each other, and I was so glad he was back in my life—hopefully to stay this time. My guess was Agnes wouldn't let him go without a fight.

My cell phone rang. "Thanks again, Abe. I'll let you know when I get started." Once Abe exited my office, I answered the call. "Hey, Vernon. Good morning."

"Not unless you have some carbs and refined sugar along with caffeine on hand." He grumbled.

"I've got caffeine, and I can get the rest. Do you have anything for me?"

"My contacts say they are still getting information on the crime organization, and that could take some time."

"Oh, ok…" I was really hoping he would have some info for me.

"Don't be so glum. I'm not empty handed. Miss Serena did offer up her plans for the diamonds and the confession of the murder pretty promptly."

"I'm all ears!"

He sighed. "Maybe you should just read mystery and crime novels instead of trying to live one. Some day you might not be so lucky. Anyway, when Camilla apparently reached out to procure some conflict diamonds, she demanded not only normal ones but the pink and blue hues as well."

"I think those are even more rare and valuable, right?"

"From what they tell me. What I know about jewelry… So Camilla apparently just wanted the deal and had no idea what to do with them after."

I was right about that point at least. "Not surprising. Money wasn't what motivated her."

"Probably 'cause she had more than she could need. Miss Serena on the other hand…"

"Desperately needed money."

"Right. So she came up with the plan to have Winchester cut the diamonds, and then they were going to have them made into fancy-shmansy necklaces and then transport them out of the country, stating they were part of the Cartwright collection."

"And once out of the country, she could sell them on the black market at a hefty profit."

He laughed. "Exactly. And since Camilla had technically paid to procure the uncut diamonds in the first place, Serena's payoff would be huge."

"Too bad it required her killing Camilla for it to work."

"I don't think she would've killed her if she would have been included in the plan and the payout. Camilla forgot that money is a strong motivator, especially to those who don't have enough."

"Did the coroner ever figure out the sequence of events?"

"It's pretty disturbing. You sure you want to hear?"

I wasn't, but for some reason I wanted to know. "I'm sure."

"You were right about the chloroform. Camilla fought until she lost consciousness. Then Serena suffocated her. Once she was dead, she hit her on the head with the bat in order to frame Jack."

A shudder ran down my spine at the calculated coldness of it all. "So Jack wasn't involved then?"

"No, he's been cleared of any involvement."

"Lilly! Someone here to see you," Mandi called from the front.

"I need to go. Thanks, Vernon."

"You're welcome. Seriously, though, try to stay away from this kind of stuff.

"That's my goal. I promise."

I made my way to the front where Candace and Billy were sitting at the bar. To say I was shocked at seeing Billy again would be an understatement. "Hello." Normally I would've offered them something to eat or drink, but since we weren't open yet, I passed on that. Candace was ok in my book, but Billy had abandoned us in our hour of need. It would take me a day or four to forgive.

Billy raised his hand and offered a shy grin. "So sorry, Miss Lilly. I got scared. Been nothing but trouble since I got here. Didn' wanna end up in the slammer in a small town."

He said it as if that was somehow worse than being in jail in a big town. I'd avoided jail entirely, so I couldn't comment. The interview room was more than enough for me. "Since everyone I care about is safe and the bad people have been caught, I suppose I can let your hasty departure slide." It was the best I could offer under the circumstances.

"Well, I've decided to put his nefarious ways to good use," Candace commented with a smile.

"Oh?" She'd aroused my curiosity—not that it was hard to do.

"Billy's methods aren't always the best, but his intentions are well meant. In an effort to make sure our patients are safe, I've hired him as a consultant to test our security measures and find areas where we could improve."

Billy was practically beaming at her praise. I couldn't help but smile. "Sounds right up your alley." I was also certain working closely with Candace suited him fine too.

He nodded. "Yes. It's a chance for this old, crooked man to redeem himself."

Something inside of me softened as I thought about Billy not having to worry about where his next meal came from. Perhaps good would come from all of this mess. "I'm happy to hear that, Billy. You take care of yourself and Ms. Cartwright's nursing home."

I looked at Candace. "Thank you for taking care of Serena's aunt. That was very magnanimous." Abe could skip vocabulary—I'd been studying the word-a-day calendar Mandi gave me for my birthday and putting it to good use. Go me!

Candace nodded. "It seemed the right thing to do, even under the circumstances." She grinned. "Convincing mother might take a day or two though."

We both laughed thinking of the elder Cartwright woman, realizing she would be housing someone for free. "I'm certain you'll manage. You can be very persuasive."

"Thank you. Well, Billy, we should be on our way. Our flight leaves from Seattle in a few hours. Take care, Lilly."

"You too."

Our first patron of the day was none other than Jessica Byers. The smile on her refreshed face indicated she'd got a much better night's sleep than the rest of us. "Hi, Jessica. What can I get started for you today?"

"I'd like another one of those hurricanes, since the first one was so good, and you can offer up some good wishes."

As I made the hurricane, I asked, "Wishes for the auction tomorrow?"

She grinned. "With Camilla, Serena, and Jack out of the field, I'm feeling pretty confident. I think I can convince Adam to stand down as well. I found another piece of property that I think will interest him even more."

"I hope it all works out for you then."

She nodded. "Thanks. I'm meeting with the real estate person tomorrow morning first thing to talk price. Given there was a recent *incident* there, I'm hoping to have them practically give me Shady Pines."

My appreciation for her not saying *murder* was significant. "That's great news. You'll be able to get started on the renovations right away with the extra money and make your dream of a place to help those less fortunate a reality even sooner. Congratulations."

Jessica nodded. "Thank you. I plan on holding you to your promise to help out."

"Of course. We'll coordinate with the soup kitchen and other area businesses to see how we can pitch in to make this a success."

"Thanks, Lilly. Danger Cove is the best."

Sam entered through the kitchen door. "Lilly, can I speak with you for a moment?"

The serious look on her face made me withhold any teasing about her coming in on her day off. "Of course. Jessica, will you excuse me?"

Jessica nodded and went to work on her hurricane as she surveyed the menu. Sam and I moved to the end of the bar. As it was still early, no patrons were sitting in the area. "Everything ok?"

Sam pulled her bottom lip between her teeth for a moment then exhaled a long breath. "I know you contacted my former employer."

"It's standard to verify employment and check references." I nodded, curious to hear what she had to say about the missing diamonds.

"First, I want you to know that I didn't take the diamonds."

"I believe you." And, I really did.

She offered a nod, "But, I was responsible."

"Because you were the security at the time?"

Sam plopped down onto one of the bar stools. "Mostly, but there's another reason." She lifted her head and gazed directly at me. "I was in a bad relationship, and didn't have the courage to leave because he had been good to me and my son. Sometimes love makes you do crazy things, even when it defies all logic."

I reached out and clasped her hand. "I totally understand. So what happened?"

"The only thing I can think is that my ex overheard a conversation or saw my notes about the security plan for the diamonds. He had to have used that knowledge to arrange a small heist. I think it was a test. He took a few to see if he could get away with it. If he was successful, my theory was he'd use me to gain access to more."

"Did you turn him in?" It made sense, mostly. I wanted to know if she pursued justice as hard as I did.

"I didn't really have any proof, but I did confront him. He got angry and threatened me and my son. When he left for work the next day, I packed up everything I could, grabbed my son from school, and stopped at the police station and told them everything I knew. My next stop was my parents' house. They live just outside of Danger Cove and have agreed to help me with Reid while I get back on my feet."

I pulled Sam into a hug. "You're part of our family now, too. We will help whenever and however we can. You need to bring your parents and Reid by soon so we can meet them."

"Thanks for understanding and for giving me a second chance."

I couldn't help the smile that spread across my face. "We're all about second chances here. Now go home and be with your son. We'll see you Tuesday evening."

"Thanks, Lilly." Sam offered as she stood and headed toward the door, the smile on her face warmed my heart.

Before I could reminisce about all the second chances life had given me, Tanner emerged from the kitchen and waved me over. I put other thoughts aside as I wanted to make our last hours together before he headed back to Seattle full of warm fuzzies. He'd stayed with Ashley last night, so we'd missed out on snuggle time. Maybe after the lunch rush we could take a few minutes to sit on our favorite bench out back and just visit.

"Can I steal you for a moment?" Tanner asked as he grabbed my hand.

"Tanner, as much as I'd love to visit with you, I can't leave the bar."

Abe emerged from the kitchen. "I've got you covered. Take a few minutes with him before he has to leave."

For a second time that day, I didn't argue. This had to be some kind of record. See what sleep deprivation does to a gal. "Ok, thanks."

A gentle breeze rustled through the trees. The afternoon sun highlighted the grounds with rays of warmth. With Tanner's arm around me, all felt right in the world once again. "Mmm, thank you for suggesting this."

"Thank you for understanding about me staying with Ashley last night."

"No prob. Is she doing ok?"

He chuckled. "She's fine. She loved that you made Winchester wince. Also telling him he should be glad Ashley wasn't there made her laugh and feel better."

"Glad I'm finally in her good graces."

"For at least a week or two." He laughed. "How are you doing?"

I snuggled in. "I'm ok. Just bummed I've lost my bracelet."

Tanner moved so he could face me. He lifted my chin until our lips met. Yeah, this was nice. When the kiss ended, he reached into his pocket and pulled out something silver and shiny. It couldn't be...

He held the bracelet up for my inspection. "I wanted to surprise you. I took it the morning I slept over. I didn't mean to worry you. I'd wanted to give it to you sooner, but then everything happened. I had it cleaned and inspected to make sure the charms were secure. I know how important this is to you."

Tears flooded my eyes as I noted there was a third charm added. There nestled between the circle charms belonging to my grandfather and grandmother was a new one. This one was a heart with an inscription. This time I knew exactly what those three words meant. "Oh Tanner, thank you so much. I love it, and I love you too."

"I'm hoping you'll still feel that way after I share my news with you."

His words caught me by surprise. "News? What news?" I had no idea what he might say, so I decided to not say anything more and just wait for him to share.

"I applied for a position at a school just outside Danger Cove. While I love the job in Seattle, I don't like being even that far away from my family or"—he leaned forward and kissed my forehead—"you."

Joy started to swell within my soul. Could that mean? "Are you moving back to Danger Cove?"

He flashed me that toothpaste-white smile that started melting my heart from the first time we met. "I'd like to settle in this little sky blue cottage just outside the city limits. I'm hoping there's still some space available despite the fact a new tenant moved in just this week."

Thoughts of having both Tanner and Watson to come home to every night brought my peace, love, and happiness factor to an all time high. "Just so we're clear, you're asking to officially move in with me?"

The smile faded the tiniest of bits from his face. "As long as you're comfortable with that. I know how you are with commitment."

My hands framed his face, and I pulled him into a kiss that shared all the love I held in my heart for him. For the first time in my life, the idea of upping my level of commitment in a relationship didn't bring me fear or even give me pause. I pulled away and gazed into his crystal blue eyes. "As long as you are the one I'm committing to, I'm completely comfortable."

He kissed me one more time, and then we resumed our position of me snuggled up against him as we watched the breeze blow through the trees. Contentment settled in my soul as I knew I'd finally found home.

ABOUT THE AUTHORS

Nicole is the *USA Today* bestselling author of the contemporary romance series, *Heroes of the Night*. She has been an avid reader and lover of books from a very young age. Starting with Encyclopedia Brown, Nancy Drew, and Black Beauty, her love for mysteries grew and expanded to include romance and suspense. A Midwest girl, born and raised, her stories capture the love and laughter in her real world heroes and heroines.

Visit Nicole online at: http://www.nicoleleiren.com

USA Today bestselling author Elizabeth Ashby was born and raised in Danger Cove and now uses her literary talent to tell stories about the town she knows and loves. Ms. Ashby has penned several Danger Cove Mysteries, which are published by Gemma Halliday Publishing. While she does admit to taking some poetic license in her storytelling, she loves to incorporate the real people and places of her hometown into her stories. She says anyone who visits Danger Cove is fair game for her poisoned pen, so tourists beware! When she's not writing, Ms. Ashby enjoys gardening, taking long walks along the Pacific coastline, and curling up with a hot cup of tea, her cat, Sherlock, and a thrilling novel. She is also completely fictional.

Visit

DANGER COVE ⚓

We're a sleepy little town in the Pacific Northwest and home to renowned mystery novelist, Elizabeth Ashby. Don't let out name fool you—we are the friendliest (if deadliest) small town you'll ever visit!

Meet the local residents, explore our interactive town map, and read about the next Danger Cove mystery!

www.dangercovemysteries.com

If you enjoyed *Dark Rum Revenge*, be sure to pick up all of the Danger Cove Cocktail Mysteries!

www.GemmaHallidayPublishing.com

CPSIA information can be obtained
at www.ICGtesting.com
Printed in the USA
LVHW090956210220
PP15709500002B/2